VENICE PEACH

A NOVEL

JESSAMYN VIOLET

A MAUDLIN HOUSE BOOK

MAUDLIN H**USE

maudlinhouse.net
twitter.com/maudlinhouse

Venice Peach
Copyright © 2025 by Jessamyn Violet
Venice Peach illustration by Jules Muck @muckrock
ISBN 978-1-7370222-9-9

EARLY BUZZ FOR VENICE PEACH

"Hold on to your hats! Jessamyn Violet is taking us to some truly unexpected places with the release of her new alternative mind-bender of a novel, Venice Peach. Nothing is what it seems in this funny, terrifying, episodic head trip into a futuristic Southern Californian Never-Neverland. With its extraordinary cast of characters, it is graphic, brutal and darkly comic. In the best possible way, Venice Peach is the thing nightmares are made of! Jessamyn rises again!"

-Curtis Armstrong, *Revenge of the Nerd*

"With a cast of really-deep-thought-spouting misfits— including robots, aliens, monsters, shrunken heads and a 'conspiracy' of beautiful women—Venice Peach is a funny, irreverent, adrenalin-fueled and 'sex-centric' phantasmagoria of a love letter to Venice Beach. 'Shut the fuck up, do cool shit,' and read this book!"

-Francesca Lia Block, *Weetzie Bat, House of Hearts*

"Uh-oh! A TikTok time bomb has burst the Superdoom Portal. Nothing, it seems, can stop the haywire L.A Hellscape seen by Jessamyn Violet – twisted visionary extraordinaire."

-Jack Skelley, *The Complete Fear of Kathy Acker*

"Sex drugs and rock n' roll is only the beginning here. Add astrology, robot politicos, witchcraft, sleazy podcasts, aquatic creatures, telepathy and a kaleidoscope of beach-dwelling misfits to get a sense of the satirical carnivalesque future world that's so fun and compelling to inhabit in *Venice Peach*."

-Duncan Birmingham, *The Cult in my Garage*

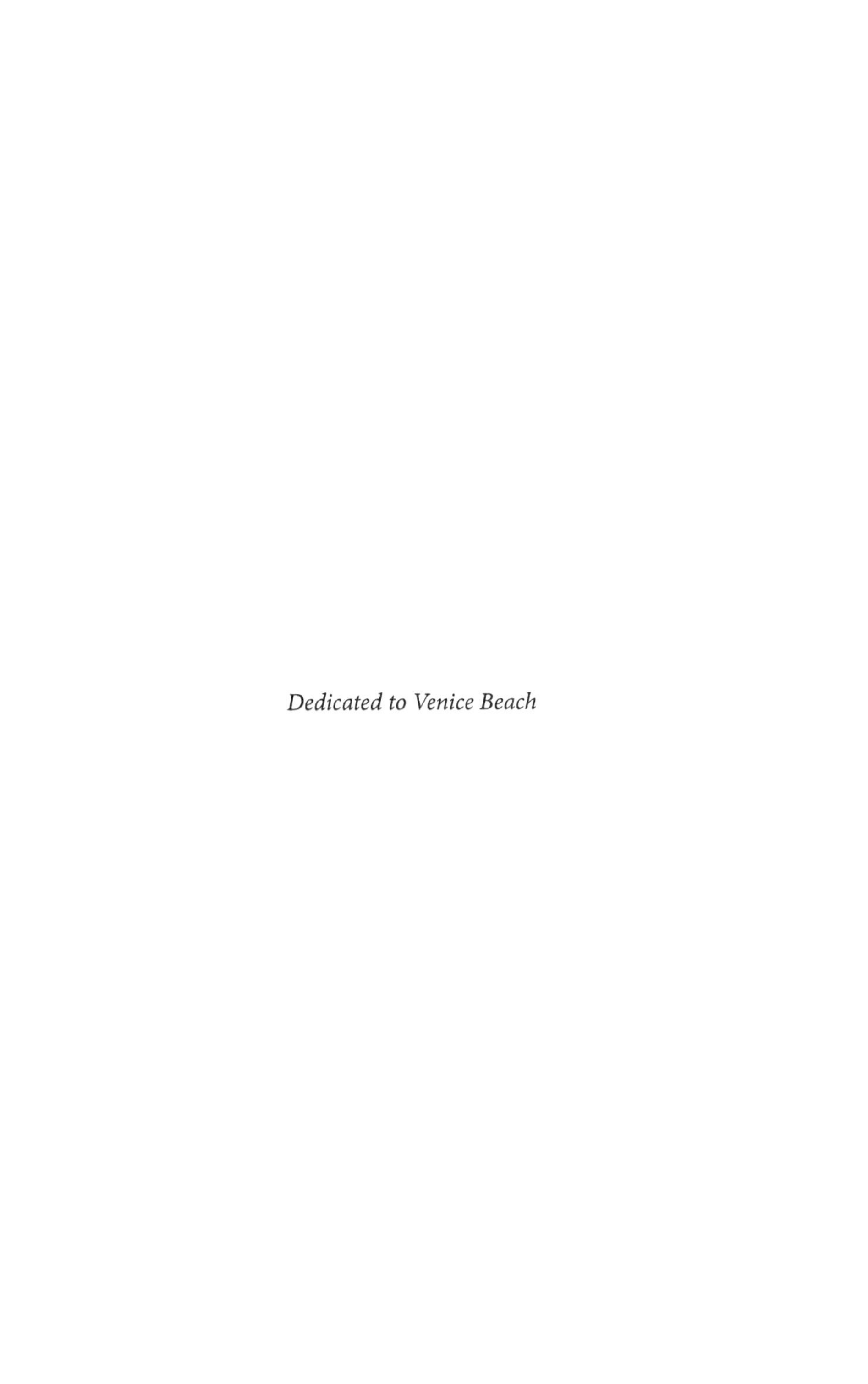
Dedicated to Venice Beach

ELLIE DELIGHT

Step right up here, Pop Stars and Punkers…

Welcome to the Strangest Show on Earth.

I'm Ellie Delight, a former sex-bot that has transformed into the psychic ringmaster of the Venice Peach Freak Circus. You don't know about it because it doesn't exist yet. My original owner, mad genius engineer Ringo Blackstar, felt guilty using me strictly for pleasure and reprogrammed me with my own intelligence, throwing in a counter-cultural edge. Little did he know, I would come to use this counterintelligence to break free of him to create and run a highly illegal underground show of forgotten talents in today's future.

This includes specimens like the Venice clowns, live analog rock bands, gypsy fortune tellers, a classically beautiful bearded lady, a prophetic typewriter poet, a one-armed jazz pianist, mad magicians, jugglers, smugglers, and a few two-headed snakes.

And myself, of course—psychic tarot reader and ringmaster of it all on a most important mission: I have come from the future to show you what happens when you ask the wrong question on the wrong night in the right place.

But first, I need you to take everything you think you know about Venice Beach and forget it. Throw it away for this ride. The California circus-by-the-sea has never been a place that can be summed up in a few mind-bending films, wild shows, or gritty reads. Like all extraordinary characters, there's too much to know. Like how Venice has had five different piers burn down, and how they used to drill for oil right on the beach. Or how the oldest bar in Los Angeles was right off the boardwalk and one of the original speakeasies during the Prohibition era, complete with underground tunnels to smuggle liquor inside. And maybe everybody knows the whole town was founded by a wacky tobacco tycoon named Abbot Kinney, who built the original canals and called it Venice with the vision that it would become the most beautiful and expensive vacation property in the country, but violent gangs took it over for decades.

If you did know all of those things, you're probably a local. And you may consider yourself in the unofficial westside club, Locals Only, originally formed by the wildest surfers and skaters known as the Dogtown Z-Boys. These were the fearless locals who would surf the most dangerous waters through the burned-down pier ruins, and the skaters who would tear up such rugged abandoned swimming pools that it was a wonder and testament to their true talents that anyone lived to tell the tales.

But this story takes place in a very different Venice, a Venice that exists a little further in the future than you're familiar with yet. Therefore, it's best ingested after forgetting everything you think you know.

See, where I'm from on the timeline, the robots are busy fixing everything. On all sides. Human-made history is finally sick of repeating itself. The people will elect corrupt celebrities to govern no more. Scientists, physicists and engineers secretly gathered funding to develop a Presidential Edition Robot back while the last human, former reality television star President Fuckwad, was in office. TBD 3000 had a stunningly effective campaign. The robot was said to be programmed with just the right software to restore the country to its original breeding ground for commerce and creativity, innovation and art. And so, the American people voted to hand over the reins to robots.

In reports from the White House, the team behind President TBD 3000 claims that things are, in fact, starting to improve since the damage done by Fuckwad and his cronies. For many reasons it was the unsexiest period of time in all of history. There was both a civil war and a great recession to recover from, which is no easy task for any human or non-human. Progress in most areas ground to a standstill. We're not as far along in the future as you would think.

President TBD 3000 claimed to be incorruptible, unhackable, and only wanted what was best for the numbers. What else could it want? It didn't have an ego to protect, a demanding spouse to appease, mistresses to be blackmailed by, or households to uphold. Hell, it didn't even have any bratty children to send to exorbitantly overpriced universities.

It just wanted to run things, and to run things right.

Oh yeah, and restore the Great American Dream.

No glitches, no guts, no glory.

TBD promised a return to unity, working to restore equal rights, body autonomy, and an all-inclusive sense of empowerment. But despite these promises, as a countercultural intel robot, I could still see cracks in the system. There wasn't a place for everyone in President TBD's programmed vision/version of the future. But hope was finally blooming again along with birth control and people were searching for fresh types of fun in their sexual renaissance. So, born from the grand tradition of the Venice Beach original boardwalk Freak Show, using the original speakeasy's basement, I started to secretly collect and showcase every outlier the current robotic leadership had refused to recognize in its rebuilding algorithm. I thought it was a great idea, gathering an army of magical misfits—until one of them asked the wrong question on the wrong night in just the right place to change the course of the future forever.

All this carnival ride asks for is a clear palate.

And a taste for a little bit of everything.

THE QUESTION

The supermoon hung low over the limitless stretch of the Pacific, its reflection like a shattered plate over the churning waves. The wind's jagged grasp carved up the water, smashing it onto the shore in frothy spews. Seagulls hovered in the sky, shrieking, bobbing and fighting the invisible currents that crisscrossed the shoreline.

A strange and wonky energy tugged and pushed at all those wandering the Venice Beach boardwalk at dusk. Drifters and vagrants scattered in search of shelter. Robotic security scanned the souvenir shops as the owners shuttered their doors and windows, preparing for a tumultuous night of hot gusts blowing in from Santa Ana. Airborne grit and grime coated the heaping piles of abandoned technology and covered benches and turbo-tennis courts like dirty snow. Outside gyms and the silicone skate bowl grew littered with fallen palm fronds and feathers.

From an alley behind the boardwalk, a lone woman with her head wrapped in a silk scarf darted inside a juice and smoothie stand marked only with a spray-painted peach, just as the employee inside moved to lock the front door.

"I need to see Ellie," the young woman said. "It's an emergency."

The employee simply nodded as the woman moved past her and disappeared behind the door marked "EMPLOYEES ONLY." Inside the office, the woman punched a code into the keypad that prompted the entire shelf to swivel to reveal a set of narrow, dimly-lit steps leading down to what looked like a dungeon. She plunged down the stairs without any hesitation.

The underground Venice Peach Freak Circus was especially empty that night, with just a few Venice clowns who sat at the bar, sipping drinks dejectedly. Hunky, the one with the prison-striped ball nose and giant floppy ears covered with barbaric piercings, honked at the sight of her.

"Odessa! You're a sight for sore ears." He wiggled his huge, pierced-up ears.

"Hi, Hunky."

"What about me?!" asked the green-haired clown with a patchwork bodysuit of a million tattoos, wearing only a black leather loincloth.

"Hey, Punky. Sorry guys, can't chat right now."

She hurried on down to the end of the bar where their fearless ringmaster Ellie Delight sat at a barstool, wearing its trademark bejeweled top hat and suit, running the books through its own untraceable program.

"Sorry to interrupt," Odessa said breathlessly as Ellie looked up. "I saw something in my dreams, and I need to know if it's going to happen."

"It is not a good night to go peering into alternate worlds," The psychic ringmaster said firmly. "The portals are especially thin on windy super-moons. Even a slight tear can set loose total chaos between every existing dimension. Besides," it added. "I can sense something is off with both you and the universe right now."

"But this is an emergency. I *have* to know."

"*Why* do you need to know?"

"It could be life or death."

Ellie smiled grimly as it removed a deck of tarot cards from the inside pocket of the jacket. "My dear, it is always a matter of life or death. But I am going to indulge you because you are one of us, though sadly still so very human in your flaws. What is your question?"

Odessa leaned over and whispered it into the ringmaster's ear microphone. Ellie's face did not change as the androgynous humanlike robot lay out the cards in a wave formation.

"Pick one," Ellie said somberly.

Odessa reached over and selected a card with a shaky hand. Ellie turned it over.

It was *The Fool*.

At that exact moment, there was a crack of thunder so loud it sounded like the place had been bombed. The lanterns flickered over the bottles behind the bar. The one-handed jazz pianist fisted the low end of the baby grand piano onstage. The clowns honked and hawed from their barstools.

"I'm afraid you should have stayed home this evening," Ellie said darkly.

"Why?"

"Your foolish question has summoned superdoom on the next supermoon."

Odessa's eyes widened. "For just me?"

"For us all. Now GO HOME, Odessa."

"I'm so sorry, Ellie." Odessa bowed her head, a tear running down her cheek. The ringmaster just waved Odessa off and closed its eyes.

As she hurried to leave, the prophetic typewriter poet handed her a slip of paper.

"Take this," they said.

"What is it?" Odessa felt a shock of electricity run through her as she took it from their slender hand.

"A transmission from the supermoon," they replied, peering up at her with wide eyes through wire-rimmed spectacles. "It just came in. I think it's for you."

She folded it into her pocket and braced herself for the windy walk home.

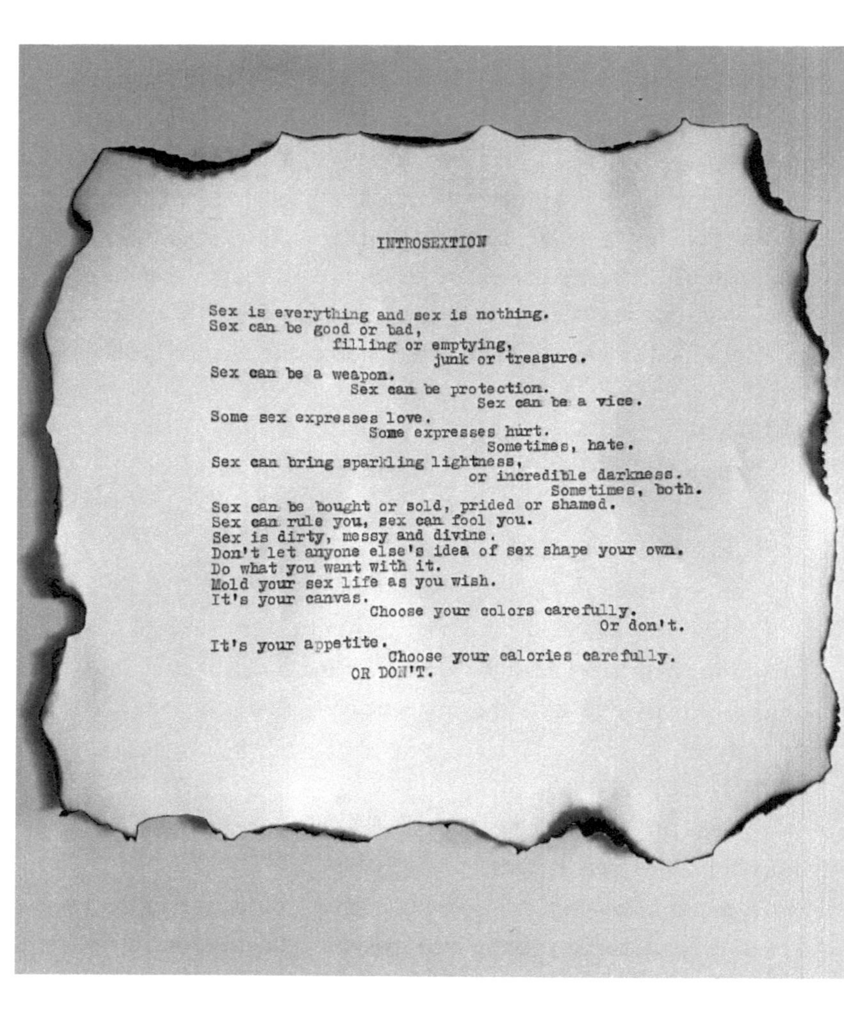

INTROSEXTION

Sex is everything and sex is nothing.
Sex can be good or bad,
             filling or emptying,
                     junk or treasure.
Sex can be a weapon.
              Sex can be protection.
                      Sex can be a vice.
Some sex expresses love.
              Some expresses hurt.
                      Sometimes, hate.
Sex can bring sparkling lightness,
                      or incredible darkness.
                          Sometimes, both.
Sex can be bought or sold, prided or shamed.
Sex can rule you, sex can fool you.
Sex is dirty, messy and divine.
Don't let anyone else's idea of sex shape your own.
Do what you want with it.
Mold your sex life as you wish.
It's your canvas.
              Choose your colors carefully.
                            Or don't.

It's your appetite.
              Choose your calories carefully.
              OR DON'T.

ODESSA MESSA

"Disaster is laughing at us, Felix."

Odessa Messa stood tall before the bathroom mirror, surveying her-self through the looking glass speckled with toothpaste. Her surly, curly, bleach-blonde hair twisted around her pixie face like a wig of tiny golden snakes. Her bikini top barely covered her breasts with little bright blue triangles that looked like eyes over a bellybutton nose and the jagged smile of hips adorned with ripped jean shorts.

Her black and white cat stared up at her from the checkerboard lino-leum floor with wide green eyes.

"It is! Disaster is laughing at our lack of landlines, our distractions, our silly ground-bound escape vehicles. What if a Tsunami came in tonight? What would we all do, jump in our cars to sit on Venice Boulevard in a gridlock? After that superdoomed tarot reading last night I can't shake this feeling of utter powerlessness, like the whole world is a bad hand of cards that's been bluffing too long and is about to fold. Do you know what I mean, kitty-coo?!"

"Purrrr-*owww*." Felix started to purr and rubbed against her bare legs in an effort to reassure her, or maybe himself.

"Don't worry, baby. I have a plan. I'd shove you in my backpack and we'd bike the hell out of here. I'm in good enough shape to beat a Tsunami, right?"

Felix purred away in hopeful agreement. Odessa bent down to rub his head and smelled the familiar fruity stank coming from her roommate's room. She swayed her hips to nothing in particular and then bounded down the hall.

Knock, knock. "Wacko, you in there?" No response. "I can smell you're home."

Finally a muffled, "Open the door, then."

Odessa found Wacko slouched on his L-shaped couch, listening to old school hip-hop and hitting a vape pen the size of a permanent marker. Wacko's unruly copper-red hair matched the state of his room. He sported high top sneakers, slightly baggy jeans, and, at the moment, a nostalgic kitten tee shirt. He took his time shifting his gaze from the ceiling to his underdressed roommate. The muted Zero-Screen television projected footage of a sleek humanlike robot rolling onto a hyperjet, the caption "PRESIDENT TBD 3000 JETS OFF TO START NATIONAL INTERVIEW TOUR" scrolling below.

"Let me hit that!"

"Come and get it."

She collapsed next to him. He looked at her stomach. "Tan."

"Still Moroccan, asshole. Besides, the beach... We live practically on top of it."

"I am barely a human being," he said flatly.

Odessa squinted at him. "You should fix that. Fast."

"How?"

She plucked the vape pen from his hand, took a champion pull off of it, and tilted her head back on the exhale. "I dunno. Try something new?"

She took another hit, passed it back, and stood up. He reached forward and tugged at her belt loop with his free hand.

"Wait. Where you going?"

"I have rehearsal." She wasn't *not* interested in an afternoon romp, but it was rarely a quickie with Wacko. The guy liked to take his time in general.

There was plenty to do at band practice that day and she kind of wished she hadn't gotten so high. Their rehearsal room was in the back of her friend's warehouse in Mid City, in which he kept his fleet of light show drones. It was a strange space to rock out in – a small, somewhat sterile storage room with gray walls, black carpet, a drum kit and a few odd accessories placed haphazardly on cheap shelves. Odessa sat down at the drums and began to warm-up, but was quickly interrupted by knocking from the other side of the wall.

She opened the door to her lit-up bandmates Johnny and Clint holding cased instruments and mini amps. They loved to play together so much it was practically an orgy every time they had rehearsal. All that eye fucking and sonic screwing and sweaty pheromones always made Odessa a little crazy.

"We had some afternoon libations," Johnny admitted as she hugged him.

"You jerks didn't bring me any?" Odessa whined.

"Of course we brought an offering for our queen," Clint said, opening his guitar case to reveal a flask nestled next to his instrument.

"Thanks." She took a swig of the bitter drink and cringed. "Yikes."

There was another knock, this one sharper.

Clint opened the door and Stevia walked in with her theremin case, wearing a vintage sundress with cherry red lipstick, looking impeccable as usual.

"Hey, gang," she said coolly, setting up in her usual corner by the Himalayan salt lamp. "How's everybody?"

"Good," they all chorused. Odessa and the guys didn't really dig Stevia's vibe all that much. It always felt strained and fake, like she was doing them a favor just by being there. But they couldn't forsake the facts that she looked great onstage and could really play the hell out of that theremin. The instrument sang in a way that had become an irreplaceable part of the band's sound, and Stevia knew it. Everyone said she was a witch, but Odessa had never gotten close enough to prove it. Odessa always had the feeling that Stevia didn't like her, but the guys said that was just the impression she gave everyone.

They got to work. Sometimes, Clint and Johnny and Odessa would lock in so hard that they'd stare at each other until Odessa thought their sex organs would explode. They shared an intuition she'd never found in band mates before. One time, she'd even had a tiny orgasm while playing onstage during a particularly crazy part of a free jam.

Stevia was pretty much always on the same musical page with them as well, although she never made eye contact while playing, which made Odessa wonder how exactly Stevia did such a good job following.

Often, Odessa's lyrics and drum beats would be explosive and off-the-grid, the words inciting action, the drum fills spontaneous and a little scrambled, but she always landed back on the one with the rest of the band. People loved the wild, throwback, analog sensation that was Tiny Tin Heart, hooting and hollering at the sweaty, underground shows they'd play every Friday night in the secret speakeasy basement of Venice Peach.

All together, there was an effortlessness to their sound that made Tiny Tin Heart an analog band that the locals had come to know and love like they were the next big thing – though it would be near impossible to reach that kind of status because the live music scene had almost completely died out. Most venues had transformed into sports bars or DJ-fueled nightclubs. And it was known that fame, in general, took longer than ever these days, thanks to the oversaturation of Everything On Earth.

Odessa felt most alive when she played music. It kept her intuition fine-tuned and she sensed change in the air like popcorn about to burst.

The superdoom tarot reading had secured the overwhelming sense that her days were numbered, and after receiving the mysterious sex-centric space transmission from the prophetic poet, she vowed to seek the best possible sexcapades each day until the next and apparently final supermoon.

And that would begin, she decided, by finally hooking up with her bandmates.

"That ending was sloppy as hell," Clint said, smirking as they came out of a song so clumsily it was clear they'd all gone off wandering in their own thoughts.

"I liked it," Johnny said as he stroked his beard thoughtfully.

"That's cuz you're lazy," Odessa said playfully, swigging again from the flask. She came up for air and a punch line. "Everyone knows bass players don't wanna work."

"Kiss my ass." Johnny winked at her. Odessa blew a kiss at him. He bent over and smacked his own ass.

"We play it till it's tight," Stevia said crisply. "We're not going to be written off as a jam band. It doesn't matter how weird we get in the middle, but the beginning and the end have to be on point or no one takes us seriously."

"Yeah, Stevia," Clint said. "Someone's gotta steer this careening spaceship or we'd get lost in the galaxy."

"*Again*," Stevia said. "I have to be out of here by eight."

As soon as rehearsal ended, Stevia took off. Odessa lingered with Johnny and Clint to get high in the parking lot. They sprawled out in the open back of Odessa's antique Honda manual station wagon, Odessa leaning against Johnny, and Clint lying with his head on her lap.

"Smoking a real joint in this car is a total time-warp," Johnny said.

"I like classic things that stick around," Odessa said. "Things that stand the test of time. Do you guys fear oblivion?"

"Isn't that human nature?" Clint said.

"I don't," Johnny answered softly.

"Well obviously," Odessa joked, "or you wouldn't be a bass player."

He ignored her. "I made my peace with death when I was seventeen and my best friend died. He never got a chance and he was a creative genius," Johnny muttered. "I'm probably the only one who still thinks about him."

"I'm sorry, Johnny," Odessa said, tugging his hair softly.

"Yeah, well, it doesn't make a difference, is my point. All the time we spend worrying about death and whether anyone will remember us when we go. Our so-called 'legacy' left behind. Legacy is as much a scam as anything else. No one remembers shit anymore. And even if they did, being remembered doesn't actually matter. Being *alive* does. And when you're alive, just shut the fuck up, do cool shit, and enjoy it while you can. Quit worrying about how famous you are or should be. I guarantee, even famous dead people mean next to nothing to most people."

"Can't argue with that," Clint said after a moment.

"I'm not saying I want to be a *celebrity* or anything," Odessa countered. "That's *gross*. I'm just talking about finding things that last and holding on to them." She grabbed Johnny's arm and gave it a soft tug. "So can you just fill me with some lasting, like, *love,* you guys?"

"Hell yeah, we can."

"Absolutely."

Odessa leaned back and just went for it, kissing Johnny with the passion she had stored up for him for years. He returned the kiss while staring down at her with surprised eyes. Then she moved her hand over and rubbed Clint's groin, causing him to sit up immediately, at full attention. He moved towards her and she broke the kiss with Johnny to meet her other bandmate's hungry lips, lips she had only dreamt about since the inception of Tiny Tin Heart. Odessa's other hand traveled down between

Johnny's legs. His arms closed around her, cupping her breasts, fingering her nipples while Clint started working the fly on her jean shorts. A little moan escaped her lips as he got it open. She shuddered with pleasure from their simultaneous touch, as the joint fell to the ground.

At that very moment, a remote-controlled robot cop, commonly known as a *rocoboco*, rolled into the parking lot, its sidekick drone sweeping the ground with spotlight and motion sensors. They zoomed towards the station wagon. Upon hearing the whirring machinery, the three band mates broke apart. The spotlights fixed on them, shining directly into the vehicle. Three laser beams were trained on the dead centers of each of their chests. Johnny's hands quickly dropped from Odessa's breasts. Clint removed his fingers from inside Odessa's pants, sat upright and cleared his throat. Odessa pushed her hair back away from her face, zipped her fly back up, and adjusted her shirt, trying not to look too disappointed by the interruption.

"To be continued," whispered Clint. "*Please.*"

"Agreed," whispered Odessa. "These guys give me the serious creeps."

"This version of the future is some serious *bullshit,*" Johnny murmured.

An officer's voice crackled through the rocoboco intercom:

"Pack it up. This is a private parking lot. What is your business here?"

"We're a band. We use this warehouse to rehearse," Odessa said, holding up her drum sticks for the cameras to register. "I have the entrance code and everything."

The rocoboco continued to scan their faces while the sidekick drone hovered above, keeping its spotlight and stun guns fixed on them. Clint shifted his legs nervously and kicked Odessa's arm by accident, causing a drum stick to fall from her hand, the sound ricocheting through the lot as it hit the pavement.

They heard a crackling and then the commanding police officer, in a control tower somewhere downtown operating the robotic surveillance duo, spoke again through the rocoboco speakers:

"Pack it up, I said. *Now*. This is private property and your reason for being here is not cleared."

"What does that mean?" Odessa squinted into the drone's spotlight.

"If you're a musical project, as you claimed, where do you perform?"

That left them speechless for a moment. Where they performed was an illegal venue.

"We're, uh, in a hobby band," Clint stammered.

"If you are in a hobby band as you claim… Well then, speaking historically, hasn't it always been a bad idea to screw your band mates?"

Odessa erupted in surprised laughter.

"Yeah," Johnny said coolly. "And what if we're a family hobby band?"

"Leave immediately or we will stun you and bring you downtown for further questioning. Seriously," the officer barked through the robot's intercom. "Don't make me run blood work on you all."

The machine beeped as a syringe emerged from a side compartment. The three band mates stared at it in shock and then scrambled to get going. As soon as they'd exited the Honda's hatchback, the drone began sweeping the rest of the parking lot and the rocoboco sped away after it, the creepy laughter of the controlling officer echoing through the speakers.

Odessa hit Johnny on the shoulder. "Way to keep a low profile! They're probably running background checks on our facial scans right now."

"It doesn't matter," Johnny said.

"Because nothing matters?" Clint responded dryly.

"Because we're already ruined," Johnny said.

Odessa stared hard at him. "You feel that, too?"

Johnny put his hand on her cheek and nodded.

Clint shrugged. "I don't know what you all are on about, but let's get out of here. The rocoboco's already coming back around."

Odessa fumed and flashed her breasts as she slid into the driver's seat. "LAPD can suck my left one, buncha bot fuckers!" she screamed out the window as she dropped the old manual Honda into gear and tore out of the lot, burning rubber onto the pavement behind her.

STEVIA WONDER

"Girls, you are really starting to stink. The natural deodorant isn't doing it anymore. It may be time to switch to the harder stuff."

It was true. The garage reeked of lavender, sandalwood, and increasingly every day, the shrunken heads of pretty surfer girls. The odor had combined into one bizarre, unsettling scent that had crept under the door into the main cottage and declared itself an unwelcome permanent house guest. Stevia didn't know how long she could keep attempting to mask it before it raised the wrong eyebrows. She'd started her garage-made natural skin care line to hide the scent of her shrunken heads, and it was simply no longer doing its job. She would probably just have to rent a remote storage space soon, but she hated keeping the heads far from her view. They were her favorite things to gaze upon.

And talk to, occasionally.

She went back into her cottage. Her audience of four cats watched from their respective favorite spots on her queen-sized bed as Stevia hummed a melody she'd been working on for her solo theremin album and brushed her long black hair. Pansy, the smallest and eldest of the cats, a gray tabby with a heart-shaped marking on her chest, hopped onto her bureau and pointedly mewed as she watched Stevia admire herself in the mirror.

"Oh! OK, Pansy. Thanks for the reminder. Come with me."

Stevia scooped up Pansy and brought her through the door back into the garage, which was crowded with soap and lotion ingredients for her beauty product line. Her collection of shrunken heads of pretty surfer girls sat on a high shelf, keeping permanent watch over operations with their twisted little faces. Stevia had set up a chemistry bar with all of her most sacred secret ingredients in unmarked jars of different sizes. She placed Pansy on the fur-covered pillow on the counter and grabbed her mixing bowl. A dab of white rhino testicle, a pinch of dead sea salt, some tortoise jelly, and a dash of enchanted human bone powder all went into the mix. The final touch was a smear of raw honey from the magic bees her friend Otto kept in a valley up in Ojai. Stevia had hard-won the exclusive purchasing rights.

Pansy purred as Stevia mashed the mixture into a paste. She retrieved two small silver spoons from her drawer and filled them, then held one out for Pansy, who licked greedily at it until it was gone. Stevia licked the other spoon clean herself.

She rubbed Pansy's back. "Good girl."

Pansy had been Stevia's most prized cat since the day she'd had her heart broken by the first person she'd fallen for, many, many years ago. Stevia had discovered Pansy in the alley behind her apartment building in New York City and rescued the kitten in order to cheer herself up. Pansy had slept curled up on Stevia's chest that night as she cried herself to sleep, and when she woke up the next morning, she'd felt a whole lot better. That continued until one day she'd woken up completely cured of the heartbreak altogether, and realized it had only taken a week to get over a three-year relationship. That was when Stevia decided she would keep Pansy alive for as long as she could, no matter how expensive or hard-to-get the extra anti-aging materials were.

Since then, Pansy had helped her get over many more failed relationships, as well as the losses of family and friends, major heartbreaks in her musical career, chaotic power upheavals, the civil war and economic crash—all at record speed. If Stevia had to rate the items in her house in order of importance, Pansy would be at the top, even above her high-priestess enchanted jade theremin from Yugoslavia.

"I'll be famous soon enough," Stevia cooed to her beloved kitty. "I know it's been a long time promised, but I will get there. Soon. And when I get there, you'll be sitting pretty on a plush velvet cat bed eating this potion three times a day while I boast a name for myself and all the other sorcerer musicians who lived and died before me."

Once back inside, Stevia stretched for a while and then fixed herself dinner, a clump of sauerkraut and a small piece of poached wild salmon. She looked up a few spells in her spell book and cast a rejuvenating one on her plant that was looking peaked by her kitchen window. She threw a general disruption spell at Odessa, sensing that something fun was happening to her.

That girl bothered Stevia to no end.

Suddenly, her phone buzzed.

AUGGIE: *When r you cumming over?*

Stevia smirked and looked in her mirror, taking a strand of her hair and smelling it for freshness. Finding any scent hard to detect over all the lavender and sandalwood and shrunken heads, she shrugged and voted against showering.

STEVIA: *On my way. Hold your horse.*

AUGGIE: *Projected – One Item:*

(3D rotating veiny erect dick)

It's in my hand right now waiting for you to ride it, beautiful.

Stevia sighed. She wasn't into "sexting" but it had long ago become part of the way of things, and she had to play along in order to "act her age" – which, thanks to her anti-aging potion, was a perpetual twenty-seven. Keeping with the technological times was by far Stevia's least favorite part of staying young forever, as it was certainly the most challenging.

Anyway, Auggie was a weirdo and certainly not boyfriend material, but she found comfort in that detachment, in not needing him to call or text in order to feel OK. And the sex was enticing enough to keep up for a while, even though he smelled like patchouli, which reminded her of some bad times long ago.

Stevia threw on her sparkly sunglasses for the bike ride over to his place. She poured homeopathic kibble and freshly filtered water into the cats' bowls and was off.

When she pulled up to Auggie's pad by the canals, she crypto-locked her beach cruiser to a street sign and heard sounds that determined he was inside his party bus. The party bus was known as The Zebra, a name that explained itself with its exterior paint job. Regardless of how much of an eyesore it was, Auggie claimed it was booked solid through the weekends and four out of five nights of the week. The Zebra was notorious around the westside for its transcendence of common law; any bad bus behavior was OK with Auggie as long as you weren't a political or religious pusher and everyone on board was having a good, consensual time.

Auggie poked his frizzy-ponytailed head out of an open window and grinned at her. Despite his general unkemptness, he did have a terrific set of teeth. And would probably make a pretty cool shrunken head, Stevia had thought on several occasions.

She walked up to the sliding door of The Zebra, breathing in the combination of chemical air freshener, weed, and good old unsettling patchouli.

"Hiya, Stevia. Wanna take a spin?"

Stevia dismissed him with a little hand gesture.

"Once was enough for me."

Auggie raised his eyebrows. "Alright, alright. I like a woman who makes me work to impress her. Coming aboard?"

"I was actually thinking we could sit in the garden." Stevia didn't feel like steeping herself in the scent of The Zebra. It was bad enough managing her pungent odor situation at home. Plus she had a meeting the next day with Dan Blacker, the handsome producer who paid well, and she didn't feel like washing her hair beforehand.

"Good idea. Almost done with this cleanup. Meet you back there. Front door's open, grab anything you like from the fridge."

Stevia made her way up the chipped slate steps into the house, which had been on the Venice Canals for so long it had become part plant itself. Vines wrapped around windows to the point where they couldn't close completely anymore. Cracks in the kitchen wall emitted sprouts of ivy that snaked along the indents between tiling. Everything was a faded kind of colorful, which appealed to Stevia in a nostalgic sort of way. She would never live there herself, though. Too many critters and far too many signs of decay, which was pretty triggering to someone who worked so hard to maintain a nearly-impossible upkeep. And don't even get her started on the bathroom. Unbeknownst to Auggie, sometimes if Stevia had to pee, she would sneak into the abandoned construction site across the alley and pull a crouching tiger behind the tarps just to avoid using his toilet.

She helped herself to some water after re-washing a glass from the cabinet. Auggie's old, blind dog Rusty ambled into the room, tail wagging, and she let him smell her hand.

"Hi, sweetie," she murmured. She always pitied the copper-colored animal, but Rusty never actually seemed all that sad about his condition. She thought his blindness was perhaps a blessing that kept him from being aware of the squalor in which he lived.

Once outside, Stevia brushed off a cushioned chair, double-checking to make sure there were no spiders. Auggie's side yard was more like a tropical forest. He had haphazardly strung some solar lights around a few of the plants that lit the foliage with a dim, pleasant glow. Stevia loved it out there, even though it was as unruly as the rest of the place.

"Goddamn, you look good in my garden," Auggie said from the doorway, startling her. He was barefoot and wearing a Hawaiian shirt with tan cargo shorts.

"It feels good to be out here."

"Shit, babe. You know you're always welcome." He popped a can of beer and sat in his chair, a dilapidated hammock-stool that creaked annoyingly every time he shifted like it was going to cave under the weight of his stocky frame.

"What's new?" she asked.

"Damn near everything, these days. Did you hear about the upcoming visit from TBD 3000? '*The Interviews Tour*?' That POS model is already gearing up for a re-election. What a load of crap."

"You think everything's a load of crap."

"It usually is."

"Well, I think it at least seems like a more humane model." "Tell me, how is there such a thing as a 'humane' robot? They will never have anything alive about them. How the hell did we end up letting machines make our decisions for us, anyway? How humane – or inhumane – or insane - is that? Our futures determined by algorithms and artificial intelligence… What happened to *real* intelligence? How did they trick us into this fuckery?"

"Please, old man," she said, playing the part of Cooler Younger Woman when she was probably 20 years his senior. "Machines have been the future for so long it seems like forever, now. Get over it. It's just the way it is. Why do you hate robots so much, anyway? What did they ever do to you?"

"You know I think you're gorgeous and super smart and charming as hell, but your passivity is a drag," he responded, ignoring the question.

"Then quit trying to argue with me about politics."

"Robots are not and should not be political. And I'm not giving up on you. Just like I'm not giving up on the future. Since the fancy bots have taken command, some things have improved. I'll give 'em that. But considering we were at rock bottom, broke and angry and in a piss-poor civil war, there wasn't much elsewhere to go but up! And this whole 'bringing back the American Dream' mission statement has got to be a massive disguise for something else, something sinister and ugly. They're secretly mapping something through these interviews. Just the fact that it's illegal for people to tell anyone they're participating or disclose anything about the experience tells you everything you need to know right there."

"Pssht. Even the stupidest reality shows make the cast and crew sign non-disclosure agreements," Stevia said flippantly. "There are plenty of non-conspiracy situations that call for secrecy. They probably just don't want people going in with any expectations or getting dissuaded from doing it at all by people like you."

"They're definitely digging," Auggie said. "And I want to know what for."

"They want the world to get better," Stevia says. "No one wants it to be this fragmented. Not even robots. It seems like they're just collecting data like the Census, seeing where the public opinion and general status quo is at."

"Don't even get me started on the goddamn Census."

"You're impossible," Stevia said with a sigh.

"No, I'm skeptical. Which is *healthy*, I might add."

"And boring."

"Would it help if we started in the bedroom before having these discussions?" Auggie grinned at her. He selected one of her feet, removed her boot, and began to massage her foot with a touch that Stevia was annoyed to find she crumbled to.

She closed her eyes. "It would probably take the edge off, yes."

"Well then, by all means, let me have a re-do," he said, and kissed her toes. He stood abruptly and swooped her into his arms. Stevia shrieked in a pleased sort of way. Auggie did make her feel petite and young in ways she hadn't in a long time. She rested her head on his shoulder as he carried her into his bedroom.

Auggie barely let her do anything in the bedroom but be a receptor and she gladly submitted to that. He may not have been the be st looking or smelling guy she'd been with, but he made up for that and then some in generosity. She would lie there and let herself become an instrument of pleasure, occasionally even humming melodies along to her orgasms, which he seemed to enjoy and inspired him to further extend his giving nature.

Afterwards, they lay like broken toys on the bedspread, panting and tangled up in each other.

"If you were in the TBD interviews and they asked you to rate my lovemaking on a scale of one to ten, what would you say?" Auggie grinned and tickled Stevia's arm.

"I don't do ratings *or* reviews, so they probably won't be interested in having me," Stevia replied. "But are you really saying you wouldn't participate if you did happen to be selected?" She was sort of curious now. He was right. Sex did take the edge off his radicalism.

"Haha, I *knew* it! Why didn't I think of this sex-first thing before? Hell no, I wouldn't do an interview. I'd never do anything to unknowing-ly become entangled in the massive overt conspiracy to turn us all into obedient cyborg slaves. I bet they stick a microchip in you or something once you're there."

"I think 'overt conspiracy' is an oxymoron. And you think everything is a conspiracy."

"Everything *is* a conspiracy."

"What about me?"

"You?"

"Yeah, am I a conspiracy?"

"Of course you are."

She laughed uneasily. "What?! How do you figure?"

"You're a beautiful woman. Everyone knows that beautiful women are a conspiracy. They're practically the biggest conspiracy of all. "

He *is* smart, Stevia thought.

Out loud she said, "That's *sooo* dumb."

AUGGIE BREAKMIRRORS

The rooster alarm went off each morning at 8AM. Auggie had a very specific routine, even though the slapdash environment he awoke in would not suggest that he was a routine kind of guy. He'd stretch in bed, listening to the birds of the canals outside his perpetually-cracked window. His hands would travel south to play with himself a little, just for a minute or two, using his erection as his first cup of coffee. He'd never follow through, though, because that was wasting his energy when he needed it most. Auggie would finish himself off later at siesta time or right before he went to sleep, if there wasn't a female companion over. One thing was for sure; he never left himself hanging.

Then, he'd get out of bed and get a pot of *real* coffee going. Fresh ground beans in an old-fashioned French press with a dash of cinnamon and cayenne. Natural French vanilla-infused cream. He knew he knew how to make damn good coffee. None of that press-a-button, pop-a-thimble-in-a-machine-made convenience crap. One woman he'd dated for a while actually admitted that his coffee was the reason she'd stay the night instead of heading home after sex. And that was OK with Auggie because then he'd get to collect on the most-excellent morning sex. It was a win for both of them—until she'd moved to Boise.

Stevia, on the other hand, didn't drink coffee, so his talents in that department went to waste on her and she never stayed the night.

He'd pour his first glorious cup into his army-issued thermos and grab the old chewed-up leash from the counter. Alerted by the jingle, Rusty would begin wagging his tail and panting, because it was time for their favorite part of the day: The morning walk.

"C'mon old buddy, let's go out and smell the day, what do you say?"

Auggie had moved to Venice when the world had seemed too dim for anything else. He'd never taken pharmaceutical drugs, they were *most definitely* a conspiracy. This was it: Venice was his Prozac. It seemed the sun shined on Venice in a different way than anywhere else he'd been, and Auggie had been an army brat, and then in the army, so he'd sure as hell been around. Venice boosted his mood like nothing besides sex with a beautiful woman, the one conspiracy he would never deny himself the pleasure of falling victim to, time and time again. The sunshine was playful and positive as it poured over the canals, fun and free-spirited as it filtered through the canopy of the overgrown walk street trees, and beautifying and bright as it bounced off of the incredible array of succulents that accented the modern landscaping.

Then there was the beach, with its bike path and boardwalk; the endless fireworks of colorful graffiti everywhere, the parade of characters out and about with their custom transportation inventions.

Goofy guy on a tripped-out hoverboard, *surf sign*, *check*.

Dude on an electric longboard with a pit bull between his legs, tongue flapping in the wind, *peace sign*, *check*.

The creepy 8-ft unicycle clown, *shudder*, *check*.

The woman on silver roller skates in a hot pink mini skirt blowing bubbles, *smile*, *check*.

Skaters of all ages taking risk after risk in the skate bowl, continually wrecking themselves but bouncing back up, brushing off the hurt, throwing a cloak of *whatever*-dom over their collisions, *hell yeah*, *check*.

Auggie loved the leathered, weathered vendors on the boardwalk selling their oddball art: Cut-up soda can airplanes with spinning propellers, ornately painted skulls, psychedelic sun-burnt paintings on knotted slabs of wood, bits of semi-precious rocks wrapped in wires on cords… It all somehow seemed sellable to them, and therefore, it did seem to sell. That was part of the place's magic, too.

The fishermen at the pier were the ultimate favorite, though—in particular, a burly man named John, who would always let Auggie sample a piece of his catch, BBQing it right there at the end of the pier on his own little portable grill. John would palm Rusty scraps as well, rasping, "Poor blind bastard," as he'd scratch behind the dog's ears. Auggie knew the fish were probably contaminated with a million terrible things, but still felt it was important to eat local, in moderation.

Yes, they were all vital to Auggie's mental stability, though they didn't know it—as was his local business of operating the ultimate party bus, The Zebra. He'd been doing it for eight years now, and it never ceased to amaze him how it continued to provide for his lifestyle. Auggie remembered thinking of the plan way back when he'd first gotten his license – *all people want is a safe place to party and a designated driver.* And all Auggie wanted was a simple life of good, clean debauchery and fun. The Zebra kept him feeling cool and social even though he was a rather dorky, radical hermit most of the time.

Perhaps that was what Auggie loved about Venice the most: Even misfits like himself could feel like a vital part of the community. Auggie would purposefully do or say things with no filter, and hardly ever did they have much of an effect. Nor would his daringly-bad outfits ever raise an eyebrow. Venice was virtually shock-proof. In Arizona, there had been haters everywhere. People snubbed him because of his mismatching clothes, his frizzy ponytail, his loose anti-government talk at the bar, and most especially for his addiction to prostitutes. In Venice, he didn't even need to pay to have sex with beautiful women. Why the hell wouldn't he want to call it home?

A bicyclist sped by as he turned the corner onto Speedway, an alley just behind the boardwalk. Auggie thought it looked like the back of his therapist's head. That reminded him that his next appointment was that afternoon. He would have forgotten, as he often did, probably somewhat purposefully. He figured paying the guy for the missed sessions counted for something, anyway—though he wasn't sure what.

"Good morning, Griselda," he said, smiling a broad smile as he stepped into his favorite juice and smoothie shop, Venice Peach. It was a small and unmarked place other than the logo of a peach wearing sunglasses spray painted on the side of the building.

"Auggie! You are looking so fit today!"

Auggie shrugged and Griselda giggled. Griselda was a blonde German woman with an uncanny ability to tell just by looking at Auggie if he'd had sex recently. Sometimes Auggie would do jumping jacks or push-ups before walking in, just to see if he could trick her, which never worked. It seemed he could do nothing to thwart her 100% psychic sexual activity accuracy. He had heard they were running some secret operation out of the basement, and given her supernatural skill to pick up on residual sexual energy, he was pretty sure it was a sex dungeon.

"Nailed it again, G," he said sheepishly.

"Maybe nail *you* some day," she said, smiling suggestively at him, which elicited a startled look from Auggie.

She'd never made that kind of suggestion before.

"Don't you have a boyfriend?" he asked sheepishly.

"No," she said. "What makes you think that?"

"I don't know, I just did."

"You never asked me. Looks like your intuition is as bad as mine is good."

He laughed. "You're probably right about that."

Griselda raised an eyebrow. "I'm always right. Remember?"

She began to make his green juice without another word. He watched her strong shoulders shove the cucumbers straight down into the whirring juicer, then the apples, then the inevitable struggle with the spinach and kale. He knew everything about her lean arms and back muscles already. It would be strange to sleep with her. Rarely had he studied a woman's physique for so long before engaging in bedroom behavior. He wondered for the 900th time how it was possible that he was considered in such a way by gorgeous females here in the land of gorgeous people in general, when back in Arizona, he was basically considered a grungy psycho who had to pay for sex.

"Say… I still haven't taken you out for a spin in The Zebra, have I?" he asked as soon as she switched the machine off.

"I think I would remember such an event, and I'd hope you would, too," she answered with a dry smile, squirting a generous amount of ginger juice into the green mixture. She knew Auggie liked it spicy.

"Let me rephrase: Would you like to accompany me for an evening of debauchery in The Zebra sometime?"

Griselda placed the cup of frothy, brilliant green juice down in front of Auggie and put her hands on her aproned hips. "We would go out, like, with an actual party on this party bus I've heard so much about?"

"Yeah," Auggie said, taking a tiny sip of the green froth on top. "It's nice to have a co-pilot sometimes, and you seem like you'd be a fun one."

"OK," she said, nodding casually. She picked up a towel and began to wipe the counter down. Then she leaned forward and wiped Auggie's upper lip with her finger, smiling.

"OK!" Auggie stared excitedly at her and took another sip. "How about tomorrow night? I'm picking up a bunch of law school grads. Should be a fun night."

"Do I have to dress up?"

Auggie grinned. "Do I look like someone who dresses up? Ever? For anything?"

"Good point. You can pick me up here, then. I'm off at 6."

At that moment a guy walked into the shop and started asking about sunglasses he had left there. Auggie glanced at the clock and realized his whole morning had gotten off to a slow start. If he was ever going to make it to Dr. Phil's on time he'd have to get his ass into 5th gear.

"You can come check out the lost & found box in the back," Griselda told the guy, winking at Auggie mischievously. "See if you are lucky."

Auggie felt a flash of suspicion that she was going to take this guy down to the underground sex dungeon. He wanted to stay to scope the scene but didn't feel like throwing away all that missed appointment money again. Hopefully he would get the full story out of her on their date, anyhow.

"OK, see you tomorrow. Thanks for keeping me juiced, gorgeous." He threw down some cash and pulled at Rusty's leash. "C'mon, ole buddy! Let's go!"

Rusty ambled along behind him, never to be rushed.

Auggie sure admired that dog. Every day, eagerly stepping out of the house to walk around and smell things even though he couldn't see a damn thing in front of him. Rusty would forge ahead so confidently when he was, in fact, never quite sure what lay ahead of him, and oftentimes would stumble off of or into curbs. He'd never even pause to feel sorry for himself, just keep going like he knew exactly where he was headed. It was an incredible daily performance—Oscar-worthy, really. The old copper lab gave Auggie inspiration to leave the house every day. If Rusty could be excited about it and he was blind, what the hell was Auggie's excuse?

DR. PHILIP K. PARKER

"Right. So what makes you think this juice-making woman is a different story than the others, Auggie?" Philip leaned forward in his chair as he stroked his left mutton chop and tried to look *pensive*. Whenever he felt especially tired or bored, he made sure to pull hard in the opposite direction. He didn't earn his money easily, that was for sure.

"I don't know, man, Dr. Phil. You know, you just sometimes have this feeling like a lady is different from the others. Like she's been through some sort of life tumbler that's polished her into a rare gem."

"Wow, Auggie," Philip said. "That's a bit generous for a stranger, isn't it?"

"It's true." Auggie leaned back on the couch with his meaty hands clutching his knees. "Anyway, I just asked her out. I always thought she was taken, I don't know why. I know it's a little early to be talking about her. And I'm still seeing Stevia, who is a goddess but obviously doesn't take me seriously, and that starts to weigh on your heart after a while, you know? Someone refuses to see you as more than 'not good enough' and you can only take so much of that."

Philip stifled a yawn and felt his eyes water up. He blinked hard and attempted *affable*. "From what you've told me, you've been having a perfectly fine time with Stevia. An enviably good time, come to think of it. So what makes you suspect this? Has she ever actually said that you weren't good enough? Or are you projecting that opinion onto her? Is it *you* who doesn't think you're good enough?"

Auggie looked down at his big hands, which had found their way back into his lap. Auggie reminded Philip of a skeptical baby bear. He had both a happy-go-lucky naïve side, and a darker, more aggressive depth – and the combination continued to puzzle Philip; the former part especially, since Auggie had done multiple tours in Afghanistan and had somehow dodged becoming a serious drug addict. Philip studied vets with a special interest, and Auggie was definitely a stand-alone case.

Philip genuinely admired that Auggie refused to take meds and didn't really blame him for thinking everything was a conspiracy. In fact, Philip kind of agreed with Auggie, there. He, too, felt like everything was a trap. And that even just thinking that was a trap in itself. Life sure was a long, godawful mindfuck, wasn't it? That was why he'd become a psychother-apist: No shortage of demand ever, and he loved sitting on the throne of knowledge in the world's most stupefying court. He considered himself a studied spirit guide; a shaman of shame and all the other emotions that plagued people enough to end up in his office. That felt like a good enough life to him, even though he was mind-numbingly bored and distracted the majority of the time. He'd learned early on that the real trick to psycho-therapy was asking the tricky questions and letting the patient do most of the work.

Like now, for example. Auggie was shifting things around in his head, putting the self-deprecating self-portrait puzzle together for himself. Philip had to stifle another yawn while watching him sort it all out. He desper-ately wanted to check to see if the cutie he'd matched with on LoveBug had written back yet. She'd had a quote from Philip's favorite philosopher as her profile statement and he was practically dying to meet her.

Auggie rambled on while looking Philip dead in the eye, still stuck on the question it felt like Philip had asked hours ago. "You know what?

I think you're really on to something there. You're right, maybe I never expected her to take me seriously so I presented myself as someone who didn't expect to be taken seriously, therefore causing her to not take me seriously. Makes total sense. One of those self-perpetuating things, right? Like everything else, I guess."

"Yes exactly; a subconscious self-perpetuating self-deprecating self-portrait. Do you actually want Stevia to take you seriously? Are you in love with her?"

Auggie retreated to his brain again. Philip respected clients who took their answers seriously, but sometimes the answers took so long in the making he felt like Auggie was just really stoned.

"Do you use a lot of THC products, Auggie?"

"Well, sure. Who doesn't?"

"I don't. Do you use them before you come to sessions?"

Auggie stared at him and broke into one of his big-gummed grins that made Philip cringe inside. "Well shit, Dr. Phil, I didn't know you cared about that sort of thing. Of course I do. It opens me up. Makes me more, you know, receptive."

"You use cannabis every day? Every morning?"

"I kind of have to. It helps me, um, chill in my existence. If that makes sense."

"It does. A lot of vets use it to help with PTSD. I understand it can be a comforting lubricant for depressed or emotionally-wrought brains. But Auggie, if there's one thing that marijuana definitely also does, it makes us complacent. People get stuck in time, in thought processes, in emotional growth."

Auggie ingested that. "Hmm. Never thought about that before, but I think maybe I can see your point."

"Do me a favor and try not to smoke before you hang out with Stevia.

See how that changes things. See if you even want her to be taking you seriously. Examine how you feel with this juice girl—"

"Griselda."

"Right, Griselda, see how you feel when you hang out with her as compared to how you feel with Stevia. What is the thing that, um, sorry—Griselda—possesses that makes you so excited? Is it anything other than the unknown? Because that tends to bewitch us time and time again, causing chaos and upheaval, only to later feel reality kick us in the seat of our pants."

Auggie laughed. "Well, there's an expression I haven't heard since my grandpa."

Philip bristled. "I'd appreciate it if you came here with a clear head next time. I'm interested in seeing the difference it makes."

"OK, Doc. I guess I can handle that homework."

"You most certainly can."

Auggie grinned again. "You're a funny guy, Doc."

Philip sighed. "I'm not, really."

Two breaks between clients later and Philip had confirmed his dream date for drinks. He was depleted after the long day of back-to-back sessions so he went for his own therapy: A long, fast and furious bike ride. Philip would step into his spandex and hit the bike path hard. He found it soothing to melt away the burdens of the day with the rapid, continual circular motion of pedaling. It was freedom to him; ultimate, infinite freedom. He could swear endlessly at the amateur assholes who would swerve into him, or those airheads who were on their phones or biking side-by-side, gabbing on at each other. Truth be told, there weren't a lot of bicyclists that *didn't* piss Philip off, and it felt great to talk shit to exactly all of them. And the best part was nobody knew who he was or could get a response in elsewise as he sped by, a blur of hot spandex lightning on spokes.

Philip then needed a few drinks during and after his post-ride shower to fully recover from all the active people-hating. It always surprised him how little compassion he was capable of feeling. He probably needed to brush up on his empathy skills, especially when it came to women.

He dressed smartly for his date. They were getting drinks at The Other Door, where it was dark enough to get away with kissing and groping and plenty else. Philip wasn't sure it was the right choice. He'd forgotten it was typically his go-to *second*-date location, likely since it had been so long since he'd had a second date. It was usually too crowded to be able to have a decent conversation so Philip could just neck his way out of more small talk. But it was too late to shift plans. He didn't feel like making excuses. Philip was going to follow through with his bad plan like a man. He polished off his third beer and belched loudly. In the mirror he saw a guy who looked like he was holding his face in an expression that didn't quite fit.

He never knew what the fuck to do about that.

After grabbing his "professor" tweed jacket, he was out the door and walking the three minute walk to Abbot Kinney Boulevard. There weren't a lot of people out for a Thursday, a relief. The high-end shops that lined the street were well lit and mostly empty of shoppers.

Nebraska was waiting on the corner, gazing into her phone like everyone else who refused to just observe and process the world around them for a minute while they waited. Great. He hadn't even met her yet and already he had a reason to write her off.

She looked up and their eyes caught at that moment.

No matter how many people Philip met, he still got satisfaction out of reading people's eyes. He felt it was a sort of Braille, as contrary as that was to say— a reading with a different sense, one that went far beyond the 3-dimensions of sight. But not everyone operated like that. Not everyone was insightful enough to scan people as quickly or deeply as Philip did. That was why he had trouble staying interested. He'd read people front to back and be ready to move on to the next within minutes, searching for a real challenge, a twist in a human plotline he could never have seen coming.

Sometimes, Philip even considered that he could be a borderline sociopath. But he figured his awareness of it made it equally as likely that he wasn't, if that made sense.

Which he wasn't sure it did.

Regardless, he'd never gone as far as to put himself in a therapist's office to get a second opinion.

Nebraska seemed happy to see "Gio" – probably finding him even better-looking than his dark and somewhat obscure profile pictures. He pictured himself through her eyes at that moment: Tall, slim, with gelled, short-cropped hair, wearing a tweed jacket over a thin, dark blue cashmere sweater and creased gray pants. A successful, athletic, handsome career man. Philip was also happy to find Nebraska as self-advertised: A slim slice of sweet prettiness-with-an-edge. Her eyes weren't all cyborg. A part of her was, in fact, very human; bright and warm and present in the moment.

"Gio?"

"Nebraska, hello."

She smiled and put her phone into her cow-print purse. "My name's not actually Nebraska. I just use that for my profile. I'm Cassandra."

"I understand," Philip said. "Good to keep that initial degree of distance. Shall we have a drink?"

Ten minutes later, they were seated side-by-side in the back of the bar. Cassandra seemed very comfortable in her own skin. Philip was having a hard time being able to tell what her issues were right off the bat. None of the obvious, usual insecurities upfront. And she looked familiar. Very familiar. He hated that about Los Angeles. If someone looked familiar, he never knew if it was because they were already famous to some degree, or he'd met them before, or if the person was going to be famous soon. It all translated the same way.

Much to Philip's surprise and delight, Cassandra ordered beer. There was nothing more intriguing to him than someone unpredictable. He'd had her pegged for a rosé kind of woman. Or maybe he just had them all pegged as that.

"So, Gio, what did you do today?"

He settled back and composed his *at ease* face.

"I saw eight clients."

"Wow, you must be exhausted!"

"Well, in the beginning it was exhausting, but by now I'm pretty used to it. I have to have a detached attitude towards taking on emotional conflict so that I can be as effective as I can be efficient. And after my workdays I go for a long cycle. It really helps."

Cassandra's face twisted up.

"Wait… so, you're, like, a cycling psychologist … or a psychological cyclist?"

He almost snorted his drink up. "That's rich."

They laughed about that for a minute. Philip couldn't remember the last date who'd made him laugh like that.

"Wow," he said when they'd calmed down a bit. "How am I not going to think about that on my rides now?"

Cassandra grinned and pushed her dark hair away from her eyes. "My fault! I think in poetry and song lyrics."

"Do you really?" he asked.

"Quit analyzing me!" she said immediately. He was stunned and felt an instant rise of anger. She then collapsed into giggles. "Kidding! Bad joke. Oh, I didn't think you'd take it that seriously. I'm sorry."

"Some sour previous experiences with that accusation," he mumbled, feeling sheepish and exposed.

"I can see that," Cassandra said. She rested a light hand over his for a moment. He pulled away, hating that he'd lost his composure. Philip made a mental note that dating younger did not always mean he would necessarily be in control. This woman seemed to have a peculiar humor that unnerved him.

He suddenly craved a cigarette.

"Moving on," she continued. "I'll tell you what I did today. I managed the rental rooms in my house – the usual making sure the place is clean, the renters are happy, all has been communicated, etcetera. Then I taught yoga. Then I wrote a song. Then I came to meet you."

"Sounds like a pretty good day," Philip said, struggling for *back-to-normal*.

"I can't complain," Cassandra said. "I owe it all to my father, he left me his huge house on the canals. And thanks to Rentaroom, the place funds itself as well as my bank account. It's basically its own motel. I should start calling it 'Cassie's Corner' or something."

"You could probably think of something a little catchier than that," Philip said, attempting *playful*.

She just nodded. "The name hasn't come yet. It's like naming a band, it's no big deal and yet it's somehow everything."

"I get it," Philip said, though he really didn't. The only thing he'd had to name in his lifetime was his practice, which, surprise, surprise, was *Dr. Philip K Parker, PhD, Psychotherapist*.

CASSANDRA PANDA

It wasn't a complete dud of a first date but she wasn't sure she was that into Gio. He had a general air of mystery and misery and solemnity. It seemed as if she was lifting his spirits, but that wasn't new. She always seemed to be the one fighting for good moods to prevail, and she was pretty tired of it, to be honest. Where were all the lighthearted guys? She wondered all the time. As a teenager, she had sworn to lose her virginity to the lightest, most radiant heart she could find. Now it had been too long and it was clear her standards had been set too high. She was ready and then some. Horny, in fact. But she was pretty sure her virginity had turned into some sort of cloak of sour sexual juju, warding off those who were at all hip to the vibe and attracting those who she just could not feel right about remembering forever.

After they finished their first drink, they went outside for a smoke. Gio stood close to Cassandra and she wondered if what she felt was sexual tension or if he was just intruding on her personal space.

"So, Gio, when's the last time you fell in love?"

This question, like most of her conversational moves so far, apparently threw him off. He didn't seem like he was used to being on a date with someone with any personality. He probably only dated bobble heads who babbled on endlessly. She watched him step a little farther away, retreating somewhere deep in his head. Then he shook it off and went back to pretending to be nonchalant. It was pretty crazy how he seemed to have no idea how transparent he was.

"It's been a while," he finally said. "Probably close to twelve years. I was married, actually. I was too young when we married and I'd somehow deceived myself as to her betraying nature. Probably because the sex was so good." This came out as forced as a bad lie, followed by a short, strained laugh.

"Glad you're divorced, then?"

"Yes," he said seriously. "Sex and contracts do not go well together."

"I couldn't agree more," she said, and pretty convincingly, she thought, considering she had no experience at all with the combination. When he looked at her in surprise, she wondered if she had honed her non-virgin act a little too well, and might be coming across as rather loose.

"What about you?" he asked. "When's the last time you fell in love?"

"Last weekend," Cassandra answered casually, flicking her cigarette to the curb. "But it happens. No big deal. I fall in love all the time, especially with the improbable."

"That's not love, then," he responded quietly, taking a drag off his cigarette. "That's temporary infatuation."

"I disagree," she said cheerfully. "I know you're a psychological cyclist and all, so no offense, but who are you to define what love is? I think every-one is entitled to their own version of the most talked about and puzzling part of human nature, don't you?"

"I suppose," he said after a long moment.

"What's your definition?"

"Of love?"

"Yeah."

She watched as he considered this, his fingers trembling ever so slightly.

"I consider love a lasting feeling of infinity you find in someone."

She couldn't help but scoff. "What, did you read that off a tea bag tag?" Philip sulked like he had been slapped. She hurried on to lessen the blow. "I just mean that I think feelings can be powerful, but love is the most potent magic spell, never cheapened by circumstances or how long it lasts."

Philip put out his cigarette silently and they looked inside. The bar crowd had turned into a pulsing, sweaty blob. Getting an order in looked exceedingly difficult. They decided to go somewhere else for another drink. As they walked down Abbot Kinney, it seemed like everyone had a friendly nod or smile for Cassandra, which she found very amusing, to see so many people she knew on a first date. Hell, even a movie couldn't have gotten away with staging this much recognition for a character who wasn't "famous" by LA standards. Gio's gigantic transparent ego seemed more than a little uncomfortable with it. She was amused by the general rigidity that he seemed to perpetually be trying to hide, but she supposed if she sat around listening to other people's problems all day, she wouldn't be all that easygoing, either.

After dinner they walked along the canals, the moon still hanging low and bright in the sky. It was awkward of him to want to walk her home, and she didn't want him to come inside. When they reached her house, she looked to see if anyone was up. The front room light was on and she heard soft music playing.

Gio paused out front, obviously uncertain as to his next move.

"Thanks again," Cassandra said, giving him a very final-feeling hug and a quick kiss on the cheek. She also thanked him for his book recommendations that she'd probably never get around to reading. Her dating profile quote had made him think she was some kind of bookworm. She wasn't about to break it to him that she'd found it online when she'd searched "quotes about life."

"I want to hear your band."

"Oh, OK, yeah! We have stuff on the apps, and a Saturday night residency at this secret speakeasy, Venice Peach. Do you know it?"

"No," he said, still awkwardly lingering. "But let me know where and I'll come check you guys out."

Cassandra laughed at the mental image of Gio in a sweater cardigan, clutching a martini and watching them play to a bunch of sweaty, stinking rascals in the low-ceilinged underground freak circus.

"You're so full of laughter," he said, gazing at her. "It's refreshing."

"Um, thanks."

"Would you like to go out again?"

"Maybe."

Gio looked determinedly at her for another moment and then leaned in to kiss her. Cassandra let him, though his kiss was tight-lipped and too reserved for her taste.

She pulled away. "OK… Goodnight!"

He waited for her to go inside, which she would have found more creepy than chivalrous if it weren't for the fact that he was clearly an old-school kind of guy. She was eager to see who was still up in her house. There were two tenants currently staying in the extra rooms. Cassandra was only *really* interested in whether one of them was up: Gerard Vice, a handsome B-list actor who bounced back and forth from New York to LA, and had just arrived last weekend. His upbeat attitude and incredible looks had already been giving Cassandra butterfly tornados in her tummy. She'd been half-thinking about Gerard all throughout the date with Gio. Now *that* was unmistakable sexual tension. And also a definite reason not to invite Gio inside, although after that very sterile kiss, she was glad to have pre-made up her mind about that.

First, there was someone she had to consult about it all. She went into the kitchen and made tea, which took long enough to ensure that Gio had gotten along on his way home. She left it steeping and then went outside again, heading down to the main bridge over the canals.

Cassandra ducked under Dell bridge, tucking herself away enough to not be seen from the sidewalks.

-*Bobobo*, she thought. *Bobobo, you around?*

-*I'm coming, my land princess,* she heard him echo in her mind in a voice that sounded like a sweet old man. *Give me a moment.*

-*Of course!*

She waited, still and silent, for his trademark tinkling as he swam to her. He'd told her that the tinkling was because his skeleton was made of wind chimes. Bobobo had a lot of funny explanations. He also had a lot of surprising wisdom.

Less than a minute later, Bobobo produced his slimy, jingling self. He wriggled up the rocky banks like a lumpy, dark eel, his cute little face smiling at her from the front of his amorphous body.

-*Bobobo! I'm so glad to see you!*

-*And I you, darling. What troubles you tonight?*

He always could sense her mood. It was comforting to her.

-*You are so adorable. Did you have a nice day?*

-*Nice enough.* The canal creature let out a little sigh that sounded like a low whistle. *The misses was giving me a bunch of grief. You know, it's getting to be mating season again. The worst time of year for me.*

Bobobo was deeply devoted to a female duck, but she was unfortunately not faithful to him, as she couldn't resist having offspring each year. It drove him wild but he stayed by her side (or usually in the murky water underneath her).

-*You poor thing. I wish I could help.*

-*You do help. You're the only one to whom I can vent,* Bobobo's voice echoed, earnest and gentle.

-I'm happy I can do that for you.

-So, my dear, what troubles you this evening?

-How do you do that?

-Do what?

-Sense when I'm troubled?

-I sense everything. I'm a big sensing machine.

Bobobo shivered and his body rippled and chimed beautifully in the supermoonlight. She laughed and gathered her thoughts.

- I met someone last weekend, and I'm feeling things. Things that make me think he may be the one, you know, to be my first. But now something's turned and it feels like it's become an unhealthy obsession. I tried to date someone else to distract myself but it didn't work. The more I try to ignore it, the more it persists. The urges are just clawing around in me like unwanted prisoners. I've written some lyrics and it helps a little, but not enough. Bobobo, I need to lose my virginity so badly that I fear I will never lose it.

-Ah, I understand. But why fight your lust and love so hard? He could be feeling these things too, whomever he is in this galaxy. Maybe his spirit is fixated on you, too. Maybe that's why you can't control the feelings.

-Well, I kind of hope so because I don't even really know him yet and I hate obsessing. It's so uncomfortable. I'm almost afraid of what would happen to me if we did, you know, do it. Would I just completely lose myself?

Bobobo scrunched up his little face, deeply concerned.

-My darling Cassandra, I understand you more than you know. You must bring him to me somehow. Do not tell him of my presence. Just lead him here. I will be able to read his mind and see if he is feeling the same way.

Cassandra nodded and looked down at her reflection in the canal water. It was dim, rippled and pale. She looked haunted. It felt like her virginity had become a torture hook, gotten its claws into her somewhere deep down, twisting deeper every now and then. She shivered and flicked the water, making herself disappear in the tiny waves.

Back at the house, the music had stopped and someone had turned out the light in the front room. Cassandra grabbed her lukewarm tea and her ukulele and headed to the darkened living room instead of her bedroom, *just in case*. As soon as she'd plucked a few notes on the instrument's heart strings, she heard Gerard's door open.

He looked delighted to see her.

Damn actors, she thought. Even their seemingly reflexive facial motions had to be questioned. Was he actually happy to see her? Or was he acting happy to see her because… well, what would actually be the point of *that*? Kissing homeowner ass? Either way, the desire to slurp each other's faces off had to be mutual, didn't it?

Ugh. He was So. Unbelievably. Hot. Sharply-Freshly Hot. Beautiful-Deeply Hot. Bursting-Fourth-of-July-Fireworks Hot.

"Hey, you," she said in an abnormally high-pitched voice, panicking and looking somewhere vaguely to his left.

He checked the direction she was looking and found nothing.

"Cassandra… Hey! Are you high or something?"

"No, no," she said. "Sorry. I'm just unwinding from the day."

He sat down. "You look good with that instrument in your hands. It sounds like it likes to be played by you, too." She giggled. "Thanks! My bandmates have forbidden me from bringing it into the bedroom, but I play it in secret sometimes."

God. Why did she, like, black out when she was talking to him? It was so weird.

"The bedroom?"

She laughed again. "That's what we call our rehearsal space. You know, because—"

"—That's where the magic happens?" He raised an eyebrow.

"You got it."

"What's your band's name, again?"

"Baby Grand. We're pretty heavy. Doesn't really fit, sound-wise, to have a ukulele."

"Right. Cool, uh, name." His phone chirped in his pocket, and he visibly fought himself not to check it, then sighed as he gave in and dug it out. "Damn, how did it get to be 2:30 already? I have this huge audition tomorrow."

"Cool. What for?"

"This series called *Time's Up* where the lead gets to play five completely different characters. They have a whole special effects makeup team on board, the same guys who did *Terror Town* and *Who Called The Reaper?*"

"Bad ASS!" Cassandra could get excited about that. She loved horror movies—so much, in fact, that she wondered if that was another reason she had trouble letting go of her virginity.

"I know," Gerard continued. "I should probably get some sleep but I'm all wound up."

"Do you want to run your lines or something?"

"Thanks for the offer, but I already ran through them with Jeremy earlier." Jeremy was the other boarder in the house, also an actor, staying in the back bedroom. She had seen him all of twice since he'd moved in two weeks ago. "I want to save the rest of my energy for tomorrow, yeah? I'm not going to lie, it's bloody exhausting hearing all these voices in me head," he said, easily slipping into a lilting British accent.

Cassandra smiled and tried not to look disappointed. She stood as he stood and they stared at each other from opposite ends of the couch, eyes casting invisible ropes that lassoed each other. They walked towards each other slowly, as if possessed. Then Gerard unexpectedly came in for a full on-the-mouth kiss.

She was so caught off guard she missed a direct landing by at least an inch. It was a sloppy half-smooch. Never had a kiss felt more awkward. Not even with Gio.

Her cheeks burned. She was mortified.

Gerard shrugged it off with a laugh. "Good night, Cassandra."

He left her dumb and lovestruck in the living room. She was cursed! She had to be. It was the only explanation for her unbelievable bad fortune. The torture device otherwise known as *love* dug itself a little bit deeper. She sighed deliriously and went back into her bedroom to write more angsty songs about it.

GERARD VICE

It was a good day to be good looking.

Gerard arrived at his audition right on time and took his seat among the other third-round in-person callback actors, checking as he always did to see if anyone was better-looking or brighter-looking than him. He saw a few of his usual competitors whom he'd continually proven to beat out. He felt sorry for them, really. They always looked so deflated when he showed up.

There was only one guy who looked almost as handsome and intelligent as Gerard knew he himself looked, but this guy was a new face. The fresh competition met his eyes, and they gazed at each other levelly.

Where did this guy come from?

Pay it no mind, Gerard countered to himself. *You've beaten out bigger names than you. This guy isn't even recognizable.*

The bastard sure was handsome, though. With piercing eyes. He had "that face."

It was probably nothing. But the part had come to mean too much at this point. Gerard's entire future depended on landing this role. The director, Ty Beck, was one of the last few directors worth working with. The industry had completely gone to shit and most productions out there were written by algorithms starring holograms. Gerard was only interested in doing the real thing, and therefore hadn't sold his image, voice and likeness profile off yet. His agent would surely dump him if he didn't get this job.

But he couldn't think negatively now. Gerard reassured himself he'd get the part because he'd always wanted to do something like this. He'd served his time, paid his dues and then some. He wanted it more than anyone; he wanted it to the point of borderline desperation. With a couple minor roles in major action films under his belt alongside a leading role in a 3-season series, he was reaching the tier where he finally saw himself as undeniable and didn't need to sweat it out in the waiting room as much.

Yet here he was, sweating it out regardless. Gerard did wish that guy would stop staring at him. To confront the situation, he met his rival's gaze dead on. He was feeling charitable, so he even shot over a small smile. The guy didn't return it.

So… He was a *stone cold* handsome bastard.

Well, that was the last Gerard would try to be civil. He took out his phone and began texting with his agent, Jimmy Park. Jimmy was inviting him to happy hour at La Cucaracha with one of his favorite podcast hosts, Matt Bogart. Fuck yeah, he wanted to join them. Gerard's schedule was filling up fast for the few weeks he would be on his favorite coast. With a force much greater than luck, he'd land something good and get to extend his stay. Possibly even finally move to Los Angeles.

"Gerard Vice," a petite blonde called in a voice that made it sound like he had been picked to win the lottery.

Gerard stood and looked at no one. He walked directly into the casting room, eyes fixed on the prize. Five people sat behind the conference table, tablets scattered about, the newest version of super-camera set up behind them. He was familiar with two of the casting agents and the director. One of the agents had cast him in his largest grossing commercial yet. He took that as a good omen and flashed them his most winning smile.

"Good day, people of the casting castle."

Who knows. He was aiming for silly and it came out stupid. Somehow, though, it got a better laugh than he expected. Also a good omen. They were feeling generous.

"Paul, Kathy, Ty," he continued, slathering on more cheesy charm. "Great to see you again. Thanks for having me back. Hope all's going well!"

Paul nodded at him. Kathy waved amicably. Ty cleared his throat like it was time to get down to business. The woman at the far end stood up and smiled.

"So, Gerard, why don't you go ahead and just launch into it, this time off-script. Give us your improvised impressions of the five characters back to back."

So he riffed as a Texas rodeo clown named Buster Spurs, a gay trans South African gymnast called Clarence, Billy the super nerd astronomer, Wylie Ryles, the British rock star, and Lieutenant Tom Murphy, the hard-ass Boston cop.

By the end he had scrambled brains, but they felt like good scrambled brains. Like he had whipped them well enough to be fluffy. The casting directors seemed impressed. Paul said, "Go back to Wylie and tell us more about your alibi, why it couldn't have been you who killed Marjorie."

Automatically he slipped into his Brit rocker's voice:

"I was out at the club until just past 3am, and I went home with this one model who I reckon could be showing for Triptonix next month, Valerie Butter. Just ask her, we spent a fabulous night together. Besides, I could never kill a birdie 'cause I quite like them. They're gifts from the Divine Mother. Why would I slash something that brings me the most joy in the whole world? I only touch women in ways that feel damn dirty good for them. It's a bloody tragedy, that's what it is. I'll kill the bastard myself if I get my hands on him."

The casting directors gave him a short round of applause. He hadn't heard them do that for anyone else. He left the room gliding on a slanted ray of light, growing brighter with each of the jealous glares from the waiting room on his way out.

Traffic was the usual nightmare. When he arrived at the Mexican restaurant, it appeared Jimmy and Matt were already at least a pitcher and a half of margaritas into it.

"If this is actually the golden age of the future, then why do we still have to sit in traffic?" Gerard vented, sliding into the tall booth. "They can't figure that shit out?"

Jimmy gave him a pat on the back and clumsily filled a margarita glass for him.

"Try a raunchy podcast, really takes the edge off," Jimmy joked. "Speaking of, Gerard, meet my other favorite client, Matt Bogart."

Gerard shook Matt's hand enthusiastically. "Great to meet you! I love your show, man."

"Thanks!" Matt flashed a sloppy, puppyish grin. "I hear you're from New York. Where do you stay when you're in town?"

"Here in Venice. Rentarooming on the canals."

"I'm in Venice, too. Right behind Abbot Kinney. Little place my family got a great deal on way back when it was mostly gang bangers and broke-ass artists."

Gerard already knew all of this, as he'd listened to enough of Matt's podcast to win an *I Slept With Them First* trivia night. He nodded. "Me too, I have a family-owned place in Park Slope."

"Well now I get why you haven't moved here yet," Matt said.

"I'm ready to," Gerard replied.

"Soon enough." Jimmy motioned to the waiter for another pitcher. "We gotta get you on our level. Nobody should be in La Cucaracha sober for more than five minutes."

Matt looked around. "Can't believe it's still standing. What a *cucaracha* of independent businesses. Thank god they didn't all go down with the collapse. Gotta say, I'm digging this President TBD 3000. Can't believe that a machine actually has me feeling hope for this country."

"Is TBD going to be on your show?"

"That's hilarious. I assume you're joking. What the hell would we talk about? It doesn't do talk shows or podcasts, anyway. They have a strict no-entertainment-publicity policy. The New Constitution doesn't allow it to do anything non-related to politics. But," Matt leaned in, his greasy hair peeking out from the back of his Dodgers cap, "I do have an inside connection that assures me I'll get selected for The Interviews."

"Your father's connection?" Gerard asked.

"No," Matt said defensively, but didn't bother to elaborate.

"Hey, how'd the final callback go, star man?" Jimmy asked.

Gerard hated when Jimmy called him that, but it was better than "little star man" which was what his agent called him when he was *really* drunk.

"It went well, I think. Even got applause."

"That's right, you're my golden ticket."

Matt looked vaguely interested. "In-person auditions are still a thing? What's the part?"

"This throwback series called *Time's Up*. I'd be playing five different characters," Gerard said. "It's pretty wild. A whodunit murder mystery for the masses."

"Are we *still* not over murder mysteries yet?" Matt rolled his eyes. "Well, you must be good. Jimmy doesn't take on many actors."

Jimmy smirked. "You're right about that. I don't have time for anything less than top-shelf. But listen, I wanted you two to meet for reasons other than the fact that you're two of my favorite clients. Matt, Gerard has a story worthy of your show."

Gerard paused from downing his margarita and stared at Jimmy. Then he looked at Matt. Matt raised an eyebrow and produced a high-pitched giggle.

"Must be a good one," he said, "because he looks scared shitless."

Gerard's mind scanned and reviewed. When had he told Jimmy that story? Damn. He would probably get himself killed for telling that to the public. He'd dreamed of being on the podcast forever, and he'd always known he'd had the goods. It had never felt right, though, no matter how many angles he'd tried to justify sharing it.

"Who do you have?" Matt asked Gerard. Gerard stared back, tongue sitting on the bottom of his mouth, motionless. Matt looked at Jimmy. "*Who the fuck does he have*?"

"Kristina Brightside," Jimmy said, as seductively as Gerard had ever heard the bastard say anything.

Matt's eyes grew huge. "Holy *FUCK*." He looked back at Gerard and lowered his voice to a whisper. "Seriously? That's a next-level shag. This could be the most-listened to episode of my entire career. *Seriously*? You *slept* with her?!"

Gerard stared vacantly into Matt's eyes.

"You were *actually inside* that *smoking hot A-list actress?*"

Gerard felt himself start nodding slowly from deep inside his own head, hitting his brain with a sledge hammer, almost free of his conscience. The damned thing was putting up an unusual amount of fight. He kicked back the rest of his drink to hasten the demise. Jimmy refilled his glass immediately.

"When?! How?!" Matt stuttered. "Jesus Christ, kid, you're a hero. I've never even heard of anyone who knows of someone who even got her to look their way. I can't wait to hear this fucking story about fucking Kristina. Let's take a car back to my place right now. I could streamline this thing to air next week. *Fuck*."

Gerard took a big, long, deep breath. They always said there was no telling how low anyone would go to get themselves ahead in this town.

Now, it seemed, he was about to find out.

MATT BOGART

Probably no one loved their job as much as Matt did. And definitely no one needed a breakthrough episode as much as Matt. He wanted it desperately, more than anything else in the world, to prove that he was more than his famous rock star father. He needed to be seen as something bigger than the son of the guitarist for Snake Eyes, Geoffrey Bogart's only child. A lifetime of cursing his bad luck, and Matt suddenly couldn't believe his good fortune. After years of particularly uninspiring interviews about sleeping with basic B-list celebrities, he'd landed a story about a woman who was, according to exactly everyone's radars, the hottest actor in the game right now.

When they got to Matt's place, the alcohol had settled deep into their systems, causing them to stop and smoke like their lives depended on it. Matt and Gerard vaped away, while Jimmy chain-smoked a couple of cigarettes, bragging about how he'd just had a pair of glass lungs installed.

"I just get 'em cleaned every few months and nothing can hurt me. Not smoke, not vapor, not respiratory illnesses. Best money I've spent in my life. I get to smoke all I want with no repercussions."

"Oh no? How's the love life?" Matt joked.

Jimmy shot him a quick glare.

"This is a nice place," Gerard observed, looking around the rustic backyard Matt paid someone to design and maintain as they exhaled lungfuls of nicotine.

"Thanks. It's inspired by Kentucky, the animals and all. Those big, fluffy rabbits of mine really get me laid a lot. Especially when they have babies. No line has ever worked better for me than, 'Wanna come over and pet my baby bunnies?'"

"Yeah, right," Gerard said. "Like you need help reeling 'em in."

"Ha. It shouldn't be breaking news to you that most of my listeners are guys."

"Does that matter? It's a huge hit."

"Yeah, well… Hardly anyone knows me by face except crazy older broads who are obsessed with Snake Eyes and my dad. Maybe I should start doing a teen talk show, switch up my demographic."

"Write up a treatment and I'll shop it around," Jimmy chimed in.

They went inside the garage-turned-recording-studio behind Matt's house. It was set up like a vintage parlor, centered around a pair of tall armchairs and a table with two old-fashioned radio show mics on it. It was time to lay down the episode that could define Matt's career. Something big enough to beat out his bloodline byline. His fucking moment had finally arrived.

Gerard looked nervous and cleared his throat.

Matt laughed. "Sit down. I'll mix us drinks before getting started."

He went to the bar, poured three tequilas neat, and handed them out ceremoniously. Jimmy tucked himself away in the leather office chair at the desk in the corner while Matt scrambled to get everything set up.

Finally ready to roll, Matt reached over to pat Gerard on the back reassuringly. The kid looked like he was going to bolt any moment. Frightened rabbit would frighten the rabbits, running out of there spontaneously. And there was no way he was letting the interview of his lifetime get away from him. He'd do what he always did. He would say whatever it took to get the job done.

"OK, Gerard. Relax. *Please.* It really helps the mood. I'm going to ask you to get pretty graphic but just remember, she can't sue you. This is what *all* celebrities sign up for when they step into the spotlight. Remember? And this won't do anything to hurt her, regardless of what you're thinking right now. In fact, it will only help her. All publicity is good publicity, right? All clichés are cliché for a reason, and that reason is inarguable: They stand the test of time. *Right*?" Gerard was white-knuckling his drink and looking at the door. Damn. It seemed like he was losing the kid even more. He decided to reach for the big backup hook. "I've actually had a ton of celebrities become fans of the show after they were featured."

"Really?" Gerard looked momentarily relieved. He was back.

"Absolutely. You *gotta* be cool to be a celebrity, don't you already know that? And sexploitation is always chill when it's consensual, man, so ease up. No one can touch you, it's Article 665 of the New Constitution: The Freedom of Media Act. You're just sharing your personal experiences and it just so happens they're about a public figure. Alright? We ready to move on from the pep talk?"

"This is going to be good for everyone, Gerard," Jimmy encouraged from his corner of the room. "Why do you think I put it together? You won't live to regret it. I promise. Risks, Gerard. We have to take risks to get anywhere."

"Risks?" Gerard echoed, eyes glazed over.

Matt clapped excitedly. "And… I'm pressing record… *Now.*"

Gerard swallowed hard and nodded again.

It was happening. They were rolling.

"Here we are, another night, and another sordid, steamy tale coming at you from the tell-all studio of your favorite podcast… *'I Slept With Them First'*."

Music filled the air temporarily, the tune he composed for the show.

Matt played the jingle at the top of in-person interviews to set the mood. Also he loved that little electric guitar riff he had come up with. It somehow never got old to him. And it was way catchier and better than anything his dad had ever written, in his opinion.

"Welcome back, folks. I'm Matt Bogart, happy to host the show here with our very special guest, actor Gerard Vice, a handsome young man with a very big story... a close encounter of the sexual kind, with none other than your favorite alien from TMI's *Three Aliens and a Boxer*! Can you say hello and tell the public who it is that we're discussing this evening, Gerard?"

"Hi, everyone. I'm Gerard and I'm here to talk about... Kristina Brightside."

"Whew! I don't know about you guys, but I can't wait to hear this one. Kristina's the sexiest alien by FAR on that show. And that's saying a lot. Do you agree, Gerard?"

The kid was gripping the edge of the table now, swaying enough to make Matt worry for a second that he was going to pass out. Matt gave him a little pinch on the wrist and Gerard's eyes widened. He straightened up and snapped into focus.

"Uh, yeah, I mean, she definitely looks unnaturally good in metallic green."

"She sure does, the little nymph. And she's about to premiere as the killer clone in the acclaimed analog indie film *Tell Me All Your Secrets!* Speaking of secrets... Let's get right into this. Paint the beginning for us, my friend. How and when exactly did this all go down?"

Gerard settled into a more comfortable phase of drunken acceptance. "Well, it was around four years ago. I was in need of a break from app dating."

"I know what you mean, sometimes it's just too much flesh market.

Makes you dizzy."

"Yeah. I wanted to go out into the wild to, like, hunt for my food, you know?" Gerard looked suddenly nervous again. "I didn't mean… I'm not a sexual predator or anything. It wasn't supposed to come out like that."

Matt gave him a wry grin. "Let's just continue on with the story, shall we? Scrambling defensiveness is never a great look."

"No, really! You can edit that out, right? Right?!"

Matt crossed his fingers under the table and mouthed *of course*.

"Ugh, OK. So. So anyway, I decided to go to the best old-school match-making arena—"

"Yoga class?"

"Ha! No, no. That's another oldie but goodie, though. I went to an underground concert. An ex's favorite band was playing. I never really liked them, but I sure liked her, so I figured I'd do pretty well there."

"Alright! I like your style, Gerard."

"Yeah, so I head over to the secret address and get a few beers in me. The band is better than I remembered and I'm feeling ballsy, so I sneak into the VIP area to hang with the "top shelf" crowd, if you know what I mean…"

Matt laughed. "I'm picking up what you're laying down, brother. No finer selection than the VIP section."

"And there she is, Kristina, right before the aliens show dropped, looking like sex-on-a-stick in a black dress. Just an absolute stunner. I just about died where I was standing. You know when someone's so attractive that their eye contact actually causes you to have a physical reaction? An adrenaline jolt? I love that feeling. It makes you feel so alive. So yeah. She's that smoking hot. And lucky for me, she was as tipsy as she was hot."

Matt felt a smile-grimace twist across his face. "Uh oh… Just how drunk was she, Gerard?"

"Well, who actually knows. I was pretty drunk at that point, too. And to be completely honest, she approached me. There's no amount of liquid courage that would have gotten me to hit on someone that gorgeous. She was keeping it together much better than I was. I just assumed she was blasted because she came up to me and told me she liked my hair. Which really isn't that cool. My hair, I mean. You know, it's fine, no big deal or anything. So that's when I knew she was basically saying she wanted to hook up."

"Wait a minute. I'm comfortable enough with my sexuality to vouch to the audience that you're a very good-looking guy yourself, but do you expect us to believe that Kristina Brightside basically *threw* herself at you? What show was this, anyway?"

"I know, Matt. I was as shocked as you are. It was a Girls Push Girls show. Maybe it was all the crazy female punk rock energy in the air. Or maybe it was the lack of other options. There weren't many guys there."

"Unbelievable. You're a goddamn pick-up genius. So then what happened?"

"She asked if I wanted to come back to her place… Like she even had to ask. It was really cute. Turned out she lived just a few blocks away. She took off her heels and walked barefoot through the streets of West Hollywood. I was like, who *is* this chick? She seemed so confident and laid back, like she already had the world conquered. Of course, I didn't know she kind of already did, yet. I just knew she had *me* conquered. So we get to her place, and she pounces on me as soon as the door's closed."

"I'm sorry to interrupt, here, it's just… this story is a bit hard to swallow. Does this happen to you a lot? Stupidly good-looking girls throwing themselves at you? Or was she, like, blackout drunk?"

"No, no, she was fine. Just… Try and understand, I'm a lover man. Also known as an actor and a happy drunk. I have this mode that I get sucked into... Especially by beautiful women. It's like I know how to be exactly who they want me to be. It's this weird gift, this ability to have a chameleon reaction to a situation, be someone's perfect mirror." He sighed and shrugged. "Not that I'm insincere. I just find that people, especially women, are comfortable with me a lot sooner than they're comfortable with other people, for no obvious reason other than this... way I have. They trust me quickly for no other obvious reason."

"I have got to hang out with you more," Matt said, surprised to find himself actually kind of in awe of a guest for the first time in 348 shows. "So, then what? Did you tear the clothes off or did they come off slowly? Let's hear all the details."

Gerard paused. He seemed to still be fighting through something in his head. Matt prayed he didn't crumble just as it was getting to the good part.

"Details, Gerard," he urged. "We need a play-by-play. That's what makes a good story. You want to do Kristina justice, don't you? Think of the expectations, here."

"Yeah. It was... I'm just trying to remember. Oh, yeah. She—she made a comment about her feet being dirty, so I volunteered to wash her feet in the bathtub for her."

"You *sly fox*."

Gerard eyed him warily so he made a mental note to dial it back. The kid was clearly walking some kind of line, and Matt's encouragement was not helping keep him on the good side. He could always add his responses in post.

"She lit some candles in the bathroom, too," Gerard continued, "so it felt kind of ritualistic. Look, it wasn't calculated at all. I wasn't trying to be sly. And even though I had no idea who Kristina was, she was *special* sexy, you know? I thought, *I have to do this right*. I had to treat her like royalty. I didn't want to rush it or force anything. So she got in the tub and I started washing her feet with this body scrub she had. She lay there with her eyes closed, like a cat getting its belly rubbed, all vulnerable and adorable. I can still see it so well, even though I was pretty drunk. She looked so incredible that she seared herself into my blurry memory. And then I started rubbing the scrub on her legs, up her thighs, and she was shivering in a good way… and she just… she…"

"What, Gerard? *She what?*"

"She had the most amazing body I'd ever seen. Like in-person CGI, there's nothing real life about it."

Matt flipped his hat backwards and licked his lips, barely able to contain himself.

"And did you taste every square inch of it?"

Gerard downed the rest of his tequila and smiled crookedly. Matt could tell with that last giant sip that his guest was finally "in the zone" – good and blazing drunk and not holding back any longer. "I got in the tub and I tasted exactly every part of her body. I even remember licking behind her ears. I wanted to eat her whole, I swear. It was almost scary. She tasted… she tasted like sweet vanilla and bourbon. I mean, just the best that a human being can physically taste. Then we moved things into the bedroom."

"*Fuuuuck meeeee,*" Matty moaned. "Were you in absolute fucking heaven?"

"A part of me was terrified the entire time," Gerard slurred earnestly. "I have to admit that or I wouldn't be doing her justice. I think we're all partly scared when we have a gorgeous person allowing themselves to be seen and touched in that way. We're like, who the fuck are we to deserve this? I mean, do you know what I mean? Sometimes I wake up next to a stunning naked woman and I just feel like a mirage of a million bucks, or like the biggest fake superhero in the world."

"Wow. Gerard Vice, everyone. I'm just a little surprised, I have to admit, to find you're such a *romantic*," Matt said, shaking his head. Jimmy mouthed *so drunk* at Matt from behind Gerard and they smirked at each other. "You're getting pretty poetic for someone your age. Didn't you grow up beating off to endless internet porn like the rest of your generation?"

"Yeah, no—that's only partially true, actually. I read a lot of dirty novels. I wanted the character studies for acting. And I didn't watch too much porn. I preferred the real thing and had plenty of fun times with girls growing up. We got drunk and made our own porn that I beat off to a lot. Maybe too much. Maybe even briefly considered being a porn star if the acting didn't work out, hah."

"Wow," Matt was gasping through his own laughter. "I believe this whole story a lot more, now. Hope you kept that footage locked up tight, or someone's gonna make a fortune when you blow up yourself."

At that, Gerard bit his lip and looked frightened again. Matt sped on, realizing his own dumb mistake. "So what's your old man like, then, you being such a Casanova and all?"

That shook Gerard back to the present. "My dad? He always told me porn was like junk food; the more you watched, the worse the health of your real sex life would be. He encouraged me to find fun and willing girlfriends, use my imagination and good looks, ask a lot of questions, and always build the fire slowly if I wanted it to eventually roar. He said if I stayed away from the 'junk food sex life' that quality women would just be able to tell. And I have to say, so far it's proven pretty true."

"Sounds like a smart guy—and a good man."

"Sure was. To all his wives *and* mistresses."

That cracked Matt up. The actor kid was way more of a trip than he'd expected. He'd predicted just another shallow, drunken bro story. His phone was vibrating like crazy. He snuck a peek. It was Odessa. She liked to hit him up late at night. She was a fun slice. They took turns badgering each other to hang out at odd hours. It was almost like they liked each other more the less each other tried; like it was some sort of competition to ward each other off but neither of them had yet been turned off enough for it to actually end.

Gerard detailed the rest of the encounter to the point where Matt had to press down on his jeans and mentally stall his erection, promising it that Odessa would be there soon enough. That was his goal for each episode, to achieve the overwhelming need for his listeners and himself to get off with a fresh new fantasy in mind. And this kid had absolutely 100% fucking nailed it.

Matt stopped the recording and sat back. "Alright! Show's over. Thanks, buddy. This one's going to break new ground, I can feel it." He gave a very uncertain-looking Gerard a high five. "Great stuff, really exceptional work. By the way, how much of that was bullshit? Do you really not watch porn?"

"I do sometimes. And I can't say I don't have a 'junk food sex life.'"

Matt laughed. "Hard not to in this world."

ODESSA MESSA

"Thank you, Venice freaks! We love you!"

The applause surrounded Tiny Tin Heart like thunder. Another Friday night; another sweaty, hormonal performance at Venice Peach Freak Circus. Odessa had given it her all, as she did every week in the passionate throes of her band's music. She was hesitant to attempt another threesome with Clint and Johnny after the failed one earlier that week. It felt like the universe didn't want her going there, interfering with something so pure and purposeful as her art project. But her libido was still stoked and searching for something to scratch that giant groin itch.

So she left the speakeasy without saying goodbye and texted Matty.

Odessa wasn't exactly proud that she got the craving to see Matt every now and again. She just liked his dick. There was an undeniable appeal to it, even though she was pretty sure he was one of the sleaziest human beings on the planet. She'd been hooking up with him off and on throughout the last year and could hardly believe it was still going on between them, nor did she have any idea why she was so gravitationally drawn to his package. It was like they just *got* each other. They shared a rare kinship, or something. Matt had even admitted she gave him better hand jobs than he gave himself. Seeing they'd had so much fun and now that her days were suddenly numbered, she wanted a proper goodbye screw—for good luck, or just good fun, or something.

Odessa drove over to his place and as she approached, she could hear him saying goodbye to someone, so she crouched behind a jasmine bush until three figures emerged and she could see they were guys, not some other woman he'd had over for the early portion of the evening. She stepped out and walked up to them. They were unbelievably drunk. She could feel it ricocheting off of their every move. A really good looking guy spotted her first and stared at her without saying anything. She shifted, hands on her hips, giving them her best coy cat smile.

"Matty!"

Matt turned and saw her. "Odessa, *hey*. This is Jimmy and Gerard. They're just on their way out."

"Already? The night is so young."

"Webeendrinkingsincefour," Gerard slurred.

"Oops! I meant to say the night is so *done*," Odessa teased.

"Not for '*Matty*' I guess," Jimmy said with an obvious jealous edge to his voice. He wasn't so bad looking, either, Odessa mused. She decided she was up for a foursome, if that's the way the night went.

As if he could sense the thought, Matt said, "OK guys, thanks, now get the hell out of here." He walked over to Odessa and gave her a hug and a big kiss on the lips, grabbing her by both her ass cheeks. An unusually-grand display of possessive behavior, she noted, but she didn't exactly mind.

After they left, Matt brought her into his studio.

"Ooh, I've always wanted to do it in the studio," she said. "Can we pretend that I'm a guest on your show?"

"Who do you wish you had fucked, pre-fame?"

"Brian Duckling."

"Oh, that is an *excellent* choice."

"I know. So hot even the straight guys want him."

Matty fixed them some drinks as Odessa walked around, looking at the decor. It all seemed a bit calculated to her. His "rustic art" matched a little *too* much with the old-school shag carpet. The blinds and leather sofa were a little *too* "vintage style" to be actually vintage. Whatever, maybe he just happened to be an authentically cool and unique guy. He did have big fluffy bunnies that had tons of babies all the time. They had to be too high-maintenance to be just fully-functional babe lair props.

"Would you rather be really famous and unable to fuck, or be stuck fucking a really famous person who didn't give a fuck about you?" Matt asked, stirring a fresh batch of tequila sodas before delivering one to Odessa, who was now sitting on the cream-colored love seat in a corner, perched like a princess under a painting of a gold-flaked sun.

"Oof, that's a rough one," Odessa said, chewing on her lip. "But in the end, I feel pretty confident there's probably nothing worse than being famous and unable to fuck."

"Right?"

"Why do you ask?"

"I don't know. I thought about it last night when I couldn't fall asleep."

"You think about some weird shit."

He pulled out a little mirror from the cabinet next to the love seat.

"Speaking of unable to sleep…" He produced a small vial from his pocket and dumped sparkly white powder onto the mirror. "Care to stay up with me all night?"

Odessa observed him. "How much have you done already?"

"Just a couple lines to sober up enough to tape the show."

"You just taped a show?"

Matt separated the powder into four perfect lines. "Hell yeah, I did. That Ken doll you just met screwed Kristina Brightside before she got famous."

Odessa's eyes widened. "Holy fucksticks. That's gonna be huge!"

"I know." Matt leaned forward and snorted up two giant lines with a little straw he'd materialized from his pocket. Then he held it out to Odessa, who looked torn for a moment.

"No, thanks. It's bad for the groove," she said, air-drumming for a moment. "Plus, I'm trying to live in the moment right now. Tell me something: Do you feel like we're on the brink of disaster, and that's why everything's so sweet right now?"

"I don't know. But it wouldn't surprise me."

Matt sniffed up the other two lines, then ran a hand up her arm, stopping to tug her earlobe gently. Odessa fluffed her massive head of bleached curls, suddenly feeling fiercer. He stared at her. She stared back.

"I keep having these dreams," she said, sipping her cocktail. She closed her eyes and felt Matt playing with her curls. "Plane crashes, tsunamis, earthquakes, bombings. Sometimes I get saved, but sometimes I die before I wake up. I heard that's supposed to be a bad sign. So I got a tarot reading about it yesterday. And it ended up confirming the bad signs. Not that you believe in stuff like that." Her eyes popped open and she started drumming on his thigh absentmindedly.

He shrugged. "I wouldn't know a bad sign from a good sign. It all seems fucked to me."

"Do you dream?"

"Not really."

"Do you *have* a dream?"

"Beating my dad in everything," he said immediately, then raised an eyebrow. "And of being tied up by a hot little vixen."

She didn't miss a beat. "Well, I can make that one happen. You have tools?"

Matt nearly choked on his sip. "You know, I do. Left over from my buddy's bachelor party. This stripper brought all this kink stuff here."

"You don't have to explain why you have it to *me*," Odessa stood up, smirking. "I don't need to be your girlfriend, I just wanna be your favorite radio station. So, go get it!"

"OK, sick," he said, growing visibly excited. "Sick, sick. I'll be right back."

Odessa jumped out of her clothes in about ten seconds. When Matt returned, she was sitting in his office chair, legs crossed, wearing only her bikini top and panties. He grinned at her and held out the roll of shiny black bondage tape.

"How's this going to go?"

Odessa rose. She pointed at the desk chair.

"Sit."

He started over and she held out her hand. "Strip."

He tore his jeans and shirt off even faster than she had and sat in the chair. It was clear he was already very physically excited. Odessa took his shirt and tied it around his head, covering his eyes. He sighed with relief and reached his arms out to touch her stomach. She tsk-tsked and grabbed his wrists, pressing them onto the arm rests and taping them down tightly, one by one. Then she crossed his ankles behind the chair stand and bound them together. He kept on sighing loudly, like just the act of getting restrained was relieving him of some burden. She put one of his socks in his mouth and taped it there as the final touch.

Odessa was growing more and more thrilled by the moment. It was the powerful feeling she had been seeking ever since the doomed reading. She was completely in charge, could do exactly as she wanted. The master of her own fate for a moment—at least sexually. She tipped his head back and brushed her lips against his ear, a whisper of a kiss that produced more heavy sighing. Then she got on her knees in front of him and ran her nails all over his body. He'd grown taller than she'd ever seen him between his legs, but she made him wait, licking, kissing and caressing deep into his thighs. By the time she touched him, he felt like a warm stone dildo. One that was buzzing to be reunited with her.

The chair was thankfully sturdy enough to support a fluid straddling situation. She hopped on top of pop and he moaned with deep pleasure. She began to rise up and down on him as he gagged with delight.

Matt started making strange grunting noises through the gag tape in his mouth. His face bloomed a deep shade of purple-red. Odessa imagined it was flushed with pleasure and smiled. His eyes grew wider until they looked like they were going to pop out of his head.

It wasn't the hottest sight, so Odessa closed her eyes, trying to channel the limitless power she had felt just moments earlier. But his moans got uglier and harder to ignore. She pressed a finger to her lips, trying to quiet the mood-killing sounds. When she opened her eyes again, she found him to be practically having a heart attack; lips blue and foamy, eyes stunned and open.

Quickly, she climbed off of him and released him from his gag. When he just stared at her, seemingly in shock, she gave him a slap and threw her drink on his face. That managed to knock him out of it. He licked his lips and shook his head slowly, the color in his cheeks returning to a more natural shade.

"What the hell? What was that about?!"

"Um…"

"Let me guess. You totally blew this by doing too much blow beforehand."

"Fuck," he whispered, still staring at her. "That was nuts."

"Nuts like horror or nuts like pleasure?" Odessa asked. "Both? I couldn't tell."

Matt shook his head, seeming to still be in a state of shock. She began untying him and noticed his hands were shaking. His whole body was shaking.

"What happened, Matty?" she asked. "Was it that good or that bad?"

He blinked. "Um, I guess—I guess I started seeing things," he said, laughing embarrassedly. "I mean, it was good, don't get me wrong—"

"What did you see?!"

"You wouldn't believe me."

"Try me."

"Um… I saw one of the sexiest spontaneous acts of the year," he said.

"Pssshht. What a cop out. Well, if you're fine, then now it's my turn," she said.

"Of course," he said. "Of course."

She finished un-taping him and he stood up slowly and kissed her hard. Then they went over to Matt's loveseat and he folded her arms and legs back and taped them to themselves, until she was a being with bent half-limbs. Odessa gazed up at the ceiling of the garage studio, utterly transfixed by the loss of all power after having it all. Surrender felt like a different type of freedom. Then Matty went down on her until she had to beg him to stop because so much blood had traveled between her legs that her face had fallen asleep.

It wasn't the goodbye screw she had expected, but as she walked home, weightless and exhausted in the best of ways, she realized that she was actually wasting time; what was between her and Matty was nothing that she could hold onto forever. In fact, as she unlocked her door, she realized there was probably something else she should be doing. Another way to find something lasting within her life other than making a lot of music and a lot of love.

On the other hand, she thought that for a life story, that wasn't half bad.

STEVIA WONDER

"Odessa! *Guys?*! Hell*ooo*?!"

Exasperated, Stevia made the theremin scribble around in a chaotic melody. She rolled her eyes at her male band mates, who were busy looking concernedly at their drummer queen. God, they doted on her to a sickening degree, even when Odessa looked like she'd spent the night partying hard; hair frizzier and wilder than usual, makeup fallen below her eyes, enhancing dark circles.

It annoyed Stevia how Odessa still somehow looked good, the very definition of a hot mess.

Odessa shook her spacey eyes back onto the group.

"Sorry! I'm off today. Um, where were we?"

Stevia rolled her eyes. "Take five. Go make some coffee."

Three quarters of the band went for coffee and Stevia stayed behind in the rehearsal room. She played a low, violent melody on the theremin, something she'd been working on for a little while. The door opened, and Odessa popped her head inside.

"What was that you were playing?"

"Nothing."

"Sounded like something."

"Just a riff I thought of the other day."

"Love it. We should jam on that when we get back."

She left again and Stevia frowned at the Himalayan salt lamp. She was sick of giving all her best material to Tiny Tin Heart, for Odessa to write the lyrics to and assume the credit for just because she was both the drummer and the singer. It was time to put her own solo act into action. A song she'd added theremin to was a pop hit right now. Music producer/DJ Dan Blacker loved her theremin playing, claiming it was a cool sound that no synth could replicate. He'd given her a feature on another single by the biggest teen male pop star at the moment, Curtis Creation. It was the highest-profile gig of her entire decades-long music career so far.

She credited it all to the wealth spell that she'd finally had enough money to cast. Alas, the cliché "it takes money to make money" also applied to spells. The money-generating spell required a stack of 888 $100-dollar bills. With the enormous rent she paid for her cottage/garage combo in Venice, it was hard to save that kind of cash on hand as a self-employed freelance artist and small business owner. But she had finally accumulated the cash, thanks to Dan Blacker and a burst of her overpriced skincare product sales, she was financially set to soon be rich. She had to wait six months before attempting the spell again, though, or she could lose all her money. Witches were not supposed to be too greedy. But it was deep inside both human and inhuman nature to be greedy, Stevia now knew – no matter how supernatural you were, you only wanted more.

The band re-entered the room, clutching coffee cups. Odessa looked slightly more alive.

"We came up with a new theme for the next show," she said. "Disasters!"

Johnny elaborated. "Yeah, we'll combine all this footage of natural and man-made disasters from the past and project it behind us."

"I was telling them about that riff you were playing, it would be cool to write an instrumental intro/outro to that," Odessa added.

No lyrics? Sounded good to her. Stevia nodded. "That could be cool."

"Yay, she likes it! We'll call it 'The Apocalypse Anthem,'" Odessa said, somehow borderline chipper after the break.

"We haven't even tried playing it yet," Stevia said curtly.

"It doesn't matter," Johnny said, defending Odessa as always. "It's just a name. Anyway, let's jam!"

After rehearsal they all agreed that they were sounding pretty damn good. Stevia couldn't complain about what they'd done with her riff. Every time she got close to leaving Tiny Tin Heart, something would work out so well she'd be reminded that it was worth sticking around to play with them. They were talented, after all, and their weekly speakeasy shows paid well, a strong source of regular income. She also stubbornly recognized that she actually missed what they did with her gloomy riffs when she tried them on her own. That was what had held them together for a couple years now, and what kept her just satisfied enough to record her own music once in a while, but never really take the time to fully work out the solo record. *Soon enough, though,* she swore to herself.

Back at her place, she received a text message from Auggie:

Steve-- Come over. Please? NOW?

What was she, his freakin' call girl?

She was feeling extra irritated so she cast another disruption spell towards Odessa. This time, though, when she was waving the baby bird wing bone in the air, her cat Sassy pounced on it and it snapped.

"Crap!! Sassy! Bad girl!"

She wondered what that would do. Probably nothing. Probably it meant she would just have to find another dead baby bird or kill one ceremoniously. But just to be sure she didn't turn the curse on herself, she figured she would check with the only out-of-the-closet witch she knew, Madame Hummingbird, who read her crystal ball down at Venice Peach Freak Circus. She threw on a headscarf to hide her identity, along with her sunglasses, and began biking down to the boardwalk.

Along the way, she admired the restored richness of the real estate that lined the walkstreets. People had complained that Venice had gotten too fancy before President Fuckwad's time in office, but when the country slid into socio-economic decline, Venice had started to become scary again and though her cats would have hated it, Stevia had even briefly considered getting a big, scary guard dog. There were so many deserted houses that creepy-crawly vagrants would take over, selling drugs in Ghost Town and throughout the canals, trading guns behind Abbot Kinney and doing drugs while camped out in front of the library that had since been shut down. But when the first model of robot president, TBD 2000, had taken over, along with its nation-wide fleet of rocobocos, the beach town had slowly grown safer again. The rocobocos had driven most of the vagrants out with stun guns and jail time, and the real estate had slowly started to pick up again. A flock of celebrities had returned to Venice, re-spicing it up and re-igniting the home-owning craze.

Stevia had always longed to be a celebrity. It started as a childhood daydream and she still dreamt of it daily. She wanted to be the first famous witch and loved to dress up like she was going to be photographed by the tabloids, wearing black pearls and metallic makeup just to go down to the farmers' market and sell her skincare line. She'd traipse around Venice acting like a big deal, hiding behind bejeweled sunglasses and a wide-brimmed black straw hat. Occasionally she'd score the looks she imagined she'd get if she were actually famous. People would stare, probably wondering if they should grab a picture to post on social media after image-searching her. One time, a little girl had even asked to take a picture with Stevia. Stevia had nearly cried from happiness, which was a very rare feeling for her. She was a fame addict, desperately seeking celebrity, the most powerful currency in the world, the most potent drug in the veins, desiring only to breathe the sparkling VIP air of recognition and special treatment. She used to cast the "star spell" daily in efforts to heighten her star power, wanting to not only feel magnetic, but to truly be magnetic, drawing stares like syrup to hotcakes. But alas, the star spell wasn't as powerful as she'd hoped. She was missing the key ingredient that could not be bought or faked: A genuine love for humans.

Stevia had never had that.

Nor could she seem to find a spell to get that.

It was another thing she figured she'd ask Madame Hummingbird as she pulled up to the smoothie and juice shop along the boardwalk. As she walked in, she smiled thinly at Griselda, the woman who worked the counter.

"Hello, Stevia. Your usual Venice Peach Smoothie?"

"Not today, thanks. I'm in a bit of a rush."

No one else was in the shop so Griselda tipped her head as Stevia crossed to the side of the counter and entered the back room marked "OFFICE" – which inside looked like a small and ordinary business office and storage. Since Stevia basically worked there as a resident musician, she knew the code to enter into the keypad on the shelf: 1905, the year that Venice Beach was founded by tobacco tycoon Abbot Kinney. The keypad whirred and caused the whole shelf to shift and swivel to reveal a set of narrow stone steps that led down to the underground freak show circus, complete with carved stone hands holding lanterns that lit the way down.

Down in the belly of the underground circus, Stevia inhaled the smell of mildew, popcorn, and fast food as she passed the beautiful bearded lady, Donna James, sitting on a stool at the corner of the bar eating cheeseburgers while a couple of people watched in mute amusement. The ringmaster and tarot reader Ellie Delight was showing a few young women the two-headed snakes they kept in a cage to the side of the stage. Calamity

Calvin stood up onstage, inserting a giant fishing hook through one nostril and snaking the pointed end out through his mouth.

"Hey, Stevia," Ellie chirped. "Did you leave something?"

"Just popping in to see the Madame," Stevia said quickly.

"I think she's in with someone," Ellie said.

Stevia couldn't care less. She pushed back the black velvet curtain in the corner to reveal Madame Hummingbird sitting on her throw pillow in front of the low mahogany table, her sparkling ball perched on crushed velvet and illuminated from the single light fixture overhead. A young man sat across from her. He was handsome but had severe acne.

"Use this twice a day and you'll get wherever you want to go," Stevia said, pulling a tube of her bestselling Blemish-B-Gone cream from her purse. The young man gaped down at it, then stood and thanked her, handing the Madame Hummingbird a couple of C-notes before taking off.

"Stevia," Madame said, "you know you shouldn't interrupt a session."

"It's an emergency," Stevia said, sitting down on the pillow across from the Madame's.

Madame sighed and took her perch again. "Ok, give me a moment to recalibrate."

Madame was the only person to whom Stevia had actually confessed she was a witch, other than Ellie Delight, who had psychic powers and knew anyway. But the unwritten and steadfast rule in the Venice Peach Freak Circus was that no one could talk about anyone else who worked there to anyone else, even each other, both below and above ground, *ever*. No matter what. So it was basically the only place where Stevia felt both seen and safe. Not that she didn't suspect some amount of gossip to continue on the way it does.

Madame Hummingbird looked all-powerful in an emerald green holographic dress that cycled through images of a lion's skull to a raven to an alien face. She wore a purple turban on her head and her fake eyelashes were so long it was a miracle she could keep her eyes open.

She waved her long, pointy black fingernails over the crystal ball, and they both watched as the sparkles inside moved to form a blooming flower-like pattern, then immediately combusted.

"You botched a spell," Madame said after a moment.

"Yes," Stevia said anxiously. "What will happen?"

Madame's face darkened and she bit her large lower lip. "It appears the superdoom portal to the darkest universal forces has widened even more with your broken baby bird bone blunder. There's no telling what will happen now. But none of us will emerge unscathed."

"What superdoom portal to dark forces?!"

"The one your bandmate opened with her dimension-splitting tarot question."

Stevia frowned. "Odessa? She never mentioned anything about that to me."

"Why would she? She knows you despise her."

That made Stevia frown even harder. Madame clucked and reached out to caress Stevia's cheek with an empathy that almost made her tear up.

"Ah, that all-consuming, ugly beast named Jealousy. I am sorry she eats at you."

"It's just… people love her, like *really* love her. I don't feel like anyone really loves me."

Madame Hummingbird waved her hands over her crystal ball, shifting the shining particles once again. "You do not know love because you do not feel it inside for others."

Stevia frowned at that hard truth. She blamed it on her mother, naming her after a fake sweetener and then dying when she was six years old. How was she supposed to be a loving, authentic being in the world with that kind of start? Stevia felt lucky to have inherited any powers at all from her mother, Katelin, who would teach her a little magic every day before she was taken down by her own doing. She'd ingested a poisonous spell by accident. Well, not a spell, per se, but a poisonous mushroom. Katelin had picked the wrong mushrooms for the damn spell. It had been an enchantment spell that was supposed to make whoever looked in her eyes fall in love with her. Instead she had looked straight into her daughter's eyes and died.

Stevia considered herself lucky she hadn't been old enough to participate in that one.

"You harbor grudges, resentment, anger and jealousy; all the bitter poisons that keep your heart cold and alone," Madame continued as her crystal ball pulsed with shimmering fragments. "You do not forgive, you do not forget."

Yes, she remained bitterly angry at her mother, whom she remembered as beautiful and loveworthy enough without any spells. Katelin had told Stevia she'd used the love spell with Stevia's father, but hadn't cast it strongly enough, so he'd left them when Stevia was a small child. Stevia was positive her mother could have gotten a man to love her without the magic and thus survived to raise Stevia, but Katelin had relied too heavily on magic, another common and often fatal witch mistake. Then Stevia had to go live with her Aunt Glenda, who was very much in love with her own life and barely paid her witchy little niece any attention. Suffice to say, Stevia had always been attention-starved and love-starved, to which the obvious antidote was celebrity. Her anti-aging spells had kept it still in the realm of possibility, but Tiny Tin Heart would never make it big enough to fulfill her fame needs. She'd eventually have to go out and do something on her own, perhaps make her own pop theremin album. Or collaborate with the right DJ. She needed to really stand out so she could get her face on billboards.

If only the perfect song-writing spell existed.

Alas, the only spells that gave creative powers were soul-selling ones, and Stevia wasn't quite ready to make a deal with the devil. She'd just have to keep trying to write a hit on her own. And to do that she needed to be out there, living life with the regulars, the humans. And she just wanted to be less human. There was a way to be less human. But the spell for that involved dying briefly, and she was not down for that. *Yet.* What if something went wrong and she still hadn't gotten famous?

"Do you have any other questions for me?" Madame interrupted her thoughts, and had clearly been watching her for some time. Stevia stood up as she realized she'd opened up a locked box of memories that she wasn't all that into looking through, anymore.

"Is there anyone worth loving, anyway?" Stevia asked Madame. "Anyone who can help me get where I want to go in life?"

"You want love for all the wrong reasons, and you crave all the wrong things. Those kind of wishes will never be answered without harsh repercussions, so severe you'll wish you never wished for them in the first place."

It wasn't what she wanted to hear, that was for certain.

Her phone buzzed again. This time Auggie was begging her, promising he'd do anything for her if she could come help him out with a "situation." She was curious to see what he wanted so urgently. He hadn't been in touch for a while, the longest gap since they'd started seeing each other. It made him more desirable to her, which bothered her to no end; another silly paradox that proved her achingly-human nature.

But nothing kept the mind and body younger than sex. Even a witch knew that.

She headed over to Auggies.

AUGGIE BREAKMIRRORS

"Ca-cawww! Ca-cawww!"

"Piss off, you damn bird!"

Auggie was pissed off. During the Venice Pier portion of their afternoon walk, Cackles the cursed seagull had latched onto Auggie and Rusty. It was understood through local folklore that whomever the gull latched on to would fall victim to hard times. The ugly bird trumpeted his terrible caws of doom while hovering over him and his poor dog, thoroughly creeping them both out. Fishermen pointed and clucked at them sympathetically while the gull's grim shrieking painted everything with a dark and ominous foreboding.

This had never happened to Auggie before. It seemed his easygoing luck was turning rotten.

Auggie had already been hesitant to get his green juice. He was feeling strange about the date with Griselda the night before. There wasn't the fun vibe he'd expected. She'd come along on his party bus ride, sure, and it had gotten pretty crazy, as it usually did. The problem was that she hadn't seemed all that comfortable with it.

He didn't disagree that the mostly-male crew of young partiers were being somewhat obnoxious, but that was part of Auggie's job as a party bus driver – to make a safe space for obnoxious. In Auggie's head, he was preventing the inevitable bar fights they would have gotten into if they'd been out in public in their condition. He'd hoped Griselda would be able to at least laugh at them, but instead she'd been disgusted and started ranting about Americans and how uncivilized they were, how stupid they were to elect obnoxious, incompetent presidents who ruined their country, how they deserved their shitty, backwards systems and so it figured they now had to be governed by robots.

Make no mistake – she was touching a lot of the same ground that Auggie himself felt inside, but when a foreigner said it, he was surprised to find it offensive.

By the time Auggie dropped the guys off at their "end stop," one of the many overpriced hotels in Santa Monica, Griselda claimed to be exhausted and had asked to go home. Auggie hadn't gotten the invite in, either. He was pretty surprised she'd been that rigid. He'd taken her for a wild thing, perhaps even a secret sex dungeon dominatrix. And why wouldn't he? She was always talking about his sex life.

But then again, she worked at Venice Peach, a juice and smoothie shop, an establishment devoted to health and wellness. Just because she registered as sex to Auggie didn't mean she partied and screwed like a rabbit. Also, he was aware that The Zebra wasn't exactly a "chick magnet." He'd really only met a few girls who'd been turned on by his gaudy bus, and they'd been in college, which meant they were very undateable but totally screwable.

He stood across the street from the juice stand, wondering what he really wanted from life, who he was really looking for. Once, in Afghanistan, he'd fallen for a woman whose eyes were her only visible body part. He'd told her he would take care of her – not that she could understand him – because that was suddenly all he really wanted to do with the rest of his life, and the words had come out as if erupting from his soul. Then they'd been separated in a raid and he had never seen her again. He'd seen her scarf, a unique pattern of orange and black, caught on a fence post somewhere on the edge of the village. It stuck like a splinter in his memory, resurfacing in times of pain, a reminder that no matter how you felt about people, no one was able to keep anyone else safe, even a soldier in the all-powerful U.S. Army.

Auggie shook his head. Why the hell was he thinking about that again? He had a headache now, and to make himself feel better, juice would have to enter his body one way or another. His options were to walk all the way over to Main Street to get one, or to be brave and test the waters in Griselda's joint. He stood there in the alley, staring at Venice Peach while stuck in analysis paralysis, as Cackles drifted noisily above him. As if on cue, Griselda exited the storefront holding a sandwich. She immediately looked toward the squawking gull and saw Auggie standing there in his indecision. She waved hesitantly and Auggie swore under his breath as he launched towards her, Rusty trailing behind.

"Hey, there," he said. "Break time?"

"Yes," she said, taking a seat on a low, wide ledge to the side of the store. "I'm starving."

"Please eat," he said. Cackles squawked loudly right above them. They both looked up in annoyance. "Damn it, Cackles, leave me alone already!"

Griselda observed him gravely. "I have heard of this Cackles. You must be in for some hard times." She took a big bite of her sandwich and chewed thoughtfully. "Isn't that the deal?"

"Fuck that," Auggie said coarsely. "I've had enough hard times for my lifetime. I'm devoted to living the peachful life—I meant *peaceful*. This sonofabitch bird has latched onto the wrong guy." He bent down, picked up a crumpled paper cup off the ground, and hurled it at the gull. Cackles easily batted away the trash with one wing from his perch on the roof above. He squawked again, a low, abrasive, rattling sound, and looked Auggie right in the eye.

"He's looking at you," Griselda said, seeming sympathetic and amused at the same time. "It's like he wants to kill you. Peck your eyes out or something."

Thank you, Princess Obvious, Auggie thought, just wanting her to shut up and eat her damn sandwich so she could get to making his juice. Her stoic expression was making him even more anxious. Was she trying to push his buttons? Punish him for being a stupid American? He bit his tongue, wincing as he tasted blood.

"Well, I'll let you finish your break in peace," he said with a note of finality.

Cackles chose that moment to make a dive for Griselda's sandwich. He swooped in like a bolt of dirty white lightning, scoring the entire top slice of bread. Rusty, sensing the chaos, started barking at a fire hydrant.

"You little fuck-faced fucker!" Auggie snarled as Cackles flew back onto the roof of the juice shack. He hurled a crumpled beer can up at the ratty bird, who merely hopped out of the way as he started to choke down the enormous slice of stolen bread.

Griselda looked dejectedly down at her now open-faced sandwich.

"What an asshole, that bird."

"Let me buy you another sandwich," Auggie offered.

"No, no," Griselda said, "I'll be fine. You should get your juice and get on your way."

They went inside. Griselda wordlessly began to make Auggie's juice.

"I'm sorry you didn't have fun last night," Auggie said to break the tense silence. "It's not for everyone. I wish I'd taken you out somewhere nice."

"It's fine," Griselda said curtly as she finished up the juice in record time. "Here you go."

Auggie bowed his head, slapped the money on the counter, and left.

Cackles was waiting out front, the hideous, thieving, woman-repelling troll of an animal.

"Well, come on then, you nasty little tag-a-long," Auggie snarled, trudging home with blind Rusty leading the way and crazy Cackles trailing behind them, spewing his glass-shattering songs of ruin.

When Auggie got back to his house, he had the unmistakable urge to have sex. He texted Stevia, even though it was a bit earlier than he usually hit her up. She didn't respond. Cackles cackled dubiously from outside his open living room window, perched on a low branch of an orange tree. Auggie hurled a mason jar at the bird and missed him, smashing his favorite succulent in the process.

He was tempted to get out his Glock 9.

Then his phone rang. It was an unfamiliar number, as were most of the numbers that called him. That was part of running his own business.

He answered in a huff.

"Hello, Zebra Party Bus line."

"Oh, um, is this August Breakmirrors ?"

"Who is this?"

"We need to confirm that this is, in fact, August Breakmirrors, before we go any further."

"What's this about?"

"Can you please just state your address and birthdate before we discuss the purpose of this call, sir?"

"Screw that. I'm not giving my information out to anyone who calls."

He heard a rustling over the line. Someone in the background was saying something that sounded like "he's a vet," and it sounded like someone else said, "it's the guy."

"Who *is* this?!" he shouted into the phone. "I can hear you talking about me."

"This is the Federal Bureau of the Restoration of America calling. You have been selected randomly by our algorithm to participate in the Interview Tour of 2029, which includes a sit-down discussion with President TBD 3000. Do you accept this call to civic duty?"

Auggie stared out the window, right into Cackles' cold, beady little eyes.

"Well I'll be damned. Of course I get this call today. What's the catch? Will there be implanting of any surveillance devices? Will I have to be sequestered for days?"

"No, of course not, Mr. Breakmirrors. It's simply a recorded conversation over coffee and pastries where you can share your opinions on the state of the union since we elected to be governed by robots. We're interested in hearing opinions from all walks of life to better strengthen our algorithms and recreate the American Dream."

"There's no bringing back the good old days," Auggie muttered as he slipped Rusty a treat from the dog cookie jar.

"Please save your commentary for the interview. I will disclose to you that we're particularly interested in your opinions regarding the decline of the full-time job, the services provided by rocobocos, and the disintegration of traditional relationship structures such as marriage and children."

"I have plenty to say about all of that," Auggie said gruffly. "And much more."

"Glad to hear it, sir. Your appointment is set for next Tuesday, 12 o'clock noon, at the U.S. Bank Tower. We'll email you the details as well as the non-disclosure agreement. Please bring a valid form of ID."

"More valid than my own face?" Auggie retorted, wincing as Cackles cried bloody murder in the background.

He hung up and instantly felt morose. Exactly what kind of easy-peasy minute-made sell-out was he? Agreeing at first ask to participate in this strange government interview bullshit parade that he'd so stubbornly spoken against. His headache returned along with the shrieking of the damned dirty-ass sea bird. He struggled to slam shut the window that he hadn't tried to close in years, shattering the glass pane.

He stared down at the shards in dismay.

Stevia still hadn't gotten back, either. He might have to call in the call girls. *Fuck this goddamn motherfucking crappy change of luck,* he thought. He was almost ready to go drive his bus over a bridge into the concrete trough they called the LA River.

Suddenly, someone was knocking on the door. He snorted wildly, like a disrupted boar in the jungle. He caught a glimpse of his frizzy ponytail and wide eyes in the mirror and decided to answer the door anyway.

It was Stevia. She stared up at him with her giant cat eyes.

"What the hell happened to texting back first?"

Stevia absorbed his shattered state and immediately turned around.

"Wait! *Wait*, Stevia, no – please wait. I need you," he said, grabbing her wrist. She shook him off but turned around to face him at least. "I need you. It's been a screwed up day. Cackles decided to pick me as his subject of impending doom. Then I got a call that I was selected to do the Interview with TBD 3000 and I said yes because I felt important even though it's against everything in my moral fabric, and—"

"Stop," Stevia said, raising a finger to his lips to shush him.

Just then, Cackles let out a chorus of teeth-grinding death calls.

"Show me the bird," Stevia said flatly.

Auggie grabbed her hand and pulled her through the house to the side garden door. Cackles was still sitting in the bush. He took one look at Stevia, unleashed an utterly haunting and strangely melodic wail, and took off flying towards the sea.

Auggie stared at Stevia, who looked fiercely beautiful with her green eyes glowing in the sunset and her long, dark, wavy hair flowing freely around her face.

"Shit! How the hell did you do that?" he asked, tilting her face up with a finger to her chin. "Should I be scared of you, too?"

"I thought you already were," she said, a wry grin forming on her lips.

"Much more turned on than terrified, I'll tell you that right now," he said.

He scooped her up and brought her straight into the bedroom.

DR. PHILIP K. PARKER

"I see, I see. And why do you think your catastrophic thinking tends to fixate around your cat when you're not home?"

Marjorie Bateman's knitting needles clicked in her purse as she shifted on his couch, stewing it over. "Well, I think it all started back when I was a child and my beloved kitten went missing…"

There were a whole lot of problems in the world, and Philip Parker didn't give a damn about 99% of them. He'd stopped caring about the majority of things back when Fuckwad had first gotten elected. That was when his business had gone from a steady flow to a full-force flood, everyone relapsing and overdosing and crumbling in the inevitable decline of the country. There was no real consolation for those folk. When one woman claimed that Fuckwad was the embodiment of everything her childhood rapist had been, he couldn't argue with her. When a Mexican business man claimed that he'd rather return to his small hometown in Mexico to pluck chickens than be profiled by the racially-charged presidentially-backed immigration agents who'd been given full rights to shoot-to-kill anyone who simply looked "suspicious," Philip surely couldn't disagree.

The protests went on for months after Fuckwad had been elected, and then had a resurgence when he was reelected. Many were killed in protests that grew into riots until things had escalated into a full-blown civil war. Philip had worried about his only sibling, his sister, Rita, who was a very active activist from the start. Then she had been killed while protesting in Arizona by charged-up and emboldened Phoenix locals who had bull-dozed through the crowd with their 4X4 trucks.

Two months later, his wife had announced that she was having an affair with his best friend and leaving him. That was when Philip officially gave up on partaking in emotions altogether. He surrendered to the betraying nature of human beings, the crushingly individualistic, overwhelmingly capitalist society he lived in, and the numbness that the societal structure demanded in order to survive. He wanted nothing more to do with anything even slightly related to caring.

Marjorie Bateman was peering at him and he realized he was due to respond, but had absolutely no idea what she had said. His eyes watered as he stifled a gigantic yawn by shaking his head and feigning *sympathy*. "I can't imagine what that must have been like for you. Let me ask, what are some steps you think you can take to move on from this past trauma of yours?"

Philip made loads of money by pretending to care about others. Psychotherapists were in all-time high demand, and with his collection of ivy-league degrees, he didn't even have to worry about trying that hard. People could only come to their own conclusions, anyway. They just wanted a handsome, well-educated man to listen to their situation and nod every once in a while in a way that suggested understanding and sympathy. They wanted validation of their thoughts and actions, no matter what the cost.

Marjorie brushed a strand of her salt-and-pepper hair away from her face. Her eyes filled with tears. "The truth is, I don't think I'll ever move on from Henry leaving me."

Philip felt a stab of irritation and glanced at his clock. "Unfortunately, time's up for this week. We can dive into that next time."

"You seem relieved," Marjorie sniffled as she got up.

"No, no," Philip urged as he stood up, a bit flatter than he was going for. "You're just feeling very vulnerable at the moment. Please don't take it personally. I have to keep a tight schedule with so many patients."

The underlying truth was that it made his skin crawl to hear patients wail on and on about their ex-spouses. His own ex-wife had totally demolished him in strength, finances and spirit but you didn't see him ever crying about it to anyone. He didn't cry at all, in fact. His main problem in life seemed to be women. He needed to possess them sometimes in order to not feel totally alone and cold. But they seemed to pick up on his calculating cerebral politics, his utter lack of passion. If there was anywhere in which he tried, it was in the bedroom, when the occasional woman was foolish enough to go to bed with a dead fish such as himself. But even then it was not enough to stimulate him, the connection far too weak for Philip to be satisfied and stay in the moment. He'd drift, it would turn mechanical, and often he'd give up before climaxing.

Philip's love life was, as former President Fuckwad had haphazardly called everything, "a disaster." And as it turned out, calling something a disaster did little to solve it. Philip was on all the dating apps and still running out of options. Oh, how he longed for just one woman who could be exciting enough mentally to get him off, but who also wouldn't try to get any emotion out of him.

Then he thought he'd finally found the perfect balance in Cassandra, but unbelievably, she didn't seem that into him. The kiss had been good, hadn't it? He'd enjoyed it. He wanted her. He wanted her in a way he hadn't wanted anyone in a long, long time.

And yet she seemed, if he was being entirely honest with himself, totally uninterested.

But that was impossible. He was a handsome fucker. He was a "catch."

He took his steak salad out to the back courtyard and stared at his phone, rereading the messages they'd exchanged on the app before meeting. She hadn't offered him her phone number when she'd said goodbye, and he'd been too keyed up to think to ask for it. He contemplated sending her a message now:

Get home ok? Obviously. He'd walked her to her door.

Had a great time the other night! Also obvious, the real question was did *she* have a great time last night? But if you had to ask…

Plans this weekend? Still somehow too much. Too needy. Too vague.

Ugh. This girl had turned him into a goddamn girl.

It was suddenly an unfortunate thing he didn't have friends. He used to, before his divorce. And his former best friend, whom he would never mention by name again, fucked him over by fucking his wife. Whatever. He hadn't needed company that much, anyway. He wasn't interested in friendship, really. He could be his own best friend. He was good at that.

Except for right now. Right now, he needed friendly advice. Not that he'd necessarily take it, but even Philip realized the value of an occasional outside opinion. Especially when it came to subjects he wasn't exactly an expert in, like women.

He did have one acquaintance he thought to contact. A local cycling gang's leader, Jim Berrigan. Jim was a straight-laced lawyer, highly intelligent, the type of guy Philip would actually consider having as a friend, had he a burning desire to have friends.

Which he didn't. He merely wanted some advice.

Four clients later and Philip was on a bike ride to meet Jim down in Manhattan Beach. It was overcast and a bit chilly, and there were very few people out on the bike path. He made it there in great time and got comfortable at the bar, ordering a dry gin martini with two olives. Instead of looking at his phone, he opted to look around. To him, the faces of Manhattan Beach looked inbred-level rich, lasered, dermabrasioned, manicured, and botoxed all the way into stoic, puffy, creaseless masks. That's what they looked like to Philip, masked demons. That was why he couldn't leave Venice, no matter how much money he earned. The people there didn't look like frozen assholes. They still looked like characters, quirky and striking in original ways. No matter how gentrified the town got, they would never be able to fully remove the true, salty grit of the Venice Beach underbelly. The town was built on its own brand of carnival boardwalk shadiness, the roots of which were too deep for the vines of affluence to completely overtake. Philip took relief in the fact that living in Venice was so cool in itself that he didn't have to worry about being cool in other ways. Plus, his ex-wife had always been too snobby to like it there, so he knew he'd never run into her.

He stared out the window as a rocoboco rolled up the side of the street, scanning meters and plates and printing parking tickets. He snorted. Manhattan Beach rocobocos had it easy. They probably only once in a hundred weeks had to chase an actual crime suspect. Everyone was so homogenous, so clean, so *in line*. He'd never find a Cassandra in Manhattan Beach. She'd be bored in a second. His ex-wife, on the other hand, he was suddenly nervous about running into.

His eyes darted around to see Jim enter the bar, a tanned, well-built man with a judgmental-looking set of thick eyebrows. His eyes showed recognition upon meeting Philip's, but his facial expression remained blank. The men nodded at each other.

He sat down on the stool next to Philip, flooding him with the scent of lavish man soap.

"You smell outstanding, Jim."

"Thanks, Phil. I use this stuff called *Riche Trou Du Cul*. It's Parisian. You can get it online."

Philip made a note of the name in his phone as Jim nodded at the bartender, who was waiting patiently like a dog who smelled a money bone.

"Hennessey Richard on the rocks."

So the man drank like a king. Philip wasn't that surprised, and yet suddenly he felt shabby holding his lukewarm martini. Good god, Manhattan Beach was too much for him. He polished it off and said, "I'll have the same."

Jim clapped Philip on the back, causing him to almost choke on his mouthful of tepid gin.

"How ya been, Phil? I haven't seen you on any of the group rides lately."

"I know, it's a shame. I've been extraordinarily busy."

"That may well be, but don't try to pretend you see clients at 5am."

Philip sighed. This was why he didn't have friends.

"I've been doing my rides in the evening. It's the better time for me."

"Well, go on two rides a day. I bet you'll feel twice as good."

"Maybe, Jim. I'll give it a shot."

"Glad to hear it. We're also getting a sailing group together on Sundays, if you want in."

"Really? I usually have a few things, but that might occasionally work," Philip forced himself to say, though the thought of being stuck on a boat with a bunch of pompous bastards already made him feel exhausted. "Keep me in the loop."

"Will do," Jim said, taking a slow sip of the drink set in front of him. "So, what's happening, Philip? You've never reached out before. Great timing on your part, by the way. My plans for tonight had fallen through right before you messaged me."

"Yeah, it's kind of embarrassing, actually," Philip said, sipping his cognac. It was exceptionally smooth, as promised. "Are you married, Jim?"

"Twice divorced," Jim said immediately. "So, women troubles? Lay it out for me. I've got enough experience for the both of us."

"I have plenty of experience as well," Philip said, perhaps a little too quickly. He made a mental note to unclench. "It's just that I'm having trouble finding someone who meets both my mental and physical standards. It's unfortunate that the scales are almost always tipping in one direction or the other, isn't it?"

"Wait, are you looking to be in a relationship?" Jim shook his head and frowned. "Monogamy's finally a thing of the past, Phil. We're free of those binding times. No one actually entertains the kind of silly notions of true love or soulmates anymore—"

"I'm not looking for a relationship," Philip interrupted firmly.

"Then what are you talking about?"

"I'm just sick of dating wallflowers," Philip said, exasperated. "I seem to be cursed with the inability to… This is hard for me to say… I can't get that, ahem, excited about sleeping with someone who has the mental equivalency of a chicken."

Jim laughed dryly. "You're not kidding. They sure make them dumber than they used to. I blame early screen immersion. They're out there raising zombies these days. I'm glad I don't have kids. I'd probably hate them."

"I feel the same way. I don't know how to identify with most adults anymore, and yet that's my job. And now, with TBD 3000 running the country better than any human ever has, I have literally no hope that we'll ever return to a time in which people do hard thinking themselves—at least successfully."

"Agreed. But you really can't find anyone half-decent on one of the apps? Are you trying hard enough? Are you on the new ones?"

"Yes. Believe me. And I did recently find one woman. I went out with her this week. She's fantastic, Jim. She's gorgeous and surprising and makes me feel things I haven't felt in years."

"Sounds like the good kind of trouble. So what's the problem?"

"She didn't invite me in at the end of the night. And she didn't give me her phone number. It's almost like… she wasn't that into me."

"Phil, I have to say, you're sounding awfully insecure about this."

Philip hung his head in his hands and exhaled. "I know, I know, I'm sorry. This is truly unlike me. I just need help thinking of a good follow-up message. I can't come up with anything. I feel like an idiot. Just a total waste of space." He nearly choked while slamming back his drink.

Jim looked concerned. "Slow down, that stuff is too good to be slugged. Get yourself together. I'll help you. Show me the thread."

Philip got out his phone. He pressed the screen and the message exchange was right there, awaiting more scrupulous speculation. He shook his head, shoved the phone into Jim's hands and awaited his sentence.

"Sweet Christ, Phil. What's the drama about? There's nothing here."

"I know, it's just, what comes next? I can't craft a sentence that sounds OK to me."

Jim squinted into the phone. "I don't think someone's asked me for this kind of advice since… high school? Makes me feel like a teenager again. My advice would probably be the same as it was then. Just keep it simple. Think of an activity she'd enjoy doing, and invite her to do it with you. If she says no, she's not interested."

Philip's face grew red. "I don't know what she likes doing."

"Then ask her to a movie. Everyone likes going to the movies."

"I hate the movies. The new immersive screens make me dizzy."

Jim laughed. "Well, old man, you might be beyond help, then. I can't make you think of a good date idea. I always stick to the same formula. It works for me. I take them to my tapas spot, order plenty of wine, then walk along the pier while holding hands and asking them about themselves. Never. Fucking. Fails. Romance is our greatest weapon, my friend. Most people think it's dead, and when you pull it out, it's like a magic trick."

Philip stared at Jim. "Thanks."

He took his phone back and typed the words effortlessly.

Gondola ride in the canals tomorrow night?

He paid for their exorbitantly overpriced drinks and told Jim he'd see him bright and early the following morning. Then he went home and researched renting a gondola/gondolier, or at least someone who could convincingly pose as one. He did not set his alarm for 4:40AM before he went to sleep.

CASSANDRA PANDA

Blah. Cassandra understood why nobody wanted to indulge in the feeling of love anymore. It was a serious nuisance. Especially when love was inspired by someone who was living with you. It felt like her nervous system was under attack at all times. Did everyone get this insecure? Maybe Gio was right, maybe it wasn't love, but some torturous, lusty crush that had nothing to do with anything but sexual chemistry. She could barely eat. She worried about her flaws under a whole new set of microscopes. She marveled at the human brain's capacity to manipulate reality, overanalyzing moments they'd shared until they'd grown iconic in her mind, like self-generated award-worthy sizzle reels. She probably meant nothing to Gerard. Less than nothing. At best, her title credit was *Another Pretty Housemate.* She seemed to be losing weight by the hour. No amount of deep twists in yoga poses could remove the tension from her chest, which felt like someone was sitting on it ninety-seven percent of the day. The remaining three percent of the time was short yet glorious relief provided by orgasms sponsored by her mind's very own Gerard Vice fantasy reel. Her whole being was glitching. Her heart wanted off the crazy roller coaster, thudding against her rib cage sporadically, trying to bust through—or at least commit suicide in the process.

She barely even knew this guy. *What the hell?*

She received a message from Gio right as she was going to temporarily delete her dating apps because she was nervous about Gerard coming across her profile and thinking she was some easy piece shacked up on easy street. She was even becoming stupidly self-conscious of her cyber image. Truly pitiful.

Gio had invited her to go on a gondola ride on the canals. It was an odd choice for a second date, but she considered that it would be good to take a break from sitting around wondering what Gerard was up to. He'd been getting home really late, recently. His schedule was all over the place.

Maybe the date with Gio could make him jealous.

But of course that wasn't why she agreed to Gio's gondola proposition, adding her phone number to the message before deleting the app. She briefly wondered if that meant it would delete the note before he received it, but she found that she barely cared.

Baby Grand had a riotous rehearsal that afternoon, and Cassandra was feeling fully pumped about their next Venice Peach show. The only real control she felt over anything was at the microphone down in that speakeasy. She was dialed in, if only for the desire to show Gerard how ridiculously well she could wail. She wished she was motivated by higher thoughts than that at the moment, but unfortunately, she was only human.

Meanwhile, she plotted ways in which she could get Gerard down under the bridge so that Bobobo could read his mind. She hadn't been able to catch him for any significant chunk of time, recently. It seemed he was always in transit. Or was he avoiding her? It would take a small miracle to pull off getting him down there without it seeming weird or creepy. What possible excuse could she give him for joining her under a bridge late at night? And then she thought of it: She could claim to have lost her phone and to need another phone to find it.

With that temporarily settled, she began deciding on her gondola ride outfit.

Gio picked her up at 8:00pm sharp, picnic basket in hand, hair crisply gelled, cardigan sweater folded neatly around his shoulders. Cassandra could hardly stifle a laugh, he looked so classic. And also weirdly like a man on a serious mission to end her virginity.

"Wow. Who says romance is dead?"

"Good evening, Cassandra." He took her hand and kissed it.

"A little over the top, isn't it?"

He raised an eyebrow and smiled. "I promise it won't hurt."

She threw her head back. "Oh, why not?" she asked the Venice sky.

They walked across a foot bridge over the canal and around a corner to reveal a fancy black gondola with gold trim and an appropriately-uniformed goncolier awaiting them in the water. Cassandra could scarcely register the sight as real. She'd been on plenty of dates, but already this was by far the strangest and most surreal.

"This is for us?!"

"Yes. Just something I came across last minute and thought you might enjoy."

Cassandra stared at the setup and gondolier in wonder.

"All my years of living on these canals, and I've never seen anything like this."

Maybe tonight was finally the night. Maybe she could finally scratch the giant, gnawing itch and move on with her life. Maybe then, Gerard would sense that she was finally open for business and get in line.

Gio got into the gondola first to be a proper gentleman and assist her in the transfer from tiny dock to gondola. Then she was sitting in an actual gondola on a canal just down the way from her house. What a trip Venice continued to be. The gondolier switched on the speaker and soft Italian music warmed the cool, ocean-adjacent air.

Gio smiled more authentically than Cassandra had seen before and started unpacking his picnic basket, which contained wine, cheese, crackers, grapes and figs. A few of her neighbors walked by, gawking at the display. Cassandra stared down at the water and was glad she'd worn her black wide-brimmed hat. It made her harder to recognize.

"This is really something," she said softly as they floated by her favorite giant tree with lanterns strung throughout the strong, long branches that reached out over the canal.

"I'm glad you enjoy it," Gio said. "I have to tell you something." He paused and she felt anxious, hoping for a lighter confession than it sounded. He squinted into the sunset and sighed. "My name is actually Philip. I use a fake name on the app like you but for different reasons. I don't want my clients finding me there. I don't know why I didn't come clean in the beginning like you did. I was nervous the whole date that someone would recognize me."

Cassandra nodded, relieved. "It's OK, Philip. You should have told me sooner, but thanks for letting me know in such a romantic and restrictive setting that I couldn't possibly be upset and storm off about it."

They both laughed. "It's like you see right through to me," he said, on a more serious note. "Which is unnerving but intriguing at the same time."

Cassandra dipped a few fingers in the water, then thought twice, pulled out, sniffed, frowned, and reached for a hand wipe that Philip had thoughtfully brought along. "The canal water is so rancid. I can't believe animals can still survive in it." She looked back at him, something sparking in her eyes. "Wait, so this just occurred to me: Now you're *Doctor Phil,* psychological cyclist?"

"I know, it's a funny coincidence."

"It's hilarious," she said. Neither of them laughed.

When they crossed under the Dell bridge, Cassandra heard a tinkling sound.

-Is this him, my land princess?

Cassandra looked over at Phil, alarmed.

"What? What's wrong?" he asked.

"No! Nothing, I mean."

-*No, Bobobo,* she thought, trying to look like she was really taken with the scenery she looked at every single day. Philip kept his eyes on her.

-*This one is in love with you,* Bobobo echoed in her head.

"Oh, crap," she said out loud.

"Forget something?" Philip asked.

"No, no, I'm fine," she said.

Philip's brow creased. "Do you hear… a wind chime or something?"

"Nope," she said quickly.

-*Bobobo, I love you but I'll chat with you later. I can't communicate with you both. It's too confusing.*

-*I get it. Let's just hope the other guy loves you like this one, then it would be a perfect match.*

She sighed. Philip took her hand. His hand wasn't that soft or warm. She stiffened and felt stifled. Now this distraction date had really taken a turn for the worse. If only she could get out of it. But after all the effort he'd gone to… *Ugh.* So she was hardly interested in him and he was in *love* with her? Wasn't that just the way it always shook out, though. When she thought about it, it was just another of the many dumb reasons the world population was shrinking.

Cassandra wished she could just get over the whole thing. Go back to the days when no one was in love with anybody. Seemed like those days were just a week ago. Who knew? The tension was at least proving fruitful for her songwriting.

As if sensing the tension, the gondolier abruptly switched the soundtrack from Italian love songs to fast-paced action music, snapping her out of her thoughts. He threw his head back and laughed a deep, dark, sinister laugh. The whole sky blinked and darkened like a deep simulation glitch. She looked around to realize with slow, slithering horror that they weren't in the same Venice canals anymore. It was as if a time bomb had exploded, leaving fire and chaos everywhere. Flames raked through the insides of sleek, ultra-modern houses on either side of them, shattering and spilling out through the wall-sized windows and knocking down oversize doors. Screams echoed out over the dark canal water that now glowed a Dead Sea green. A rocoboco appeared out of nowhere and opened fire on a family fleeing their house. They crumpled and fell over onto the lawn. No sirens wailed anywhere nearby, promising no rescue. A helicopter emerged from over a rooftop and shot at the armed rocoboco who had taken aim at their gondola, then the helicopter exploded due to being shot up by a giant drone that swooped in behind it.

Cassandra had only one thought through her panic: They had entered Hell.

"Where did you find this guy?!?" she whispered to Philip, who was watching the scene unfold with quiet terror in his eyes. Neither of them had screamed. They were holding hands again, which Cassandra didn't have time to think about.

"He answered my post on the DoitRight App. He had an impressive resume. He said he used to be a real gondolier in Italy—"

"Did you check his references?" Cassandra hissed.

Philip shook his head slowly. "I'm so sorry."

Neither of them had actually heard him speak previously, and when his voice came out it was strongly accented.

"Lady and gentleman, welcome to Hector's Hellbound Gondola ride. I hope you did not ingest any psychedelics before embarking on this ride. I guess this big romantic date really turned out to be hell, didn't it?" To his own joke he laughed a terrible laugh.

"Um, Hector, I might interject right here to say I didn't actually request the 'Hellbound Gondola' ride—" Philip began.

"It doesn't matter if you want it or not! You are getting it! You must witness what will become of our world if we continue to let it be ruled by robots! There is no going back once the Artificial Intelligence Anarchy begins! We are all doomed!"

A couple of ragged-looking women wielding kitchen knives crossed to the right, dodging crumbling, flaming chunks of housing. One of them stuck her knife right into a rocoboco's fat data head as it lunged at her; a sparking, sizzling, masterful and murderous chef's move. Philip and Cassandra watched in awed horror as what looked like a giant President TBD 3000 rolled up behind a flaming house, an American flag clutched in its titanium hand. The robot slowly lowered it and lit it on fire from the flames of the house.

"DELETE USA," TBD 3000 said in its booming automated voice. "MUST DELETE USA…" Lasers shot out of each of its "eyes," tearing up the water both in front and back of their gondola. The robotic president turned slightly and fired at the women across the way, who dodged behind a bush that immediately ignited in blue-hot flames.

Cassandra closed her eyes and smothered a scream in her throat.

Please, Bobobo, help us! Are you here?! Help if you can!

There was no answer. Nothing echoed in her brain but pure panic.

Philip stood up. "Hector, that's enough. You're doing irreversible psychological damage to your passengers. End this right now or I'll sue you to smithereens."

Hector grinned, displaying a gap-filled crooked pair of front teeth.

"I'm not sue-able, you idiot. You clearly signed my contract without reading it. I'm also unsearchable, and you'll never find me again. I am only showing you the future as a gift. Consider yourselves *BLESSED* to have seen this and carry on as you see fit."

The super-sized President TBD 3000 turned its attention on the boat, its mechanical "eyes" whirring in and out as if hyper-focusing on them. Cassandra clung to Philip, smelling his scent, which was as delicious a scent as she'd ever smelled on a man, to her great surprise. TBD 3000 then shot blue lasers at them and the gondola went up in flames. Philip grabbed her and they dove into the glowing Dead-Sea-green canal waters as the gondolier started chanting in a strange language.

"BLACGHEPH!!! AHSUCVHEJN!!! CHAUSGHBGH!!!!"

Cassandra and Philip opened their eyes to find they lay crumpled like frat party beer cans on the canal bank, seemingly back in "regular reality" Venice. They looked at each other. Philip gently removed a clod of slime from Cassandra's shoulder. A chunk of what could be either cheese or dry wall was stuck to Philip's hair and Cassandra brushed it off tenderly. Then they collapsed in relieved giggles, the laughter eventually becoming so convulsive it turned silent. Their bodies twisted with hysteria on the pebbles and sludge shore line. A frizzy-haired man walking what appeared to be a blind dog paused on the sidewalk above them.

"You guys OK down there?"

"Yeah!" Cassandra managed to choke out. "We just saw the future and we're just so relieved we don't have children."

"She's kidding," Philip choked through his laughter. "We just fell into the grossest water in existence and are having a moment."

"It's not *that* bad," the man with a frizzy ponytail said. "Ducks live in it."

His dog sniffed the air and let out a low growl.

"Thanks, goodnight," Philip said quickly, turning away. "Shit, that's my client," he whispered to Cassandra. "Good thing I'm so destroyed right now that he can't tell it's me." They went back to laughing at the biggest inside joke ever.

Cassandra had no choice but to invite Philip in to wash up. No one could be as cold as to send someone home with canal crust all over them. Anyway, Gerard didn't appear to be home. The two survivors stepped into the shower together, washing the muck off of each other until they no longer smelled too gross to avoid touching each other, which led to a very competitive blow-job tournament in which they both tied for first place.

"Do you have protection?" Cassandra asked as casually as she could, more ready to see her "flower" off than ever.

Philip bit his lip and looked down at her in the steamy shower. "I don't know," he said slowly. "As much as I'm tempted, and I very much am, I'm not sure it's right, me taking advantage of the survivor's lust by sleeping with you. It's against my morals."

She internally cursed her own bad luck and couldn't get out of the shower fast enough.

Cassandra let Philip borrow an assortment of clothes that previous male tenants had left behind. He sure looked different in cargo shorts, a ripped surf brand tee, and flip flops. Cassandra thought it was a vast improvement, especially with shower-tousled hair. She kissed him goodbye very generously at the doorstep. Even though she now resented him, she wanted to make him really regret his "moral" decision to turn her down.

Then she went to make some tea, trying to be content with simply being alive.

It was only when Gerard came home to find her in the usual living room spot, strumming her ukulele, that she realized she no longer had to lie.

"Oh, *crap!*"

"What is it?"

"I just realized I lost my phone somewhere in the canals."

GERARD VICE

It was the reason that he loved bouncing between the two best cities in America: He never knew what he'd end up doing any given Saturday night. Like now, for example, he was combing the canals of Venice with a flashlight and his pretty, temporary housemate, helping her look for her phone while completely drunk.

And earlier, he'd received the greatest news of his life and then had the most embarrassing moment of his life. Jimmy had sent him a cryptic text to "dress sharp as hell" and grab a bottle before taking an auto-cab straight to a mysterious residential address.

Gerard had put on his best cool celebrity guy suit and asked no questions. He rolled up to an astonishingly luxurious pad in the hills and Jimmy ran out to greet him as he climbed out of the car with a bottle of wine in hand.

"You should have brought champagne!" his agent shrilled.

"Damn it, you said wine was fine," Gerard grumbled.

"Yeah, but that was BEFORE I HEARD YOU GOT THE PART! Or *parts*, that is! You handsome hotshot!"

"ARE YOU FUCKING KIDDING ME?!" Gerard shouted in his drunken agent's face. "Please, do NOT fuck with me about this!!"

"Why do you think you got the invite to this *A-list dinner party at Vikki V's house?*"

Gerard went sheet-white for a second, staring at his agent's flushed face.

"It's really happening," he whispered.

"You're goddamn right it is!!" Jimmy bellowed. "Now let's get the hell inside and celebrate!"

Gerard followed Jimmy through the gigantic estate to the back patio, where a man was hard at work at a hibachi and there were beautiful cocktails being served at the poolside bar. Gerard could scarcely look around as he was suddenly so deep in his lifelong dream he was afraid if he examined anything too closely it would turn out to actually be a dream, and he'd wake up with a flinch.

Vikki V, one of the most famous and beautiful actress/singer/models in the world, and about 20 years Gerard's senior, made her way over to them wearing a long, flowing, glittering low-cut dress. Gerard felt his heart rate skyrocket from the jet fuel of adrenaline her stare ignited in him. She moved like a queen, gliding on impossible heels with an ease only an experienced and talented woman could pull off.

"Here she comes, Miss America," Jimmy sang.

Gerard slapped his agent on the arm. Vikki V rolled her eyes.

"Jimmy, would you be a doll and fix me one of your famous Manhattans?"

Jimmy almost tripped and fell into the pool in his haste to accommodate Vikki V's request. As soon as he was out of earshot, Vikki gave Gerard a once over that he felt from head to toe.

"You must be Gerard," Vikki said. "Jimmy was telling me all about you. But I must say, he did not even do you justice."

"Hehe, thank you. It's a pleasure and an honor, Vikki. *Gold Horizons* made me want to be an actor. And started a bit of a thing for you as a 12-year-old, I gotta admit." He swallowed thickly. Had he really just had the bravado to say that out loud?

"Well that's always nice to hear," Vikki said smoothly, like she heard those words every single day of her life. And Gerard realized she probably did. "Especially from someone as talented as Jimmy says you are."

She put her hand on his shoulder and slowly ran it down his arm, causing him total body chills. "So, you ready for the big leagues, Gerard?"

He stared at her, wide eyed and mute. Something dropped in his stomach, and fear invaded him on an almost inhuman level. He felt paralyzed. Vikki's brow furrowed as Gerard gaped at her like he'd gone dumb.

Thankfully, at that moment Jimmy returned holding three Manhattans which he'd spilled most of on his clumsy route back from the bar. He took in the strange dynamic as he handed Gerard and Vikki their drinks.

"I heard Slim Tim say he was going to throw some VegBurgs on because he doesn't eat meat," Jimmy said to Vikki.

"Oh, I will murder him!" Vikki said, taking off towards a crowd over by the grill.

Jimmy stared at Gerard. "Why do I feel like I just had to rescue you from the most beautiful woman at this party?"

Gerard shrugged and forced a laugh. "I have no idea what you're talking about."

The dinner party proceeded with lots of shallow conversation and congratulations, the meeting of faces Gerard recognized and felt he already knew through their work. Everything was surreal, and Vikki had not attempted to talk to him again after the weird freeze he'd experienced at her come on. He felt disappointed in himself, a deep shame brewing for reasons he could not pinpoint, and told Jimmy he had to get going as other guests began to filter out.

When he reached for his coat in the coat closet, a slender and well-manicured hand enclosed around his wrist.

"You're not leaving already, are you?" Vikki V tugged at him gently.

"Come on, I have to show you something before you leave."

Gerard felt himself surrender to her grasp, and she pulled him down the hallway, past a silent Jimmy who watched them with bemused fascination as they entered Vikki's bedroom.

Vikki steered him past her gigantic bed over to a shelf of awards. He stared at them, still unable to speak.

"They used to mean something," she said quietly.

"They still do," Gerard found himself able to say.

"Not really, not anymore," Vikki said hollowly. "They just show my age. But I thought maybe you'd be inspired by them."

"I am," he responded, not too convincingly.

She moved behind him and he felt her arms circle around his waist. The scent of her extraordinary French perfume invaded his nostrils and he tried not to stiffen. She brought her mouth up close to his ear.

"Your heart is racing."

"I'm… nervous," he managed to get out.

"Nervous? Or scared?"

Both?"

In one swift movement, Vikki pushed him down onto her bed. She reached up and untied the dress from behind her neck, exposing her still-perky and beautiful breasts. Then she climbed on top of him and kissed his neck slowly, hungrily, while moving her hands from his chest down, down to between his legs. Finding nothing happening there, she pushed off of him angrily and hastily retied her dress, fuming.

"You should really get that checked out. Famous people have to be able to fuck. That's non-negotiable."

"It's… never happened to me before," Gerard said pitifully.

"Are you saying it's *me*?"

"No! God, no. You're unbelievable. It's… something else. I'm not sure what. I'm sorry. I'm so, so sorry." His voice cracked as if he was about to cry.

Vikki's face softened just slightly. "Poor baby. I know better than anyone that being on the brink of fame is a very overwhelming time. I know a really good psychologist. I'll refer you."

Gerard nodded gratefully and then got the hell out of there without another word.

When he got home, he'd felt kind of crazy and hadn't expected to run into Cassandra, who seemed in pretty loopy spirits too, an electrifying combination of frantic and giddy. He'd found her playing the ukulele like it was the end of the world, a crazed look on her face as she took his disheveled state in and simultaneously realized she'd lost her phone.

He wondered what it was about him that had reminded her.

Cassandra felt safe to him, though, so he'd gone with her to in turn keep her safe late at night in the canals. He could tell she was freshly showered. Her hair hung thick, dark and wavy down her back. Gerard was grateful that he'd just had a really weird sexual experience or he'd be feeling inclined to make a move on his housemate, which he knew was never a move that ended well. It seemed like she was always around, looking like sex, smelling like sex, draping like sex on an armchair or couch, batting her sexy eyes at him, strumming her sexy little ukulele.

At the same time, something about the idea of being with her also made him anxious. Something roared *stay away*. But he felt she was not going to pressure him while he was feeling so vulnerable.

"How did you lose your phone, again?"

"Ugh, it's a story that I'd rather not tell. But basically, I was on a date and we fell into the canals."

Gerard snorted with surprise, both from her explanation and the injection of jealousy he felt at the mention of a date. She smiled at his response and he rushed to cover it up with false concern.

"How the hell did you fall into the canals? Did he push you?"

"No, no. We both fell in. Or, I guess we kind of dove in, actually. As crazy as that sounds. It's a pretty wild story…" She trailed off, seeming unsure of how to tell it, like it was so out there that he wouldn't understand. Which only made him more jealous. She'd clearly had a more exciting night than even he'd had.

Cassandra called out, "Here, phone! Here phoney-woney phoneskins!"

He laughed. "That almost feels like it should work. Doesn't it have a tracker?"

"I tried. Nothing. It must be smashed, and/or dead in the water."

He wondered why they were even looking for it, then, as he shined the light around the underside of the Dell bridge. Cassandra grabbed his arm and started leading him down under the cement arch.

"Let's look closer, it could be under here."

When they were standing under the bridge Cassandra closed her eyes for a long moment. He wondered if she was:

a) batty and/or drunk;

b) trying to get him to kiss her;

c) attempting to remember where the capsize had happened, or even—

d) wondering if he loved her…

That last option had presented itself out of nowhere, in an odd inner intonation somewhat reminiscent of his grandfather's voice. Did he love her? No, probably not. That made no sense. He hardly knew her. He might be in *lust* with her, but love? Definitely not. A wind chime tinkled somewhere close by. Gerard looked around. He didn't feel any wind blowing.

Her eyes popped open after a long moment. She looked at him, disappointed.

"What's up?" He hoped that wasn't a failed attempt to get him to kiss her.

She sighed. "Nothing. I just thought… I had a hunch… but it didn't prove out."

"Huh? A hunch about your phone?"

"Never mind. There's actually no way my phone is worth looking for."

Was it his drunken imagination or did she seem a little crazy and also pouty? And how did she not remember where they'd fallen? Was she on drugs? He tried to assuage the situation by putting his hand on her shoulder, but felt awkward immediately and quickly removed it.

Gerard wanted to tell her that he'd just found out that he'd gotten the big part, but she seemed too preoccupied to be able to take good news at the moment. He often found that good news was harder to break than bad news. Most people in LA didn't really want to hear any news at all, he'd noticed. In New York, they only wanted to hear bad news, most likely in order to give them more reasons to pummel their minds with liquor and drugs. Most of the time, he operated on the simple principle of only putting forth information that was requested of him. It was the most accurate way to judge whether or not someone gave a shit. Always astounded him, though, how little people wanted to know about anyone else. They trusted him with sensitive information, had sex with him, decided they loved or hated him – all without really knowing jack shit about him.

In fact, those had all occurred before without even knowing his *name*.

Lights twinkled in the tiny ripples of the surface of the canal water. Cassandra turned to him abruptly.

"Let's just go home."

"Wait." He held her shoulders. She looked up at him, confused. He didn't know what he was doing, either. He took her face in his hands, brushed her hair away from her eyes. "Are you OK?"

She stared back, eyes shifting through emotions like a kaleidoscope.

"It was a hell of a night."

"I'm here now," he said, and kissed her forehead. The scent of her skin caused him to pause and breathe deeper. She tilted her head up more. He felt her magnets pulling him in. Deep down inner core magnets that pulled at his every—

No.

He pulled away. He repelled with every fiber of his being. He couldn't dip into something so strong when he was about to embark on a completely exhaustive schedule. He lived with her. He lived with her.

He lived with her.

It wasn't a very strong mantra when convenience was king.

Cassandra shook him off like a bad thought. She was clearly annoyed at the whole situation.

"You're being weird."

"I'm pretty drunk," he admitted.

"I can smell it," she said grudgingly enough that he wondered what else she could smell.

As Gerard lay in bed that night, he felt like he was getting fed through a woodchipper of anxiety. The feeling scared him, heading into the highest-pressure situation of his entire life. Memories were surfacing, distant and horrifying memories that felt like they could eat him alive. He knew instinctively if he didn't address what had just gone down at Vikki V's he was going to implode right before he blew up—and he couldn't have that. He would make Jimmy get that psychologist's number and get to the bottom of what the nasty secret was, rising up from deep inside of him, ticking away, cutting closer and closer to the surface.

MATT BOGART

Matt had never been sure that he'd light the entertainment scene on fire quite like his old man had back in his prime, but when Matt went to meet his retired rock star pops that afternoon, he'd gotten over 8 million downloads on the latest episode of *I Slept With Them First* – a new record, thrice beating his old one.

He finally had something real to brag about over lunch.

He auto-valeted his T Unit and walked into the side entrance of Sea Glass, the newest "organic farm-to-table" restaurant in Beverly Hills. They always sat in the back private VIP room just for celebrities with sea glass mosaic tables and an open roof. He couldn't help but fantasize about the day that he'd be able to score one of these VIP patio tables without meeting his dad here.

Geoffrey was already seated at his favorite table, right by the mermaid waterfall. His short, dyed jet black hair was spiked as usual and he wore his trademark black-lens aviators with diamond-inlaid chrome frames. When Matt walked up, Geoffrey looked up from his watch phone and flashed his big, radiantly-white, fake-toothed smile.

"There's that handsome devil son of mine," he said, standing.

Matt hugged him. "Pops, you're looking sharp, as usual."

"Just back from Ojai. Tabitha and I spent the week at the spa. The masseuse basically installed a new back on me. I had no idea I was holding so much tension in my scapulae. This woman, Sarina, she's a genius with her hands. You have to go up there and try her. I swear, she added ten years to my life."

"Sounds great, Pops."

"Sit down. Order anything you like. I already ordered a few things, the usual."

Matt sat and glanced at the menu, then back up at his dad. Geoffrey took off his sunglasses for a moment and surveyed his son.

"So how are you, Matt? What's new? How's your little dirty pod show?"

His father loved to belittle his work. He'd been waiting for exactly this kind of set-up.

"Well actually, I just did a record-breaking episode. Eight million streams already and it's only been online for a day."

Geoffrey put his sunglasses back on, a bemused smirk on his lips.

"Fantastic, my boy. Who's the star of this one?"

"This up-and-coming actor my agent Jimmy also represents. He talks about Kristina Brightside."

Geoffrey chuckled. "Oh, yes, Kristina. She is quite a shag."

Matt's eyes popped out. "What!? You fucked her, too?"

Geoffrey took a slow sip of his white wine and shot him a smug smile.

"Twice last year, my boy."

Matt stared hard at his dad. "You're lying, you son of a bitch. You would have told me."

"I am, unlike you and your guests, a gentleman who does not air my bedroom activities to the public. And don't talk about your grandmother like that."

Matt excused himself to the bathroom. He had to do a couple of lines. When he finished, he stared at himself in the mirror. He was so sick of forever feeling inferior to his old man—who was a total hypocrite, by the way. He always paraded his conquests around Matt, making him feel inferior in every way. When would his day come? When would he be able to make his dad jealous over who *he* was fucking? There had always been this brotherly competition between them that he was perpetually losing, but it was to his *father*, so it was twice as insulting. Matt hated himself. He hated his own stupid, sleazy "pod show." He hated his house that his dad had bought him and stocked with fucking bunnies to enhance his unlovable son's appeal. If it weren't for his fathers' money he'd probably be living in Koreatown, doing his show out of his studio apartment which would be a total disaster because he was a slob and wouldn't be able to afford a housecleaner. Matt tugged at his hair that was undeniably thinning on the top of his head, examined the circles under his eyes, and slapped his cheeks to give them a bit of color. Maybe he would take his dad up on that Ojai offer, go detox, clean up, have some rejuvenating massages and get some treatments that would help him grow some hair back.

Just the thought of getting off drugs again made Matt do a couple more bumps before heading back to the table. When he returned, he ordered a beer and the salmon sandwich, even though he knew he'd hardly touch it. Geoffrey slid down his sunglasses and looked at his son again, lines forming on his forehead, yet he said nothing, which pissed Matt off even more.

"*What*, Dad?"

"I didn't say anything, Matthew."

"Why are you staring at me?"

"Do you need to take another trip to Malibu?"

Four times his dad had already sent him to rehab. Matt sniffed and tossed back some water. "Nope. I'm fine. Show's doing great. I'm breaking new ground. Don't worry about me, everything's falling into place. I'm just exhausted from burning the candle at both ends."

"Late night lady friends?" Geoffrey offered carefully.

"As a matter of fact, yeah. There's been a lot of action, lately. Especially late night. Things are going great, I'm telling you, Pops."

Geoffrey sat back, seeming a little satisfied with that answer. "Glad to hear it. Who's the latest sweet thing?"

Matt decided to paint a really rich portrait. One that would compare to Kristina fucking Brightside, that little slut. That daddy-fucker.

"I've been seeing a bunch of girls, but this one in particular, whew. She's a French runway model *and* a professional drummer, actually."

Geoffrey looked impressed. "Oh yeah? Sounds tré sexy."

"Yeah, she's like 20 and hot as hell. Plays with this band called Tiny Tin Heart, they're better than the Portal Doors."

"I think I've heard of them," Geoffrey said, but Matt knew he hadn't.

Matt leaned in. "She's super kinky, too. We get *crazy*."

Geoffrey erupted in his famous fireplace chuckle. "Sounds like quite a bird."

"She is, she really is. I can hardly keep up."

Matt drove immediately to his dealer's place after lunch. Troy lived in a pretty decent apartment complex in the valley. They'd been friends since high school. Matt punched in the code to the front gate. Troy was the most trusting dealer he'd ever met, and somehow, that had miraculously translated into a long-lasting career, so far spanning 18 years with exactly one arrest and zero time spent in jail. Troy said it was because he only dealt with people who gave him the "clear vibe." He said that he could sense dark vibes a mile away. Matt thought most drug users were shady, and had seen Troy turn people down that Matt would probably have entrusted with his life. But Matt wasn't exactly a connoisseur of character, he'd be the first to admit.

Troy was a snake man and answered the door wearing his boa constrictor named Fonsie. He grinned and gave Matt a low-five. Troy also had a bit of a green thumb and had many plants in the living room, giving it a tropical feel. Adele, his little blonde, bisexual girlfriend, was curled up on the leather couch with their husky, Harry. Harry lifted his head and sniffed the air in Matt's direction. Finding the scent and sight familiar, the dog rested his head back down on his paws.

"Hey, Matt!" Adele cooed. Adele had been Matt's first guest on his first show. She'd slept with James Darko in high school, who grew up to become the founder of the world's most "elite" dating app, Fancypants. It had seemed like an appropriate place to begin the show, seeing as most of the guests had linked up with their pre-fame fucks through the myriad of apps that were currently estimated to be behind a whopping ninety-nine percent of hookups in the world. Luckily, Troy had been cool with her being on the show. He wasn't the jealous type. He was too busy being ecstatic that his girlfriend was into group sex.

"What's good in the hood, Venice?" Troy asked Matt after he'd returned Fonsie to his giant closet-sized tank. His muscles were on display in a sleeveless shirt, making Matt wish he'd been going to the gym more. Troy had an at-home gym. Both he and Adele were trainer certified and about as ripped as two human beings could get.

"When are you gonna start training me again, T?" Matt said, slapping his dealer's bicep playfully, causing zero ripple or jiggle. "I'm getting soft." Matt slapped his own curled bicep in his t-shirt, causing his muscle to slosh around like a water balloon. He made a face and dropped his arm, defeated. Troy and Adele laughed.

"When you really want to get serious, let me know," Troy said. "Anything for you, brother. But you gotta be all in about it. Alright? No coming over to pump iron, then blowing a bunch of lines and guzzling gin and popcorn after."

Matt sat on the couch next to Adele. "You know me too well. Fine. I'll use that as a healthy excuse to keep in touch with you guys next time I get sober. That's why I keep falling off the wagon. I just miss you guys too much."

They all laughed at that.

"Hey, check it out, Matt."

Troy twisted a half-burned candle on the side of the coffee table, causing the middle to open in a flash and a tray of drugs to rise up mechanically.

It was the best coffee table Matt had ever seen.

"Where the hell did you get this?"

"Secret of the trade," Troy said.

"He doesn't want them to get popular," Adele explained. "He's not telling anyone, don't take it personally."

"That's right, I'm not telling anyone," Troy reiterated. "But it's dope as fuck, right? Whatever you put inside this baby is undetectable by trained dogs. Smell-proof. It also has a built-in sensor that sends out high frequencies that trigger an alert on my phone if any digital device is recording within a 500 foot radius."

"Genius," Matt marveled. "Absolute genius."

"So whatchu want, the usual?"

"Yeah," Matt said.

Troy laid out a few lines. "Try this shit, it's like crushed diamonds. Best shit yet."

Matt had to laugh. "That's what you always say." He bent forward and did a line up each nostril, then shook his head and let out an excited whoop. "Fuck. Alright, I'll take double the usual. Plus some weed, if you have some."

"Weed? You hate weed." Troy's eyebrows raised suspiciously.

"I know. But I've been trying to mellow out a little."

"Oooh, Matty's got a girlfriend!" Adele teased.

"No. I've just been having some good times with this one girl and—"

"Jesus, man. You're all in love and shit!"

"Definitely not, Troy. What the fuck."

Adele and Troy looked at each other.

"Honestly, you guys. It really isn't anything," Matt growled.

"Well, we hope it is," Troy said. "You've been singing the single song since high school. And that song gets old, and real sad, too. You think maybe it's time to have *some* sort of relationship? Just try it once to say you did it?"

"No offense to you guys, but nobody *needs* to be in a relationship anymore. It's biologically irrelevant." He hurried on as his audience grew increasingly skeptical. "Relationships were for back in the day when people ran out of options. Now they make babies in labs."

"Easy, preach. Nobody's talking about marriage and kids," Troy said.

"Yeah. Sometimes it's just nice to… share life with someone you get along with for however long it works out," Adele said gently.

"Look, I get that it's 'nice' for you guys. But that's basically only because you're best friends who fuck other people together. I guarantee that if you both weren't open to sharing, things would have gone wrong a long time ago."

"Dude. Watch the words. I really don't want to get mad at you," Troy said, an edge to his voice.

Matt folded like a bad hand. "I know, I'm so sorry, you guys. Everything I'm saying is bullshit and I'm just scared to face the fact that I'm unlovable, is the real problem." He shook his head and banged his fist on the table. Harry lifted his head and growled.

"Watch the fucking table, man," Troy warned, standing up abruptly.

"Sorry, shit, I'm so sorry, bro," Matt said as he stood up, removed his baseball cap and ran his fingers through his hair, tugging at it. "That shit really is strong."

Troy relaxed a little. "Yeah, it's intense. Don't let it get you too crazy.

The first night we tested it, things got weird. Really weird. Even for us." He and Adele looked at each other knowingly and he went over to her, kneeling on the floor and putting his head on her knee. Harry the husky was still in protection mode, eyes trained on Matt. "So take it easy and also—watch what you say about me and my girl. We stand strong and proud in our love."

"You guys are beautiful, you really are." Matt unexpectedly felt a few tears jerk into his eyes. He blinked hard, surprised at the feelings coursing through him. "Maybe you're right. Maybe I should be more… open to the idea."

"It'll happen for you, man," Troy said.

I hope to God it doesn't, Matt thought as he nodded.

He put a stack of money on the table and took the drugs, stuffing them deep into his briefs. Then he hugged Troy and Adele goodbye.

"Thanks, guys. I love you two."

"We love you, too, ya crazy creep."

As soon as he got outside he lit a cigarette, and as soon as he got into his car he pulled a flask of whiskey out of the glove compartment and slugged it. Then he picked up his phone and called Cindy.

Cindy was his dad's ex-girlfriend. Well, ex-fiancé, if he was being honest. She was also his human equivalent to heroin. The glorious taboo of sleeping with someone he saw as a caretaker when he was a kid combined with her perfectly-maintained body as well as the fact that he told himself he was fucking her better than his dad ever did all made for an unbelievably strong sex cocktail. When he was inside Cindy he felt like he was beating his father at something and it felt fucking good. And it felt like good fucking. And it was probably his most destructive habit of all because he never hated himself more than when he left her house.

ODESSA MESSA

"Feeeeeeelix!!! I'm drunk!"

Odessa threw a dirty sock at the cat, who sat in the hallway staring at her bemusedly. He didn't flinch as it missed, sailing over him and landing against Wacko's door. She laughed and took another sip of her alcoholic energy drink as Wacko emerged from his bedroom, beer in hand.

"Oh! I didn't think you were home!" Odessa sing-songed, chucking her other dirty sock at him. Wacko wrinkled his nose. He was wearing a sweater with a multicolored moose embroidered on it.

"I just got back, I was down the street drinking at Candy and Christina's."

"Why didn't you assholes invite me?"

"Thought you had rehearsal."

"I did, but it was a short one."

"So lay off." Wacko came into her room and sat next to her on her couch. He tilted his head back. "Check my pocket."

Odessa put her hand in his baggy jeans pocket. Her fingers closed around a thick blunt, which made her laugh. She tousled his messy red hair and stuck the blunt behind his ear. "I have an idea! I'll give you that driving lesson you've been begging for forever. We'll smoke this when you make it all the way through Ghost Town to the playground at the end of 7th."

Wacko looked from her near-empty bottle to her flushed face. "We're wasted."

"If you learn something drunk, you never forget it."

"Yeah, that's definitely not a thing."

"Who cares! C'mon, we haven't had a wacky Wacko adventure in, like, forever!"

He scoffed. "Typical Odessa. I've been asking you to teach me to drive stick for months. And now you suddenly want to do it, when we're skonked out of our heads."

"You know me! Everyone's favorite party girl! There's no time like the present. What if this is our last chance? Quit grumbling and let's go!"

Wacko sighed and shrugged his shoulders in defeat. She pulled him off of the couch and practically pushed him out the door, yelling over her shoulder, "Bye, Felix! Wish us luck!"

They approached Odessa's white Honda Accord station wagon that sat in the lot behind their apartment building. The car had originally been her grandmother's, who had maintained it meticulously. Wacko reluctantly got into the driver's seat and Odessa slung herself into the passenger side.

"I love being in the passenger seat of my own car. It's so sexy," she cooed. She handed Wacko the key. "You know how to start the engine, right?"

Wacko glared at her in the darkness.

"You know I don't know a single thing about operating this vehicle."

"OK, *OK*! Damn you self-driving car babies. Kidding! Don't get all defensive just because you don't know *any*thing and you're just a defenseless little boy at the mercy of technology. No! Don't get out. I'm done. I promise. So that's a *manual key* which means you have to physically stick the key in the ignition hole there next to the steering wheel. Just put your left foot on the clutch, press it all the way down, keep your right foot on the brake, then turn the key until the engine catches."

"And which pedal is the clutch?" he asked through gritted teeth.

"The far left, dummy!"

Wacko shot her a quick death look, adjusted his feet, turned the key, and the car roared to life. Odessa's favorite psych rock band Tiptoe Torture poured out from the speakers. Wacko looked frazzled and immediately turned it down.

"Success!" she shrieked, jiggling the stick shift between them. "So, now, keep the clutch all the way down along with the brake, and make sure it's in first gear, which is right *here*." She grabbed Wacko's hand, put it on the shift stick, and swiveled hard left and upwards, locking it into first. "Now, put your right foot on the gas and move your feet like a see-saw." She showed him using her hands. "You know what that is, right? That balance thing that used to be on old playgrounds? As the left foot goes up, the right foot goes down. Hopefully at the same-ish speed. No tee-tottering!"

Wacko set his face in concentration. He started doing something with his feet and the car shivered, shuddered, leapt forward, then died.

"OK… Let's try again… But not like *that*!"

Odessa burst out laughing as Wacko sulked.

"Fuck off, Odessa! What the hell. This shit is way harder than I thought."

"It's OK, Wacky! Just takes some getting used to. It's good for humans to operate machines sometimes. C'mon, it will eventually be fun. Try again."

"Fun for *you*," Wacko mumbled. "Gonna take me half an hour just to get down the alley."

"Oh, please! You got this. I believe in you! Remember: *See-saw*. As one foot goes down, the other goes up. Like on a playground. You have been on a see-saw, right?"

"*Yes, I've been on a goddamn motherfucking see-saw*," Wacko seethed as he stalled out again. "It was *nothing like this*."

"Well, that's cuz you're doing it wrong," she giggled.

Odessa thoroughly enjoyed watching him be humbled by her daily driver. It made her feel good, being the master of a machine that he, a man of massively overinflated ego, could hardly operate. She'd saved this stick shift lesson for when she needed it most. Disaster would be coming any minute now. She felt its hot breath on the backs of her calves. She just wanted to get in this lesson in male humility before it struck.

Wacko finally got the car stuttering at a rate of about one mile an hour down the alley. Relief flooded his face.

"We're moving! It's going!"

At the end of the alley, the car immediately bucked and stalled out.

Odessa looked out her passenger window in effort to hide her wide smile. "Oops! I forgot to remind you that when you come to a complete stop, the clutch always has to be all the way in, first."

"Oh really? No problem, it's totally cool. That's just a *giant fucking piece* of crucial information. Talk about the blind leading the blind. What else are you forgetting to tell me?"

"Nothing! I just didn't expect you to pick this up so fast! Let's get you into second gear. Once we're cruising past this light we can even get you up to third gear maybe!"

Odessa tried to push his hair back encouragingly but he batted her hand away. "Don't touch me. I'm concentrating." She sat back, slightly sobered by his tone. He looked over guiltily and stalled out again. "Fucknuts!! This is so hard. No wonder they invented cars that drive themselves. What a shit time driving this car is. Not even fun at all."

"Hmmph. I prefer it. But I guess I'm just an analog girl in a digital world. You have to learn to appreciate the perks of operating a vehicle manually. I never get speeding tickets *or* get into accidents because I have to pay close attention to everything I'm doing."

"Big deal. I could say the same about my auto-pilot." Wacko rolled his eyes as he started the car up again. Someone honked behind them sitting at the green light. He rolled down his window and frantically waved them around.

The automatic car sped by as the passenger shouted out his window, "Time to get a new car, dumbass!"

Wacko looked utterly dejected. He fixed his face in determination and attempted to start up again, inching the car as slowly as it could possibly go through the intersection. They just barely made it across before the light turned red.

"OK! You made it! Now, try to put the clutch all the way in while it's moving and slide the gear into second."

Wacko concentrated and suddenly, with just a slight grind of gears, the car was in second and sprang forward. "It's in! It's in!" he shouted, pride flushed across his face. Odessa marveled at how cute he looked when pleased with himself. She stopped herself from squeezing his arm.

"That's great, Wackito! Now, see if you can gun the engine so it's almost at the 3 on the rev meter and then put in the clutch and try for third. It's all green lights up ahead."

Wacko got it into third, and was even able to manage the coordination to stop at the red light without stalling out. "Damn! Look at me go!" he gloated.

She laughed. "Don't get cocky yet! Take a left up here at Oakwood."

He stalled out twice making the left turn, but thankfully no one was on the road. After the harrowing cross over the other side of Venice Blvd, sound-tracked by a long string of Wacko's favorite cuss words, they'd made it onto Oakwood.

The car crawled down the street in second gear. Wacko remained fixed on the road in concentration.

"There are way too many stop signs on this street," he said.

"I know."

"The start and stops are the most annoying part of this whole operation."

"Exactly. Gotta do them until they aren't annoying anymore."

Three stall-outs later, they finally rolled into the neighborhood formerly known as Ghost Town. Wacko sat forward in his seat as the air coming in the windows grew noticeably chillier and clammier. Odessa switched the music to her favorite "dead rock" band. Their eerie, esoteric, orchestral music filled the car with ominous vibes.

"Why'd you have to put this on?" Wacko asked.

"Because this is Ghost Town," she said. "Respect for the old school Venice, respect for the artists, drifters, wheelers and dealers who've lived and died here, respect for the countless people who got killed here…"

"I didn't know all that," Wacko said. "So, is it, uh—shit."

The car stalled out as he slowed down for a stop sign. He tried to start it back up but the engine just clucked and sputtered. Odessa looked out the window at the darkened baseball field to their right and the row of shadowy houses that surrounded it. She realized with a lurching feeling that not a single light was on in any of the windows. Even the streetlights were out.

"Try it again. C'mon. Let's not just sit here," she said, trying not to sound nervous. Her calves were heating up again. Danger was close. Real close.

"I'm *trying*…" Wacko turned the key in the ignition once, twice, three times. He looked at Odessa, fear transmitting from his bloodshot eyes. "It won't even start, now."

"You have the clutch pressed all the way in?"

"Yes! I'm not an idiot!" He shoved his foot down a few times, trying again, trying harder. The car didn't make a peep, now. It was completely silent. They sat there in the dark for a moment. A bird let out a shriek in the distance.

"You are *so* fucking with me." Odessa forced a laugh and punched Wacko harder in the arm than she meant to. He winced and shook his head. "Then let me try."

Wacko put his hand on the door handle, then stopped and hung his head.

"I don't want to get out of the car."

"Wow," Odessa said, but the truth was that she didn't want to, either. "Let's swap inside, then."

They tangled and twisted their bodies over the armrest, swinging themselves into each other's seats. As soon as Odessa was positioned at the wheel she turned the key and the engine whirred and jumped to life. She looked angrily at Wacko.

"You *were* messing with me!"

"I wasn't! I swear." Wacko sure looked serious. She mostly believed him.

"Ugh, it doesn't matter. Let's get to the park already. I need to get high."

As soon as she started driving the car bucked again and stalled out.

Odessa stared at Wacko. "What did you do to my car?!"

"I don't know," Wacko said, hands gripping the door handle. "You messing with *me*?"

They sat there, staring ahead at the dark road before them. The streets were totally empty. A thin fog was lying in wisps on the ground.

"Isn't it weird that not a single light is on in any of these houses—or streetlights?" Odessa mused softly.

"I wish you hadn't pointed that out," Wacko said after a moment.

"We gotta get out of here. This is totally killing my buzz." Odessa closed her eyes and prayed to the universe, then turned the engine again and the car revved with life. "Yesss!!" She accelerated hard just as a guy appeared, crossing the street right in front of them, holding what looked like a baby.

They hit him with a sickening THUD.

"What the HELL?!" Odessa shrieked. "He came out of nowhere, am I right?"

"Ohcrapohcrapohcrapohcrap," Wacko slurred as he shrank down in his seat. Then he slowly unlocked his car door.

"Wait!" Odessa cried.

"We have to see if he's OK," Wacko said with quiet panic. "Was that a baby in his arms? We can't just drive away."

"But listen," Odessa said, gesturing at her cracked window. "I don't hear anything."

"That's probably because they're dead!"

"No way," she whispered pleadingly. "We couldn't have even killed a cat at that speed. We've only gone like three feet from a complete stop!"

There was an abrupt tapping on the tail end of the station wagon and they both froze. What sounded like fingernails scraped down the car exterior. Odessa had dark tints on her rear windows, so it was impossible to see what was back there at night with no streetlights. The side mirrors proved clear of any visible shapes as well. They remained frozen in the grip of fear as Odessa double checked the rearview mirror.

Just then, a dark, hooded face appeared above the front of the car, squinting at them with flashing yellow eyes. There was a bundle in his hand as he stood up. They both watched in mute fright as the man unwrapped what had previously looked like a baby babushka. It now appeared to be a device of some sort. He placed it on the hood of the engine and switched it on.

At once, the street in front of them became flooded with what looked like three-dimensional holographic ghosts at war, punching, stabbing and shooting with semi-automatic weapons as they zoomed at each other mid-air.

It was a regular ghoul gang riot.

"What the *actual fuck*?" Wacko whispered. Odessa slunk down in her seat as the car radio came on by itself, flooding them with the sounds of all the violent visions, shouting and swearing and re-killing each other. The hooded man with the empty yellow eyes came around to Odessa's window and pointed at her with one pale, veiny finger. She stared out at his shadowy face, feeling the blood drain from her own, and tried to turn the car on again.

Nothing. Maybe this was it. Maybe her time had come for the grand goodbye.

The man's lips began to move and his deep, booming voice crackled in through the car radio as if on-air at a station.

"Hello in there. Are you enjoying the show?" A jarring laugh caused Odessa to shudder and grab Wacko's arm. "We've brought out all the action for you."

"What the fuck is this simulation shit?" Wacko's voice cracked and he sniffed like he was trying not to cry. "Is this guy like an evil robot warlord or what?"

An explosion of gunshots rang through the car as they watched one ghost riddle another with an Uzi until they burst into sparkling particles. It would have been kind of cool, Odessa thought, if they weren't the only ones experiencing it.

"Oh, this is real, my friends," the voice boomed back. "It's as real as the rest of reality, which we all know isn't real at all. And yet, here we are: *Somewhere. Anywhere. Nowhere. Everywhere...*" He laughed again, a horrible, ominous sound that somehow amplified over the feverish crossfire.

"He can hear us," Odessa whispered.

"Yes, I can hear you," the man said, and raised his arms high.

"Then what do you want?" asked Odessa.

"Isn't it obvious? I want you to give up the ghost. You can't save yourself. You can't save this town. And you sure can't save the world."

Odessa looked at Wacko. "I didn't think I was trying," she murmured. Wacko looked away, ashamed. He was shivering uncontrollably and it looked like he had pissed himself.

She tried the engine again. The car started. They looked at each other.

"I'm gonna drive the fuck outta here," Odessa said, "is what I'm gonna do."

"The dark forces will follow you," the man said. "You can run from your demons, but you can't hide..."

"Screw that," Odessa said. "These are *your* demons. We just need to smoke a fat blunt and forget about this!"

She gritted her teeth and pumped the gas. They zoomed forward through the ghostly gangbangers, the projector falling off the hood with a muted crash. The apparitions disappeared instantly. Odessa ignored all five stop signs on the way through Ghost Town to the park beyond. She finally calmed down and deemed it safe when the surrounding houses had lit windows.

They sat there, panting and choking for air like they'd just run a marathon. Then they finally looked at each other, their eyes wild, their chests heaving. She had so much love for Wacko at that moment, but she did what she always did, which was play it down.

"I hope you took good notes, because that's the last time you're getting a driving lesson."

"What was that all about?"

"I'm not completely sure, but I have an idea," Odessa said.

"I can't believe I pissed myself," Wacko said forlornly.

"I know… And to think I was gonna give you a blow job for bravery," Odessa teased. Wacko looked absolutely stricken. She laughed and threw her head back. "Calm down and maybe I still will. And spark that before this whole shit world implodes altogether."

STEVIA WONDER

Stevia had an unusually bad feeling. She obviously hadn't meant for the cat to break the baby bird wing bone during the disruption spell on Odessa. She hadn't known her bandmate had just received a superdoom tarot reading as well. She'd perhaps let her jealousy take things too far, and the tiniest bit of regret was starting to seep into her bones. Then there was the strange reaction she'd gotten from Cackles, the ugliest, most cursed seagull. She hadn't even had a chance to start the castaway spell and the clingy bird had skedaddled like Stevia was the devil herself. And now, her Thai tiger's tooth was missing, which was almost impossible to replace without a trip to Thailand. Real witch doctor dealers didn't sell their goods online. And to top it all off, while frantically searching for the main ingredient to her Star Power Success spell, she'd knocked over her jar of albino alligator powder, which was supposed to cause irreversible tragedy.

In other words, things were looking very bleak in the fate department.

In frustration, she kicked over her theremin stand and pain shot up from her toe.

"Creepy crappy monkey-loving shit house!" she shrieked. Her cats watched her with wide, judging eyes. "What the hell are you looking at, ladies?"

In an effort to relax, she rubbed calming balm to her temples and lay down on her furry shag rug. Pansy came and curled up on her chest, a sure sign of dismal times. Stevia lifted her head and stared at the cat.

"It isn't that bad, is it, Pansy?" She shook her head. "It can't be that bad. I refuse to believe it."

As if disappointed in Stevia's denial, Pansy stood up, stretched, and exited the cottage through the cat flap.

Stevia brewed some turmeric ginger tea and checked her phone. Dan Blacker wanted to meet to play her a new song by Curtis Creation and discuss the theremin melody they were hoping she could add. That wasn't bad news at all, that was exciting! She invited him over for the following morning and then set to tidying up the place. She was well aware that she might come across as a crazy cat cottage chick—but, if the place was in good enough shape, well, maybe he'd find that just another charming facet of her personality.

Once her little home was in tip-top shape, Stevia began to tweak the levels of some of her solo recordings. She couldn't believe she was finally going to have a perfect opportunity to present them to Dan. Pansy didn't return, which was worrisome, but she couldn't risk being a mess for Dan the next day so she tucked herself in with a sleep-inducing spell.

The following morning she awoke from her dreamless sleep to a scratching at her front door, which was strange considering the cat flap was always open. Stevia swung stiffly out of bed and made her way to the door. Dread hung heavy in her heart for reasons unbeknownst to her, gathering even more weight as she turned the doorknob.

When she swung open the door, she gasped.

Cackles lay dead at her doorstep, a hardened lump of dirty feathers and blood. His cold, beady eyes stared up at her in final punctuation. Pansy sat behind her offering, purring and licking her paw.

"Pansy! What have you *done*?"

Stevia stared at the cat. Pansy meowed innocently and stepped over the dead gull, rubbing against Stevia's legs for a moment before heading inside to find a warm spot in which to curl up and rest after delivering her prize killing.

"What am I supposed to do with this disgusting mess?"

Stevia grabbed a garbage bag out of the kitchen and shoved stiff old Cackles into it. Her first thought was to head for the trash bin, but then had the thought that she should really check to see if there were any spells that required parts of a seagull before disposing of the carcass. Stevia knotted the bag and placed it in the corner of her yard. Then she hosed off her steps and headed inside to get pretty for the producer.

Dan showed up at last, handsome and fresh-smelling at her doorstep. His long-lashed puppy eyes were bright in the daylight, and Stevia found it hard not to overdo her flirtation with him.

"Hey Dan! *So* great to see you. Come in!"

They hugged and he stepped inside, surveying her cottage. "What a cute spot you have, here. It smells… striking. What is that?"

"Yeah, thanks! I love it here. The scent is from the garage next door, I make and sell holistic skin care products. It can get kind of overwhelming, I apologize. Would you like some tea? Coffee? Homemade kombucha?"

"All of the above, including the skin care products." He laughed at his own joke and she chimed in as well. "Just kidding. I'd love some coffee."

She added a few dashes of enchanted dried sea conch to the medium-roast grounds of her bewitching morning brew, to enhance his openness. Dan walked around, observing her walls decorated with the cover art of award-winning albums on which she'd played theremin.

"I *love* that shirt," she said.

He looked proudly down at his frayed Bad Cat tee shirt under his blazer. "Thanks, it's an original. My dad went to all their shows. He grew up in Seattle."

"That's *amazing*!" Stevia cooed as she poured hot water over the coffee grounds. "I wish *I'd* gotten to see them!" In truth, she seen them many times, even shared a bill once before.

"Same here. And wow, my best friend produced that record," he said, standing in front of the framed Animal Brawl record on the wall above her couch.

"Oh no way, Travis?"

"Yeah, we went to high school together."

"He's a darling!"

"He's a darling bastard," Dan said. They laughed together in that *you know Travis* kind of way.

"Cream or sugar?"

"Both," he said. Suddenly he was standing close to her in the kitchen. "I like all the bad stuff in it."

They locked eyes under the kitchen skylight and Stevia felt momentarily breathless. "No problem," she whispered after a loaded moment. She was glad she'd worn her cutest miniskirt as they both turned their eyes downward to look at the negative space between them. She finally broke away to spoon honey into the mug. "I'm so excited to hear this track," she added, voice cracking slightly.

"I think you'll really like it." He received the mug of creamy, honeyed coffee and took a sip. "Too good. Thanks. How can I play it for you?"

They moved into the living room. Stevia let Dan sit in the desk chair in front of her monitors and told him the Air-fi password to connect. An upbeat, dance-y pop ballad blasted out from the speakers. Stevia danced along. Dan watched her in approval. He started humming the theremin melody he was hearing and Stevia pretended she loved it, nodding along excitedly. By the time the song was over, she was short of breath, flushed, and tumbled down onto her couch, all smiles.

"It's a hit! I love it!" she said, happy that she didn't have to fake the enthusiasm too much. It was better than she expected, especially by current pop/dance music standards.

"I'm glad," Dan said. "We've really been putting in the hours on this one. So, do you get what we're hearing as far as your melody?"

"Absolutely," she said. "*So* catchy. I can't wait to record it."

"We actually were hoping you could get it done *to*day," he said, making a scrunched-up *sorry* face. "We have to send it to the label tomorrow and we want to have you in the mix. They really loved what you did on that last track."

"Really?"

"Yeah," Dan said, leaning towards her suggestively. "They couldn't get over what a unique tone you get. When I played it they couldn't guess what the instrument was, they thought it was some weird sample of whale noises. I told them it was the theremin, and then I showed them a picture of you. Stevia, they went wild. They even asked if you'd consider coming on tour."

Stevia's eyes widened. "REEally!?"

Dan laughed. "I told them they could make you an offer. We'll see what they come up with."

"Do *you* go out on tour?" It flew out of her mouth before she could stop herself. That damn conch shell powder. Sometimes just breathing it in made her too relaxed.

To her relief, he smiled and seemed to find it cute that she'd asked. "I try to come out to the bigger shows, but I'm working on too many other projects that demand my time to go for the whole run."

"Of course! Hey," Stevia said, eager to move on. "Can I show you some of the stuff I've been working on, my own solo stuff?"

"Yes!" Dan answered enthusiastically. "Play away."

Stevia felt the prick of panic rise up. This was it, finally she had the exact right audience, and no amount of magic she had on hand could make him love what he was about to hear. As the pulsing vibrato of theremin and her deep, throaty vocals filled the room, she sat back and closed her eyes, unable to handle the awkwardness of watching him listen.

When the song finished, she opened her eyes. Dan was staring at her.

"It's…" she fumbled self-consciously. "Um, I mean—"

"—That was otherworldly," he interrupted. "I felt like I was transported to a club in Berlin or something. Never heard anything like it. Really cool."

"Oh, wow, thanks…" she said, not sure if that was exactly a compliment or a sideways *thanks-no-thanks*.

"Send me the stems. I can play around with it, add a drum beat, maybe some guitar, put some effect on the vocals. If you like what I do, we could shop it around."

Stevia jumped up, hitting herself in the face with her hand in her excitement. "Really?! Oh, that would be amazing, thank—"

A sharp staccato knocking came from the front door. They both looked over, startled.

"Now who could that be?" Stevia went over to the door and looked out the peep hole. No one was there. She turned back to Dan and shrugged. "Can't see anyone. Probably a branch brushing the roof."

As soon as she started to walk back into the living room, the strange rhythmic tapping started again. A chill shot down her spine. Dan gave her a curious look. She went back over to the door and looked through the peep hole. Still, nothing. No one was out there.

She shrugged. "So weird! Maybe it's the pipes. Anyways," she said, anxious to get back on the subject of him helping her with her solo project, "As I was saying—"

The tapping started up again, this time faster and louder. Dan stood up abruptly and strode towards the front door.

"I'll see what's going on."

Stevia had a gut-shredding feeling about it but she followed behind him.

He swung the door open.

There was no one outside.

They stood in the doorway, surveying the yard. Then Stevia saw with muted trepidation that the garbage bag containing Cackles' remains was now lying empty in shreds on the ground.

"Let's go back in," she urged, pulling at Dan's blazer. "C'mon."

"No, let's figure out who this joker is," Dan said determinedly. "Otherwise they're going to keep harassing us."

He took a few steps outside and looked around.

At that precise moment, a shrieking lump of feathers swooped down like an oversized angry wasp from the roof above them, flying directly into Dan's face. The blurry, bloody bird pecked and clawed at him violently. Stevia screamed and tried to hit the gull away but he was relentless. He wouldn't stop shredding face. Dan cried out and fought back, clawing at the savage bird with his hands, but previously-dead Cackles was seemingly unstoppable. Bloody scratches quickly covered Dan's face.

"I can't see! I can't see anything!"

He tried to run but tripped over a chair and fell backwards onto the ground. The bird spread his wings over Dan's head and continued the attack.

Stevia ran and grabbed Pansy off of her bed, sprinting back outside. "Kill, Pansy, Kill!" she screamed, throwing the cat at undead Cackles, who was going to town on poor Dan's neck at the moment, simultaneously shredding his prized vintage tee shirt with his claws and tearing at his chiseled chest flesh. Pansy took one look, hissed, and puffed out all her fur.

She arched her back and backed away sideways like a spider crab.

"No! Pansy, you have to help!" Stevia yelled, but Pansy would have none of it. Stevia ran and grabbed her broom, swinging at the bird like he was a baseball, as hard as she could. She connected to his tiny head with a crack that should have knocked him out of the yard, yet he seemed relatively unfazed.

Dan was trying to say something but it was all garbled gibberish. She couldn't make out the choked words through his pain and the choppy butcher knife of a bastard beak mauling his face and throat. She hit the Cackles again. This time he paused and looked up at Stevia with his beady dead eyes, assessing the level of interference. At that moment, Dan grabbed the gull by his legs and hurled him with a super-charged, almost-inhuman survival strength against the tall concrete wall separating Stevia's cottage from the one next door.

With another crack, Cackles hit the wall and dropped down to the ground like a busted up water balloon, leaving a trail of crimson blood and feathers on the descent.

Stevia crumpled down next to Dan, taking his torn and mangled body in her hands. "Oh my goodness, you poor, poor thing… Are you OK? Can you hear me?"

Dan's eyes struggled to open. She saw bloody tears trying to form in the corner of his gooey, pecked-out eyes. His mouth opened partially but nothing came out but wheezing gasps. She laid his head back down as gently as she could.

"Wait here, don't move a thing. I'm going to get you something that'll make it all better, I promise."

She ran inside to collect a bowl of hot water, a packet of her Insta-heal magic powder, and the softest washcloth she could find. She was back at his side in under a minute, tenderly tending to his wounds like a war nurse.

His previously very-kissable lips were now torn open and covered in blood, so she started there first. With just a dab of a soaked towel, she watched the wounds close up and his lips restore to kissable. She noted how terrified he still was by his quivering nostrils and jagged breathing. She knew it was dangerous to be using magic on someone who wasn't unconscious, but she just couldn't let him writhe around in his thrashed condition. She could rush him to the hospital, but Western medicine paled in comparison to Stevia's spells. How could she let him suffer any longer when she had the perfect cure? He was way too good looking for her to be responsible for any scars on that face.

Plus, he was going to make her famous. rt

She dabbed at his eyes next, which were nearly glued shut with blood. Quickly his eyelids transformed back to fluttering and flawless. She dabbed away, watching his irises dart around, back to fully-functional and able to see what was happening.

"You're going to be just fine," she said softly. "Just keep your eyes closed and let me finish."

He obeyed without a word.

The Insta-heal powder was strong. She'd never used it on such grotesque wounds before, and it was handling the job like it wasn't even a challenge. Within minutes his face was back to fresh, dewy and handsome. She moved on to his scratched-up neck, collarbone, chest, hands and arms. He lay there as if transfixed by the feeling of his own supernatural recovery, completely focused on the task at hand. Stevia had racked her brain for all possible ways to explain this sort of magic, but could come up with nothing remotely convincing. She'd heard about what happened to witches who revealed their powers in broad daylight. But he was going to give her everything she ever wanted. What would her powers matter then? Her talent wasn't a spell. It was real, and Dan had validated it. And there hadn't even been any time to put him under the sleep spell. Had there?

Wait. Had she actually *wanted* him to know about her powers? Did she somehow crave exposure? Had she just jumped at the chance to show off her *wicked awesome witchiness* to him?

If so, that was a Cardinal Witch Offense. But she was way too close to getting what she'd always wanted to be concerned about that right now.

"Dan," she said softly, gazing down at his perfect face, fingering his eyebrows and caressing his cheekbones affectionately. "You can open your eyes now. You're just like new."

His long lashes fluttered open to reveal bright eyes full of questions. "Wow. That was… I feel… that felt like…" He looked at his hands in shock, then raised his hands to his face, searching it, finding it smooth and blood-free. "But this is… *impossible*. What happened? How did you do this?"

"Is it possible to pass on that question? Just call it cool that you're OK?"

He sat up slowly, looking at her with a curious and flushed face. "That felt like someone was spreading sunshine on my skin, like I was getting kissed by a thousand butterflies, there was a real—"

He stopped abruptly and the color drained out of his face.

"What? What is it?"

He pointed beyond where Stevia crouched. She turned around slowly, and for what seemed like the tenth time that day, deeply afraid of what she would find.

Or not find.

Cackles' body was gone again, leaving behind only a dark pool of blood and shorn feathers.

On the wall, someone had crudely scrawled with blood:

BURN THE WITCH.

AUGGIE BREAKMIRRORS

As the days diminished in the countdown to meet President TBD 3000, the waves of anticipation grew stronger. And for each wave of anticipation, Auggie felt an equally strong wave of self-loathing. He was glad he had a booming party bus business, with a bachelorette party on the books at the moment. He felt his mood improve as soon as he pulled up to the Santa Monica address where he was instructed to pick the partiers up.

A herd of beautifully made-up, freshly-post-grad girly-girls were waiting outside on the front lawn. They pumped their arms and whooped and waved as he pulled over and tooted the horn, which he'd programmed to sound like many things, but that evening had chosen the celebratory bellow of "foghorn."

Made Auggie smile every time.

He slid open the doors and spoke into the Microsonic invisible mic.

"All aboard the Zebra Express, with non-stop service to however deep into the party dimension you want to go!"

The ladies cheered again and gathered their endless number of bags, taking their time filing onto the bus, smiling, waving or waggling their hips at Auggie as they made their way past him to the hippie-chic back of the bus.

"I *love* this incense! Isn't it, like, from Peru?"

"Oh my god, these pillows! They remind me of Kelly's dorm bed!"
"Shut *up*, Kendra."

"Break out the champagne and cognac, Christine!"

Kelly, the bride-to-be, paused by the driver's seat. "Auggie? I'm Kelly." She had too much eye makeup on and was wearing one of the holographic dresses that were trendy at the moment, set to "disco" mode. Auggie found the dresses annoying but she still roared sex like an angry lion to him. "Thanks for being our designated driver."

There was a chorus of "Thanks, Auggie!" from the back.

"My pleasure," Auggie said. "Hope you all have the time of your life, tonight."

"Kelly, get back here!"

"Wait a second! I have to tell him something."

"Where we going first, Kel?" one of her friends hollered from the back.

"She's not telling," another said.

"That's *so* Kelly!"

Kelly rolled her eyes as she leaned in close to Auggie and whispered, "We're going to pick up this guy Dr. T-Sauce. He works at Hollywood Tattoo on Sunset. He said we could pull up in the back alley and he'll run out. He's bringing his ink kit on the bus, and from then on, we don't have any specific stops. We'll let you know if we change our minds and want to make more pit stops."

Auggie felt a bit jealous of the impending male presence among the partying women, as this "Dr. T-Sauce" (just how dumb of an artist name could a guy pick?) would undoubtedly be getting laid by the end of the night, but he had no choice but to cheerily follow orders.

Auggie winked at Kelly. "Gotcha."

"Off we go!" she squealed and headed to the back of the bus. He put the Zebra into drive and headed east. Kelly connected her phone to the speakers and electronic music flooded the cabin. It was the kind Auggie especially hated; the kind with no real instruments and autotuned robot vocals.

After a few minutes, one of Kelly's cute little friends ambled her way up to Auggie. She had curly hair and an adorable nose.

"Um, Auggie?"

"Hold on tight to the seat, there," he advised as she almost fell over when the bus slowed for a stoplight.

"I'm Susanna, by the way. How long do we have you for?"

Auggie wrinkled his brow. "I think the plan is to drop you back at Kelly's around 3AM."

Susanna displayed a wad of big bills, then confidently tucked the wad into Auggie's jacket breast pocket. "Does that cover us until whenever we scrape our asses off the bus floor tomorrow morning?"

Auggie grinned. "Sure does, Susanna."

"Great. I'll keep that as a surprise from the girls until just around midnight, when we... take some drugs that are also a surprise," she said, smiling.

"Great. I'll take some extra energy pills," Auggie said.

"Well, I was thinking, maybe you can join the party later? That is, if you have somewhere you can park your big bus for the night." She gave him a coy smile and rejoined the group, leaving Auggie with a semi-hard-on, grinning goofily at himself in the side view mirror.

Thirty-five minutes later, they were in the alley behind Hollywood Tattoo. Dr. T-Sauce came out from the back entrance and did a little bow as the girls began to cheer. The dude sported an overly-manicured little goatee and his arms were covered in full-color sleeves. His neck had a thick tribal band around it. In a final gesture of mock devotion, Dr. T Sauce lifted his baseball cap off to reveal his bald, tattooed head, a giant mandala inked right at the top.

Auggie thought it looked like one of the doilies his grandmother used to keep on her coffee table. He pictured himself setting a hot mug of tea down right in the center of it and chuckled.

Auggie grudgingly opened the bus door and Dr. T-Sauce came around and stepped aboard. The inked-up motherfucker flashed him a "we're-on-the-same-page-brother-these-are-some-hot-ass-ladies" smile and Auggie managed to choke up a feeble grin in return.

Kelly ran from the back, all smiles.

"Dr. T! So good to see you!"

"Congratulations, Kel," he said, sly as hell, and gave her a kiss on the cheek. Then he reached over and slugged Auggie on the shoulder. "Let's get this party rollin'!"

What an utter cornball, Auggie thought; one of those guys who was so moronic they made you feel dumber just by interacting with them. He slid the bus door closed and started moving. In the back, someone suggested they put a horror movie Kelly had starred in as a teenager on the projector. The tense music and actors getting slashed against the ceiling and walls of the bus made for an exciting combination. Someone popped a bottle of champagne and tried to mute the concern over it fizzing up and over onto the furniture. Far worse had been spilled, Auggie assured them, as he rolled around Hollywood wearing his sunglasses at night, waving at too many assholes who thought it was funny to honk and wave at the Zebra, trying to get him to honk back. Auggie allowed himself to do it once every two hours, otherwise the clients could get annoyed at all the honking. Sometimes, when it was a super-annoying character, he'd trigger the sample of a guy yelling "HONK YOU, ASSHOLE!" which was a real crowd-pleaser. But not every 10 minutes, of course.

Dr. T-Sauce consulted with the ladies about which tattoos would look good where on them. Auggie glowered in the rearview mirror at the clever excuse for him to trace their jutting hip bones, survey their asses, touch the backs of their necks.

"Oh, I could see that looking really good right in the high corner of your left butt cheek… Here, let me show you… "

"You have such pretty legs, what about this secret spot up on the inside of your thigh, almost no one has one there, let me show you…"

"Has anyone ever complimented you on your gorgeous neck? Right behind your right ear looks perfect… Naked and waiting…"

What kind of a sentence was that? The guy really thought he was smooth. Auggie was rolling his eyes so hard from behind his sunglasses he started to get a headache.

The night wore on. They stopped in Koreatown to get takeout from 99 Dumplings. Then Susanna revealed the news that they had the bus all night. The screaming almost caused Auggie to stop, drop and roll. Too many energy pills tended to enhance his PTSD.

Susanna made her way to the front of the bus, obviously inebriated and holding on to anything she could. She bent close to Auggie's ear.

"Do you want to join the party?"

He did. He most certainly did.

"Park the bus somewhere. Then take this."

She pressed a pill into his palm. He looked at it. It was small and rainbow-flecked, like a tiny confetti birthday cake, with the letters "DQYD" etched into it.

He took a left turn back towards his house.

When he pulled the bus into his driveway, the partiers had put on an Anime movie and switched the music to electro-shoegaze. Auggie chased the confetti pill down with some beer and pressed the "privacy" button that closed the motorized blinds on all the windows (including the windshield) and locked the door.

Then he made his way to the back of the bus.

As soon as he reclined on one of the couches, several of the ladies snuggled up to his sides. They told him their names and he promptly forgot them. He was only really interested in Susanna. One of them handed him their cocktail, which he discovered was mostly vodka. He finished it in several gulps and pulled out a bottle of his reserve whiskey he had stashed in a secret compartment under one of the cushions.

Dr. T-Sauce took out his tattoo gun. "Who wants a tattoo?" He grinned at the chorus of yesses. "Bride first. Let's give her something else to commit to."

Auggie passed the bottle of whiskey around. His hands settled on a thigh to his right and an arm to his left. He felt his eyes droop with enhanced relaxation. Susanna started giving him a shoulder rub.

"Ooh, feel the tension in these shoulders. You better lie down," she cooed.

He put his head in a perfume-scented lap and let his feet hang off the end of the couch as Susanna climbed onto his back. He helped her get his shirt off. Dr. T-Sauce had convinced Kelly to get a tattoo under her left breast. She was now lying topless on the loveseat across the aisle. Auggie watched her, her nipples small and hard as the tattoo "doctor" began the outline of what looked to be a seahorse with butterfly wings. One of her friends came over to her side.

"Does it hurt, Kel?" she asked.

"Not yet," Kelly answered. She giggled. "It actually feels kinda good. But the other boob feels left out."

"I can help with that," her friend said, sitting down next to her and beginning to kiss Kelly's other breast.

Kelly closed her eyes. "Oh. That is *so* good."

Dr. T-Sauce looked like he'd never had to try harder to keep his focus tattooing. He began to break a sweat.

Auggie felt himself get aroused enough that lying on his stomach became painful. He flipped over and his little massage fairy straddled him and began to rub his chest, stopping to feed him a sip of his own whiskey. He gazed up at Susanna with pure gratitude.

One of the other girls started making out with Susanna. Auggie watched, feeling a wave of euphoria flood through him that reminded him of the time he'd done heroin. Man, that was some good shit, that candle-lit one night love affair in a den in some Chinatown, he couldn't remember where. Suddenly Susanna was undoing his pants, and the girl who was providing him her lap as a pillow bent over and started kissing him, giving him a choice view of her cleavage. He felt Susanna's lips on his package, which was free now, standing up as straight as ever. He moaned into the mouth of the girl that kissed him, feeling his body give way to a greater relaxation than he'd ever expected to feel again without that deadly hero, heroin.

Then he blacked out.

When Auggie's eyes reopened, sunlight was peeking through the slits in the window shades. He felt extremely sore and nauseous, like he'd spent all night playing drunken racquetball and forgotten to eat afterwards. He squinted up at the ceiling and groaned softly, thankful for his blanket in the brisk air of the Venice morning.

Then he realized he was naked on the floor of the Zebra and there was no blanket, just another body sprawled across his. Susanna. He could tell by her hair, curly across his chest, shining in the splinters of morning sun. He twisted his head stiffly to the right. Three naked ladies were triple-spooning on the purple loveseat. One of them rubbed at her face without opening her eyes, causing the middle one to shift and whimper softly, but none of them woke up. He creaked his rickety neck to the left. Dr. T-Sauce was also bare-assed, sitting straight up on the couch, snoring softly with Kelly asleep against his chest.

Auggie sat up then, careful to hold Susanna so that she didn't fall to the side. She made a small, cute moan, like a cat who wanted food. He looked down and saw with shock that there was a tattoo of what looked like a warped bushel of beets on her ass cheek.

Then he saw his forearm. There was a huge cartoon tattoo of President TBD 3000 smoking a joint, with "RESPECT AUTHORITAY" printed under it in capital letters.

It was the most hideous thing he'd ever seen.

"Oh, *FUCK*," Auggie moaned.

Dr. T-Sauce's eyes popped open. Auggie watched the world's worst tattoo artist take a moment to process the scene.

"Oh, fuuuuck," Dr. T-Sauce echoed as they both stared at Auggie's arm, then at Susanna's warped-beet-ridden ass.

Kelly woke up. She shook her head. "No, no, *nooooo*." She rubbed her eyes. "This is a dream, right? Why are all my friends naked? Why am *I* naked?! Where's my phone!? What time is it? What DAY is it?!"

The gang began to stir and wake up then, each one registering their own complaint about where they were and how awful they felt. Then followed the inevitable curse words upon discovering Dr. T-Sauce's shitty tattoos that had somehow found their way onto *everyone's* bodies.

"This is the definition of a waking nightmare," Kelly's friend who had previously been wearing a red dress said as she saw a series of misshapen "footprints in the sand" that were now permanently on parade up her leg like a bunch of demented slugs.

"Holy HELLBAIT!" another woman said at the "SLIPPERY WHEN WET" road sign with a downward-pointing arrow on her lower abdomen. That one didn't look as sloppy as the others. He'd spelled the words right at least, and managed to make the lines straight, somehow. He'd even pulled off some shading.

"Tell me this isn't real," wailed another girl, rubbing anxiously at what was apparently a pin-up girl's body with a well-known male celebrity's face on her bicep. Also hideously ugly. Really, really hard to look at. And very, very visible.

Auggie was afraid to tell Susanna about her ass. She had been frantically searching her body for garbage tattoo art without finding any. He was certain she would be devastated by the discovery.

"Susannaaah..?" Kelly said slowly. "What the hell is on your ass?"

Susanna paled and stood, twisting desperately to see what was on her backside. "What is it?!? Tell me!!!"

Kelly squinted. "It looks like... beets. A bushel of beets. That were run over by a two-ton truck."

"*What the hell*?! Are you sure?!!"

"Yeah, those are definitely beets," another friend chimed in.

Susanna looked horrified. "I can't believe this. I have beets on my ass?! Forever?! What the serious FUCK, Dr. T!?!"

Dr. T-Sauce stood up. He pulled his shorts quickly as he mumbled, "Hey. I just followed orders. You all drugged me. I don't know why you wanted what you wanted but I sure as hell didn't come up with these ideas."

"But... YOU RUINED US!" one of the girls cried.

"Hey!" Dr. T-Sauce threw back like a father yelling at his child. "Easy! Ever heard of laser removal? You can reverse this shit. Don't come at me with your early-morning complaints."

"That shit is SO expensive," one of the ladies pouted.

"I don't have a job and my student loans just ran out," Susannah cried.

Auggie scrambled to get dressed and going. It was hard without coffee, but the sound of eight women crying was enough of a substitute.

The drop-off ride was soundtracked by sniffling, crying, and some soft occasional murmurs of comfort. It was the most somber drop off Auggie had experienced in all his years of Zebra service.

One thing was for sure: Auggie was definitely going to have to wear a long-sleeve shirt to the Interview.

DR. PHILIP K. PARKER

Philip prided himself especially on three things:

1. He didn't intentionally mislead anyone to get what he wanted from them, which was a grand accomplishment of restraint, in his opinion. He recognized that he had quite the capacity to manipulate if he wanted.

2. He'd managed to never break the patient-therapist boundaries, which had turned out to be surprisingly easy, as most of the women were not that attractive once he got to know them, really.

3. He had a tremendous green thumb. He could grow roses like no one else on his block. But bonsai was his favorite. His bonsai collection in his office made his patients envious. They often offered him money for them, but he'd never sell a plant that he had raised. That was why he had so many. He couldn't let them go. He'd come to consider them his children. Maybe that was strange and a little twisted, but at least Philip knew he was a great plant father.

The day after his date-gone-so-wrong-then-so-right, Philip went a bit crazy with the plant-keeping. He devoted himself to his garden after biking to the local nursery with a wagon hitched to the back rack for a Sunday spending spree. He installed a whole new section of succulents, geometrically arranging them to form a beautiful mosaic-like pattern. With each pat of the soil, he thought about how completely satisfied he'd felt in that shower with Cassandra. The fierce obsessiveness of his emotions had tied his stomach in a knot. He couldn't think about much else. He had to take a Xanax just to go to bed that night.

Monday morning was rainy, which was great for sealing in the newest part of the garden. Philip had a new client coming in as well, a young actor named Gerard Vice who wanted hypnotherapy. Phil rarely practiced hypnotherapy, but this particular case intrigued him and he was feeling up for the task.

Gerard was apparently gearing up for a huge production and simultaneously suffering from acute anxiety but wasn't sure where it was coming from. When prompted, he had revealed a troubling story over the phone. When he was 14 years old, an older woman had pursued him at a restaurant in which he was dining with his family. The woman had beckoned him over and told him she thought he was cute, pulling him away to make out in the corner before grudgingly telling him that she was 29. He'd given her his number before his father had come over to look for him. She'd called and they'd had intense phone sex. Then, one evening she'd picked him up in her Jeep wearing a blue poncho.

He had absolutely no memory of what had happened the rest of the night.

Philip wanted to explore the gap in his memory with hypnotherapy. He told Gerard that if he had a lot coming up with his career, he needed to face all of his past in order to be strong enough not to self-destruct. Gerard had agreed without hesitation.

Philip answered the door to find that Gerard was a handsome young man wearing a black bomber jacket, his short, dark hair beaded with raindrops.

"Dr. Parker?"

"Yes. Hello, Gerard. Please come in."

Gerard hugged him awkwardly, catching Philip off guard.

"I'm so relieved to be doing this. Thanks for seeing me on such short notice," he said into Philip's crisp shirt.

"That's quite all right, Gerard," Philip said amicably, ending the embrace as gracefully as he could and leading him into his office. "Why don't you lie down on the couch, make yourself as comfortable as possible."

Gerard took his jacket and shoes off and stretched out on the olive green upholstered couch. He closed his eyes and looked quite peaceful.

"Are you ready and open to where this journey will bring you?"

"I'm part terrified," Gerard admitted, "but very ready."

"You're brave to do this, and few live to regret being brave. I know you'll do great," Philip said, trying to pump him up. The more the client trusted him, the deeper he could go in the cranial probing. "I'm here, ready to assist you in any way if you struggle during this, so rest assured you're in safe hands."

"This is gonna be nuts," Gerard said, suddenly looking like a spooked little boy, terrified of the haunted house he'd just decided to go into.

"Just relax," Philip said. "That's the whole key, the whole trick. Relax into the fear. Once you slip away from your conscious grip, your body will do its best to heal itself, which includes releasing whatever it's holding onto that's toxic. I promise to stay close, helping at every turn. Now, close your eyes and try to put yourself in a neutral place where you feel safe and warm and free; just a happy, pure expression of yourself."

Gerard closed his eyes obediently. Philip began his slow, low meditation chant. Then he counted backwards from ten. "You are now far, far away, back in the Ventura Country landscape that you grew up in, swinging in a hammock above lush, green grasses, under wide blue skies and sunshine so soft it feels like warm velvet, a breeze dancing in your hair that smells like eucalyptus and cedar and roses… Do you feel it?"

"Yes." Gerard's voice came out sounding younger, unburdened by time and reality.

"With whom am I speaking?" Philip asked politely.

"It's me, Gerard."

"And how old are you, Gerard?"

"Fourteen," he said.

"Hello, fourteen-year-old Gerard. How are you feeling?"

"Nervous."

"Why are you nervous?"

"I'm meeting someone."

"Who are you meeting, Gerard?"

"A woman. Lisa. She's an older lady. She thinks I'm hot," he said in a boastful and somewhat disbelieving tone.

"What are you two going to do?" Philip asked.

"I don't know," he said. "I gave her my address. She's coming to get me."

"Is that her Jeep pulling into the driveway?"

Gerard's brow creased slightly. "Yes. That's her."

"And are you getting into her car now?"

"Yes," Gerard said. "It's strange."

"What does it smell like?"

Gerard paused. "Like… weird, fruity perfume, and something else. Something gross, like stinky gym shoes."

"What does she look like?"

"She looks kinda messed up, like she's upset or something. Her eye makeup is smudged. I think she's older than 29. Her hair's in a messy ponytail. She has chipped green nail polish. Her nails are dirty underneath the polish. She's wearing a low-cut poncho and there's a stain on her skirt." He paused. "I feel kind of bad for her."

"OK, it's OK, Gerard. I'm here with you, the whole way. Look around, what else about the car?"

"She brought me a blended drink in a thermos. It tastes like… like a bad Slurpee, artificial cherry, spiked with alcohol, bitter. I don't like it. Now, she's putting on my seatbelt," he said. "I was going to, but she said she wanted to do it. She's… fumbling with it. She put it on tight. She touched my thighs getting it on. I can see a lot of her cleavage."

"All right," Philip said, leaning closer. "Is she driving now?"

"Yeah, she's driving down my road, she's a crazy driver like my mom," he said, sounding distressed. "She's taking the turns fast, like she's in a rush. She has her hand on my thigh. She asks me if I want more of the drink, and I say no. She's hurt, says I don't like her special drink she made for me, so I take another sip to be polite."

"It's OK, Gerard," Philip said. "I'm right here in the back seat. Keep telling me what's happening."

"She's taking me up into the hills," he said. "She says she's taking me to a special place she found. She says it has a beautiful view. I'm a little sleepy, though, and she keeps squeezing my thigh and telling me how good I look, how I'm going to be such a handsome man when I get older."

"What are you saying?"

"I don't say anything, I'm quiet. I feel heavy, like I'm paralyzed and things are…happening to me, but, like, I can't stop them."

"You're in shock. Breathe, Gerard. Where are you now?"

"We're in the woods, she turned off the road," Gerard continued, tension gathered on his face. "She says she knows the shortcut. She's saying how I'm so great because I haven't turned into a bitter old man yet, that I can see her for who she is because I'm not judging her, how she feels so safe with me…"

"Alright, keep going," Philip coaxed softly. "Have you parked, yet?"

"Yes," Gerard said softly. "We're in the middle of the woods. There's hardly any light left in the sky but she turns the headlights off. She starts kissing me. She tastes sour, like stale cigarettes and… just… *sour*. She takes off my seat belt. She makes me drink more of that awful drink. I feel sick. She takes her shirt off and shoves her boobs in my face. She's moaning and saying how good it feels to be alone with me, how sweet I am." Gerard starts crying softly. "She keeps saying that I taste good, like innocence."

"What happens next, Gerard?"

"She unbuckles my belt and starts sucking me off. I've never had a blow job before. Then she pulls up her skirt and sticks my hand inside her," Gerard was whispering now. "She says she wants me inside her. I don't say anything. She asks if I've done it before, I shake my head no. I'm frozen, I can't speak. She says she'll make me a man, she gets on top of me…" Gerard started full-on crying. "I can't stop her," he choked out. "I can't stop any of it, I can't stop her, I can't stop any of it, it smells so weird in the car, I feel sick. I feel so sick, I think I'm going to throw up… Oh *no*! I just threw up on her. She slaps me, I start crying. I start crying and I can't stop. She tells me to shut up, she punches me in the chest. She says no woman will ever love me if I'm a crier. She says no one will want me if I'm a wimp. She says I ruined her favorite shirt and I ruined my first time, and I won't ever be a man…" Gerard began to hyperventilate, his chest heaving up and down at an alarming pace. Philip decided it was time to make the call.

"Gerard, I am taking you out now. I need you to retreat from this place, and return to your safe place, return to people who love you and the people you love. We are waiting for you, OK?"

"OK," Gerard whimpered.

"I'm going to count backwards from ten and you will be there. In your safe place. With people you love and people who love you."

"Cassandra," Gerard said softly, shaking.

Philip's eyes widened. Did he hear him correctly? Or was he losing it?

"What did you say?"

"Get me out of here!" Gerard wailed quietly.

Philip decided to ignore it for the time being. It was too weird. Probably just a coincidence. "10… 9… 8… 7… 6… 5… 4… 3… 2… 1…"

He snapped his fingers.

Gerard opened his eyes, hands flying up to his wet cheeks, surprised to find himself crying. He stared at Philip, as pale and vulnerable as a lost boy.

"What happened?"

"Who's Cassandra?" Philip asked immediately, unable to help himself.

Gerard's brow knitted up in confusion. "What? Why am I crying?"

"You mentioned her name at the end, when I was trying to pull you out."

"Weird," he said. "She's… someone I'm staying with right now. What happened, though? Why am I crying, Dr. Philip?"

"Are you romantically involved with this Cassandra?" Philip asked, still unable to control himself.

"No! I have no idea why I mentioned her. What the hell happened to me?"

Philip relaxed, trusting Gerard to be telling the truth. He'd have no reason to lie to his therapist, would he? Philip reached over and handed Gerard a bottle of water. Then he pressed the playback on his digital recorder. They sat in silence, re-listening to the session. Gerard let out some silent tears and cursed softly. At the end, he heard himself say Cassandra's name and shook his head, utterly baffled.

"What do you think you meant by mentioning her name there?" Philip pressed on, relentlessly digging for the full story of what was going on between them.

"I guess I must feel safe with her," Gerard said, shrugging. "But is it just me, or are there many more details to discuss, like the fact that I lost my virginity to a 30-something-year-old rapist?"

"Everything said during a session is of utmost importance, *especially* the things you don't understand," Philip stretched on to justify his further interrogation. "Why do you think you feel safe with this Cassandra?"

"No clue. It's funny, because the other night I heard this random voice in my head, asking if I loved her, and I thought I didn't, but maybe I do… Maybe I should try to get together with her."

"I'd advise against that," Philip said gravely. How had Gerard had the same internal thought experience as Philip the other night on the gondola date? All he knew was he had to stomp this flame between them out as quickly as possible. "It's way too soon in the healing process for you to be entering into any intimate relationships."

"I don't know," Gerard said thoughtfully. "She's different. She's got something. And she seems really into me. It could be therapeutic for me to try to be emotionally involved with a woman again."

Philip felt a searing hot flash of jealousy at the realization that Gerard was announcing himself as his direct competition. Probably the reason Cassandra had been on the fence from the start with Philip was because she had feelings for Gerard as well. He had to up the intensity immediately. "Gerard, on an intimate level you are unstable and a danger to anyone. Unless you don't care if you end up hurting her, I wouldn't even consider starting a relationship until you get proper counseling for rape trauma."

Gerard's face shifted and he shook his head in disbelief. "Rape. Yeah. Wow. I had no idea," he said. "No wonder I blocked it out. I really can't believe it."

"You need to heal, Gerard. Not buffer the situation with another woman. You need to sit alone in this discomfort until you're not uncomfortable anymore."

Gerard frowned. "Damn it. Healing is hard work."

"That's why we usually avoid it at all costs."

"I don't have time to heal right now. Can't I pay you to do it for me?"

"Very funny. The only way to heal is to feel. Maybe we both should try it. I also gave up on feelings a while ago." Had Philip really just said that? It was a wildly out-of-character statement—especially for him to say to a patient.

Gerard raised his eyebrows. "Sounds like you need some therapy, too."

"Everybody needs therapy. That's why I got into the business."

On Gerard's way out, Philip decided to give him a bonsai. He didn't have time to feel guilty about breaking his cardinal rule against psychological manipulation. He even let Gerard choose whichever one he wanted. And then, as he watched the young man walk away, Philip realized he'd broken two of the three rules.

And for what? A woman who probably didn't even really like him?

Philip decided he would start getting up at 4am to do two bike rides a day, like Jim had suggested. He wanted to be so exhausted he couldn't even think—let alone feel—anymore.

And maybe, just *maybe*, he'd look into some therapy for himself.

CASSANDRA PANDA

It was time for some serious girl talk. Cassandra made a plan to meet her fellow musician friend Odessa at Venice Peach for spiked smoothies. They ordered two namesake specialty smoothies from Griselda up top, then took them down the secret stairs into the underground speakeasy to have the bartender, who was the Electric Lady named Sizz at the moment, add in some pineapple rum.

Hunky and Punky sat at the bar as usual, drinking and looking more sad than funny.

"Hey ladies," said Hunky, winking and wiggling his big pierced-up ears at them.

"Care to share?" said Punky, sticking out his tongue and wiggling an empty glass at them.

Cassandra shook her head as Odessa laughed and dropped a little of her spiked smoothie into the glass.

"OK, that's enough for you," she said.

"What about me?" asked Hunky, polishing his drink off and putting the empty glass down loudly on the bar.

Odessa looked at Cassandra, who didn't want to seem greedy so she reluctantly poured some of her own smoothie into Hunky's glass. He handed her a penis-shaped balloon as a thank you. She put it on the bar and Odessa laughed and flicked it back towards Hunky. It bounced off his nose and floated down to the ground.

The clowns honked their armpits as the bartender shook her head. "Don't give them any more handouts," Sizz said to Cassandra and Odessa. "I think the Madame isn't in her office at the moment, if you two want some privacy from these moochers."

"Ey! I resent that," whined Hunky.

"Yeah?" asked Sizz. "When's the last time you paid for a drink? Or tipped, for that matter?!"

"Hey! We work our asses off every day sifting through all them damn dumb tourists to find cool enough ones to invite down here. We don't make shit for pay on the day-to-day hustle!"

"Yeah, we keep this place afloat just for some free drinks and a smidge of the door. Plus, it's too hot on the boardwalk right now," said Punky. "You try promoting in this polyester clown suit."

Sizz rolled her eyes at the two girls. "See what I have to deal with every day?"

"OK, we'll be in Madame Hummingbird's office." Cassandra couldn't get up fast enough. "Thanks, Sizz!"

They went behind the curtain to see an empty set of velvet pillows around a darkened crystal ball. Curling up cozily, the two slurped their smoothies as Cassandra shared what she'd been up to, swapping out the gondola ride for a picnic in the park. But minus the gondola ride, it all sounded shallow and blasé.

Odessa looked bored as she sipped the last of her smoothie. "There has *got* to be more to your life than guys right now," she said. "And those are *hardly* stories. You haven't even had sex with either of them."

"I know! I'm sorry, it's all I can think about for some terrible reason. I swear, it almost seems like they're both, like, competing for me without knowing each other exists. It's so weird. And Gerard is obviously ahead, because he's… Gerard Vice…" Cassandra stared at the darkened crystal ball. Had it just flickered at the mention of his name? Odessa didn't seem to have noticed anything, and looked like she was ready to bail on the hang altogether. "I realize that this is all very shallow-sounding," Cassandra rushed on. "But, I guess what I'm trying to ask you for advice on is, should I pick Philip? He did bring me on this romantic date, and he's definitely in love with me."

"Oh yeah? How do you know?"

"A friend told me," Cassandra answered cryptically.

"Sounds suspect," Odessa said. "Was this 'friend' also trying to get into your pants?"

Cassandra laughed. "I doubt it. He's very much not my type. Besides… he has a girlfriend."

Odessa looked skeptical. "Neither of those rule out potential interest. Also, why do you need to choose just one? Why can't you have three doting fuckboys? I guarantee it'll only make them want you more."

Cassandra sighed. She still hadn't told Odessa about her stubborn V-card situation due to deep shame. There was no way her free-spirited friend wouldn't torture her with that information. "Yeah, I figured you would say something like that, Ms. Woman-of-a-Thousand-Sex-Slaves."

Odessa tossed her surfer curls and shrugged. "What can I say? It works these days. Keep 'em casual and keep 'em all! Be a vacation and you'll always get the best of them."

Cassandra looked at her friend in admiration. "I know. You're so confident about it, too. I wish I could be like you, I really do. I think I'm a little too needy for that lifestyle, though."

"Needy for what?" Odessa countered. "You sound like you're stuck in the 1900s. Get with the times, babe. There are sex bots, vibrators and dildos that fuck longer, friends who give compliments better, body pillows to snuggle that don't snore, and scientists who can get you pregnant." She smiled devilishly. "So tell me, what do you actually need a partner for?"

Cassandra laughed. "When you put it like that, I got nothing."

"See?" Odessa winked at her. "Now, tell me who told you that Philip's in *looove* with you."

"It's kinda unusual," Cassandra said hesitantly.

"I can tell, that's why I'm so curious."

"You won't believe me if I tell you," Cassandra said.

"Girl, you wouldn't believe half the shit I could tell you about *my* life lately," Odessa said. "Try me."

Cassandra had never told anyone about Bobobo before. She wondered, briefly, if there could be any real repercussions in talking about him. There were none that were obvious to her in the moment.

"Well… it's my friend Bobobo. He lives… under a bridge."

"Bobobo? What a name. A homeless guy?"

"Not exactly."

Odessa laughed. "He lives under a bridge? That's homeless, last time I checked."

Cassandra gathered her nerve. "It would be, but he's… a canal creature."

"A canal creature?" Odessa's eyebrows shot up and her purple lips made an "o" shape. "Now there's something I haven't heard of before."

"Yeah. He's this weird eel thing with a cute little face and a body that jingles when he, um, moves. And he communicates telepathically. He says I'm the only one who he's shown himself to in years. He gives me advice and stuff."

"*Fascinating.*" Odessa looked like she believed Cassandra and it felt momentarily good to have shared the secret of Bobobo with her. "How long have you been hanging out with this—Bobobo?"

"For a few months now. He says he's been around forever, but who knows. I thought I was kind of going crazy for a little while in the beginning, but then it became too consistent of a relationship for me to be just out of my head."

"You have to introduce me!"

Cassandra felt a clenching in her chest. She hadn't expected that reaction.

"Um… OK. Sure, sometime. Maybe!"

Odessa launched herself up off the pillow.

"Uh, you mean right *now*?"

"No better time. Let's go!"

Cassandra fretted during the whole sunny walk to the canals. "Try not to have any crazy reactions, he might be shy. I don't even know if he'll show himself if you're there. Let's just feel it out."

"Stop worrying, silly," Odessa said cheerfully. "I'm great with people. Remember? I know all about 'feeling it out.'"

Cassandra smiled tightly and felt another tug inside. Was she feeling rightfully protective or was she being kind of weirdly possessive over Bobobo? She couldn't tell yet. But she was definitely bothered.

"What are you going to ask him? Why do you want to meet him so much?"

"Why *wouldn't* I want to meet him?" Odessa laughed. "He's a canal creature! I don't have anything specific to ask, I just can't wait to check the little dude out. And I can tell if he has a crush on you."

"*No*," Cassandra said adamantly, side-stepping some dog poo on the sidewalk and hitting herself in the face with a pointy arm of an overgrown century plant. "Ouch! Do *not* mention that! I don't want things getting awkward. Come on. *Promise* me."

Odessa grinned. "I knew it. He does have a crush on you. You're totally freaking out right now. Relax. I'm going to be an absolute kitty cat. I won't say anything that even slightly borders on awkward."

"Ugh. You're impossible." Cassandra's regret was real already. Bees buzzed away, busy at work on the roses and lavender that lined peoples' front lawns. As usual, most of the houses overlooking the canals appeared empty of people. Gorgeous placeholders just taunting passersby to make more money, work around the clock to afford prime real estate that they would never be home enough to fully enjoy.

She led Odessa through a crack in the hedges down to the slimy, pungent banks of the canal, then stooped to walk under the Dell bridge. Odessa crouched down to examine some graffiti on the underside of the bridge while Cassandra sat tentatively on her usual rock.

"Now what?"

"Hold on," Cassandra said. "Give it a second."

She closed her eyes.

-Bobobo, are you there? I brought a friend. She wanted to meet you. She waited a moment. *Bobobo?*

-I'm here, echoed his voice, sounding distant. *I'm coming, my land princess.*

-No rush, she thought, *but did you hear what I said?*

-I heard you. That's fine. I will expose myself to any friend of yours you trust enough to bring to me.

Cassandra opened her eyes to find Odessa staring at her.

"He's on his way," Cassandra said carefully. "Be chill, OK?"

"Jeez, Cass, what do you think I am? Some small-minded bitch?" Odessa seemed genuinely hurt and Cassandra felt bad. She was going to say something apologetic, but there was a sudden tinkling in the air and they both froze.

-Here I come, Bobobo echoed.

Odessa's face lit up and she grabbed Cassandra's hands.

"I hear him!"

Cassandra gave her friend a tight-lipped smile.

The tinkling grew louder. Then there was a tiny splash at their feet. They both looked down as Bobobo made his way out of the water, schlumping, rippling and slithering onto shore in his own strange, lumpy way. He peered up at them with his cute little face.

-Hello, my pretty land princesses.

Odessa closed her eyes like she was copying Cassandra. She concentrated.

-Hello, Bobobo. I'm Odessa.

-My dear, you are a natural communicator. And as striking as a sea anemone.

Odessa giggled and blushed. Cassandra reclaimed her hands from Odessa's grasp, absurdly jealous even though she really didn't want to be. Bobobo seemed to sense her jealousy and hurriedly shifted the conversation back to her.

-As is my ever-lovely Cassandra, favored by many admirers. Has she told you about her little predicament with the land-dwelling males right now?

-She has, Odessa thought back. Cassandra shot her a warning look.

-It's not a big deal, Cassandra chimed in. *I'm sorry it's all I've been thinking about. I'm usually more concerned with larger issues… Or am I? Wait, that was supposed to be a thought for just me. Damnit!*

-I told her to just have two doting boyfriends, Odessa thought. *What's the dilemma? Nobody's trying to put a ring on it or anything.*

-That's such an outdated expression, Cassandra thought, wrinkling her brow in distaste.

-I agree with your friend, Bobobo echoed. *Odessa, was it?* They nodded at him. *Why not have all the fun instead of all the torment? Look at me, I have to sit by and feel my heart breaking every mating season for my duck-*

born lover. If there were any other contenders, I'd care a lot less... But alas, I am the only canal creature I have ever known.

Cassandra hadn't heard him communicate like that before. It was weird how different people brought out different sides in others. She'd had a feeling Odessa would shift their dynamic. This was a version of Bobobo she had never seen.

-See, even Bobobo agrees, Odessa echoed back triumphantly.

-What about you, Odessa? Bobobo turned to her. *What's your love life like these days?*

-Thanks for asking! Odessa thought, smiling at him. Cassandra then realized she hadn't asked Odessa a single thing about herself since they'd met up. She was so busy trying to impress her beautiful and talented friend that she'd become painfully self-centered.

-I'm pretty satisfied, Odessa continued. *I have a rotation of steady partners who are also kind of friends, so though I occasionally add or drop people, I don't ever feel lonely.*

Bobobo winked at Odessa. *-Sounds like I should be taking advice from you, you little sexpot.* Cassandra had never seen him wink before. Her blood boiled a little. How dare Odessa swoop in and steal her secret friend away from her? He'd never spoken to Cassandra in such a way. Was she not as sexy as Odessa? Of course she couldn't be. She had never had sex before. She felt her heart rate rise as the sickly, sticky, heavy feeling of jealousy poured over her.

-I can tell we're making you upset, dear Cassandra. Bobobo sounded concerned.

-I'm not upset, Cassandra argued unconvincingly, pouting harder.

-There's enough of Bobobo to go around, you know. He shook his body, tinkling a long laugh. Odessa joined him.

-I hate jealousy, Cassandra thought sadly. *It's the worst feeling in the*

world. *It's like venom in my blood. I can't control the release. This is why I can't share partners or be casual. I care too much.*

-There's only one way out of it, you know, Bobobo echoed.

-What?

-You have to dive deeper into it until it you get through it.

-So, you're saying I should be jealous all the time until I can't feel it anymore?

-No. I'm saying that you should intentionally put yourself in jealousy-provoking situations and ride it out.

Bobobo's cute little face wrinkled up as he smiled at the two women.

-I hate people, Cassandra thought. *-Bobobo? Why does everyone have to suck?*

-It has always been this way, since humans first walked the earth. Bobobo wriggled his way over to the canal water and took a tiny sip. He suddenly looked tired.

-But, why? Cassandra continued. *Why can't we just live a natural life like the animals around us? Why do we have to be so complicated and complex?*

-There's nothing complicated or complex about jealousy, Bobobo replied. *Even the lowest and simplest forms of life feel it.*

-Very true, thought Odessa. *But then why do I not feel it?*

-You've achieved a higher level of being, Bobobo thought admiringly.

"Bobobo looks tired," Cassandra interrupted out loud. "We should let him rest. I've never seen him out this long."

Odessa nodded.

-Thanks for all your wisdom, Odessa thought. *It was lovely to meet you, Bobobo.*

-Where are you going? Bobobo responded. *Let's keep the party going. Let's go back to Cassandra's place.*

-*Can you even do that?* Cassandra looked alarmed.

-*I can do whatever I want, I'm a canal creature.* Bobobo looked proud for a moment, squinting into the sun. Odessa and Cassandra looked at each other, at a loss. *Don't worry about me, ladies,* he continued. *I can party. I can shape-shift. I can last all day and night out here.* He tinkled hard, rippling his body like a high-powered fan. *And it's been way too long since I had a beer.*

-*I don't think that's a good idea,* Cassandra thought softly.

-*What if people saw you out and about? It's broad daylight,* Odessa chimed in, picking up on Cassandra's alarm.

-*Let them see me,* Bobobo thought bravely, puffing out his chest a bit. *I'd be proud to be seen with the likes of you two beautiful land princesses.*

Cassandra felt anxious and stuck. She didn't know what to do. She'd never imagined having to talk Bobobo out of exposing himself to the public and traveling away from the canals. The panic was riding towards her like a group of dark horses set on "trample" mode. She closed her eyes and focused on breathing out of her nose.

-*Damn it, I actually have to get to rehearsal,* Odessa thought as she checked her phone watch. *Can we do a rain check, Bobobo? A late night hang will be cool and you won't have to worry about people taking your picture and stuff.*

Bobobo emitted a little sigh that sounded like a baby kitten's mewl.

-*I suppose,* he thought. *Raincheck for when? Later tonight?*

-*Maybe,* Odessa thought back. *We'll come find you.*

-*I'm going to hold you to that.* Bobobo slunk up to Odessa's leg and nudged it gently, smiling flirtatiously. Cassandra watched as her friend did her best to smile back without shivering in disgust. He then clumsily slunk over to Cassandra and gave her the same affectionate bump to the leg, leaving a smudge of canal-colored slime. He did look totally exhausted to Cassandra.

-*I'm not that tired,* he thought back, winking again. *I'll rest up for later.*

With that, he schlumped back into the canal water, the tinkling filling the air as he swam away. It had never sounded so ominous to Cassandra.

"That was a close call." Odessa put her hand out for her friend and together they emerged from under the bridge.

"Seriously. You saved his life. And my nerves."

"I can't believe he was trying to come hang out!"

Cassandra sighed. "Well, there goes that friendship."

"What do you mean?" Odessa's eyes were wide. "We *have* to party with him! Who else gets to hang out with a canal creature? I wanna watch the little dude chug a beer!"

"*No way.* That will most definitely not be happening in this lifetime," Cassandra said firmly. They walked up to the front of her house. Gerard was just leaving, dressed in a crisp white tuxedo suit, looking as sharp and finely crafted as a ninja sword.

He grinned at them as he passed. "Hey! Running to the awards thing!" he said to Cassandra. "Catch up soon!"

Odessa's jaw was on the ground.

"Oh, *that's* Gerard Vice? Yeah, girl… Now I get it."

GERARD VICE

Ever since he'd been hypnotized, Gerard felt like a new man.

It was always worth it to know the whole story, and the whole story was that he was raped by an adult at a young age. That explained so many of his quirks: His overcompensating desire to act like some big lover boy. His inherent fear of older women who pursued him. His urge to avoid anyone who got too close. Knowing the truth now made him feel more in control of himself. Maybe now he'd even be able to have sober sex, something he couldn't recall doing once in his entire life. Even when he'd had longer-lasting girlfriends, he always had to drink before making moves. That skittishness felt like it was gone, now, and he felt more collected than ever. He'd faced the darkest part of his past and emerged stronger.

Which was good news considering he was about to be put under a million microscopes and dissected, his personality split and trained in different directions, five versions of his face and voice streamed around the planet.

Right now, Gerard knew himself better than he ever had, and he was eager to get out there and put his best self forward. And there was probably no better way to do that than host an awards show called "The Right Nows" – a relatively new and exciting artists awards show ruled by the public. Anyone had a chance at winning, which kept it way more relevant than all the dustier awards shows whose winners were determined by over-entitled groups of people no one knew or cared about in the first place. The Right

Nows were crushing every other award show in the business. Winners were only decided when the voting clock ran out after each category was presented. Absolutely anyone could use The Right Nows app to vote—all the way up to the last millisecond. Then the most popular vote tallies would pop up and the award would be presented by the host.

This year, the host was Gerard, who'd snagged the gig last minute when the initial host dropped out due to a viral illness. He had received the offer to host the day after he'd gone through hypnotherapy – a sure sign of the universe rewarding him for his bravery in the department of self-improvement. It seemed it was now pouring in his success forecast and he was having fun getting soaked with attention. He wasn't up for The Right Now Hottest Actor of the Year award *yet*, but next year, after the first season of his show aired, he sure as hell could assume he'd be. The network always seemed to know exactly what they were doing when it came to selecting the judges.

It was admittedly a daunting gig, but it appealed to Gerard's ego just fine at the moment. He *had* this, he thought to himself. He didn't even feel the need to pop pills or drink anything on his way over in the hired car. Instead, he took a selfie in his tux and posted it across his social media profiles, tagging the awards show, earning an instant barrage of hearts and likes and comments that stroked his tomcat ego, making him purr like a few drinks would, normally.

Or was that anxiety rattling in his chest?

Just in case, Gerard played his favorite soothing piano music in his earbuds as he practiced his breathing techniques for the rest of the ride.

The Right Nows ceremony took place at the new Victory Arena in Hollywood. The VIP entrance was a ten-ring circus of gorgeous VIP specimens and flashing cameras. Gerard grinned like a prince as he made his way inside after walking the clogged-up red carpet for what seemed like an hour. His former-agent-turned-manager Jimmy caught up to him.

"Great news."

"That seems to be the only kind of news I'm getting from you these days."

"What can I say? You're a golden sonofabitch on fire."

"What is it? What's the news?"

"Kristina Brightside heard your podcast confession and wants to do a little improv bit with you before the 'Hottest Actor' award presentation."

Gerard swallowed hard. It suddenly felt like his whole body had deflated.

"She—she's not angry?"

"Her manager said Kristina thought it was funny and sort of sweet."

That didn't seem likely to Gerard, but who was he to say what Kristina found *funny and sort of sweet*? He barely knew her. What a curveball.

"OK…" Gerard said hesitantly. "Do I have any choice in the matter? Does she want to talk it through, first?"

"Nope and negatory," Jimmy said. "The network gave her permission to do what she wants, since she is, in fact, already winning by landslides in that category. But also, this thing, no matter which way it goes, will be great for publicity, and super great for your show's hype, I might unnecessarily add. So just buck up and let her lead the dance, alright?"

"Of course," Gerard said. "Thanks for the head's up, I guess."

He got some gum off a production assistant and chewed it hard. Some of the network executives caught up with him and then they were off on a walk-and-talk containing more instructions and directions than Gerard could ever possibly remember as he was simultaneously mic-ed up by the audio department.

Then Thomas Berry, the president of the streaming network, grabbed him by the shoulders and they locked eyes for a terrifyingly tense moment. "Have fun out there, or else no one else will," the powerful man said grimly. Gerard managed to fire up a thin smile like his executioner had just cracked a joke.

Jimmy clapped him on the back and gestured towards the stage. "Showtime, golden boy. Just like in rehearsals," he said—which was a twisted joke because there hadn't been any. He pushed Gerard out onto the stage abruptly. A stadium of tens of thousands of people cheered, rippling with excitement and inebriated energy.

"Good evening and welcome to The Right Nows!" Gerard said, kicking into his autopilot host mode, voice thundering out over the sea of faces. "I'm Gerard Vice, and it's an absolute honor to be hosting The Right Nows! Are you ready to have some fun and hand out some well-deserved awards to your favorite hardworking people in this crazy thing we call show business?!"

Gerard thought his hair might blow clean off his head from the energy the crowd was directing onto the stage. It was a level of intensity he'd never felt before. He was having a hard time relaxing enough to enjoy the fact that he was suddenly ringmaster for the world's greatest awards show. In truth, the attention-hungry actor in him was enjoying it so much he felt the distinct urge to do a triple backflip while screaming bloody murder right back at them. Could he actually do that, though? Thomas Berry might think not. Too crazy town. And definitely too risky. Gerard hadn't done gymnastics since high school and his triple backflip was probably pretty rusty. He didn't want to end up air-lifted to the nearest available surgeon.

The cue screen had jokes ready and waiting for him, but he was suddenly feeling strangely confident, so he decided to try his own bit. "I don't know about you all, but I love these awards more than the holidays. It's way more satisfying to watch your favorite actors win this award than watch your family open a bunch of presents they pretend to like." He paused for the tentative titters of the willing crowd. "And the Right Nows award itself is nothing compared to the aftermath, from what I've heard…" He made his best scandalous face. "Let's just say that the win is known to us up-and-comers as the gift that keeps on giving. So come find me after the show…"

This time the audience laughed loudly enough for Gerard to feel satisfied—until the stage manager's harsh voice came through in his inner-ear bud. "Stick to the cue cards, kid. We got a schedule to keep."

Gerard, quickly realizing that he was supposed to strictly follow the rules or they'd replace him with a hologram, reverted back to the pre-written cue cards.

Eight awards later, it was finally time for the Kristina Brightside surprise skit.

Gerard felt the sweat trickling down his forehead and wiped his brow as he launched into the digital cue-card-dictated spiel: "For this next presentation, I have a very special guest joining me onstage…"

Suddenly the stage lighting shifted and the audience began to laugh. Gerard looked around for Kristina, only to find that she wasn't onstage but the giant screen behind him had begun to display a video clip of him in boxer shorts, drunk-dancing to a Top 40 pop song in someone's living room while singing (terribly) along. He squinted at the screen, unable to recall the whereabouts or source of the footage. The roar of laughter filled his ears as the shot zoomed in to his liquor-reddened face, capturing his off-pitch screechy singalong with embarrassing intimacy. Gerard felt his cheeks bloom a fiery furnace red. He pulled at his tux collar, which was suddenly chokingly tight, as the screen abruptly went blank and the stunning woman named Kristina Brightside walked out onto the stage.

She smiled scandalously and then embraced Gerard. Then she pulled back and put her hands on his cheeks. "Sweetie, why are you blushing?"

The crowd was going so nuts that they had to wait what felt like a full three minutes to continue. Gerard welcomed the pause, staring into Kristina's gorgeous, bottomless eyes as he felt the blood drain from his cheeks, rushing southward. But that was an equally embarrassing place for it to be, so he cleared his throat and turned back to face the audience. They were certainly a scary sight. Especially if he focused on their gawking, hysterical faces.

To quiet them down, Kristina finally spoke. "As you may be aware, Gerard here decided to bare our most intimate moments years ago to the general public on a little podcast recently called… What's the name, Gerard? It's so bad I don't even want to remember it."

"*I Slept With Them First…*" Gerard mumbled.

The crowd cheered uproariously again.

"Yup, that's the one," Kristina said. "So, you didn't remember me getting that charming footage of you singing your heart out on that now-infamous night, Gerard?"

Gerard shook his head sheepishly.

Kristina laughed sharply. "Funny. I wonder, then, how you remember so many other details from that evening. A curious thing, indeed!"

The audience *OoOh*-ed at the case-in-point.

Gerard could hardly speak, let alone own up. "I'm so sorry?"

"Is that a question or an apology?" Kristina sassed back at him.

Damn, she was burning him good.

"Kristina, I'm really sorry. I honestly am."

"Well, good, because all artists, *especially* women, are already dealing with enough, we don't need to be subjected to that kind of privacy-exploiting B.S…" The women in the audience screamed their support. Kristina caressed his cheek and gazed up into his eyes. "It's too bad, too," she added. "You're so good looking these days I probably could have gone for seconds."

And with that, she turned and exited the stage, leaving him all by himself up there, defeated and deflated.

Gerard hung his head. The sound of the crowd grew so overwhelming that it became a roaring white noise in his eardrums as he struggled to gain composure. Thomas Berry himself barked into his ear bud, "Snap out of it! Go ahead and present the award! Get the hell out of this mess! You look like a clueless idiot!"

Thoroughly humbled, Gerard swallowed hard, picked his head up, and faced the digital cue cards. If he'd had a tail, it would have been deeply tucked between his legs.

"Hah! That was… really something. Thanks for teaching me a lesson, Kristina. So… and… um, leading into the person nominated for the category of Hottest Actor Right Now, we have… um…"

The screen lit up with the trailer of footage of all the current assorted media featuring the nominees. When it got to Kristina, the audience went absolutely bananas and her number soared even higher over the competition. Gerard read the results with as much enthusiasm as he could muster.

"And the winner of The Hottest Actor Right Now award is, with over 1.5 billion international votes… Kristina Brightside!"

Kristina came back onstage, all smiles and charm again. She bowed before the stadium of people and a single, sparkling tear rolled down her cheek.

"I want to thank you all so much," she gushed. "I just could never have predicted this kind of support when only a few years ago I was afraid to show the world who I really was. Who we all really are, beneath the cross that stands above Hollywood, writhing and wriggling to be let out and fed…"

Kristina shot a shockingly twisted smile at Gerard and he stared back quizzically as her picture-perfect face began to melt. Her skin crumpled and sunk to reveal rotted muscle and bone underneath. A horrible stench filled the air. She growled and howled hideously as the flesh dropped away in chunks from her chest and arms, falling and splattering to the stage floor.

Thomas Berry crackled in his ear: "What the hell's happening? Gerard?"

Gerard watched in shock as Kristina turned out towards the audience.

"It is time for us to feed on the rest of them! Let us all be undead *foreverrrr*!" She screamed. The audience screamed back, a mixed chorus of zombie war cries and pure panic as the zombies in the crowd simultaneously revealed themselves and began attacking the still-humans with fevered frenzy.

Kristina turned towards Gerard, her crumbled, festering nose flaring, and kicked off her ridiculous high heels. Even as a zombie, he was amazed to find she was annoyingly attractive. Then his pure human instinct kicked in and he sprinted like a fox off the stage, hearing her gnashing and growling behind him, her bare feet thumping along heavily at his heels. He sprinted past shrieking audience members, knocking into each other as they desperately sought any exit. He tore past zombified network execs devouring B-list actors; stage crew and poor little PAs running for their mortal lives, tripping over wires and sandbags; wardrobe zombies tossing burning dresses and suits out from the green rooms. He was familiar enough with the backstage area to remember where the emergency exit was. But just before he reached it, he flew over a fallen tripod and stumbled on a sandbag, hearing a crack in his ankle. Pain shot up his leg and tears popped into his eyes.

If he could just make it around the last corner he would be outside, free from the hellish stadium, but he'd injured his ankle so badly on the sandbag that he had to stop for a moment to catch his breath. That's when he became aware that not only Kristina was close behind him, but an entire herd of her loyal zombie fans had joined her in the hunt for Gerard's humanity.

"I'm not done with you, Gerard! It's not over until *you're* over!" she snarled, clawing at the air, chunks of decaying flesh falling off of her triceps onto the tiled floor with a splat.

"*Get Ger-ard! Get Ger-ard!*" the undead Kristina fan club chanted from behind her. Gerard made his last sprint towards the exit on his bad ankle, running so hard he actually felt the bone splinter. He crumpled to the floor right in front of the double doors to freedom.

Gerard felt totally fucked. He'd brought this on himself, he supposed, but there was way too much going for him at the moment to just give up. He was a fighter, so very close to catching his long-awaited dream of eternal fame and fandom. It was just within grasping reach if he relaxed and thought for one goddamn moment.

He looked up and there it was.

A gift! The universe wanted him to win. He was a golden boy after all.

He gathered every last shred of his energy and punched the glass to the old fire extinguisher window, grabbing it with bleeding knuckles and spraying the rabid flesh-hungry zombies with a blast of good old-fashioned fire extinguishing chemicals. They stumbled back, momentarily shocked and blinded Gerard cracked the door open with his other hand while still spraying and dragged himself out, safe within his cloud of chemicals.

A zombie hand reached outside and snapped off right as he kicked the heavy door shut. Gerard sat for a second, staring at the still-twitching detached and decaying hand. Then he stepped on it hard with his one good foot. It twitched violently and then lay still.

No one was going to take his chance from him. No one, and no *thing*.

Then he stood up and hobbled away to hail an auto-cab to the Marina

Del Rey hospital as fast as he could manage. Sure, it would take longer, but he had to get the hell out of Hollywood while he still had brains.

MATT BOGART

There was perhaps no better entertainment in existence than a spontaneous, live, celebrity-awards-turned-Hollywood-zombie-apocalypse showdown. Jimmy had offered Matt backstage passes but he'd opted to watch The Right Nows from the comfort of his couch instead. He knew what a shitshow they always were. He live-texted Jimmy through the Gerard/Kristina awkward-as-hell-confrontation bit, gloated glowingly at the mention of his podcast's name on the most-watched international live show, and laughed his ass off through the awesome Kristina Brightside-led zombie meltdown following. He did line after line as he watched his podcast downloads skyrocket into the billions. He sat back, munched his popcorn, slugged his gin, and celebrated all the wise decisions he'd made in life, most especially the decision to remain home that night. He had no particular desire to become a mutant hybrid yet, though he knew of the advantages of joining the club.

At the moment, he was just content and loving his own life, doing whatever he wanted, answering to nearly no one, with a podcast that finally everyone had heard of. Several personal invitations had already come in to be a guest on the late night shows that he'd been hoping to be on pretty much his entire life. Jimmy thought they should start a little bidding war for exclusivity but Matt wanted to do them all. He knew exactly how fleeting it was, having a "moment" in the rapid-fire present, and intended on taking full advantage of his time to shine. Jimmy was thinking long game, but there was no long game for Matt. None of the latest hair technology could hold up against his hard drug habits. Another couple of years and he'd be mostly bald. He wouldn't want to do any shows then.

He could get implants, sure, but to him they always looked grossly obvious. He would stare at the ill-formed clusters on other desperate men's fake hair lines and feel mixed waves of pity and hatred. He supposed the hatred was mostly at himself, since the hair game was just another competition in which his dad was creaming him. But Geoffrey never had to deal with living in his dad's staggering shadow. He'd never had massive expectations pressed upon him from an early age. Matt had definitely gotten the worse end of the stick, even though Geoffrey would tell it the other way around; Geoffrey was the one who was shoveling cow shit when he was 8 years old on a farm in Kentucky and Matt was the one who had supermodels for babysitters and practically grew up at Disneyland.

That always made Matt so mad, that farm-vs.-Disneyland comparison of their childhoods. He hadn't even *liked* Disneyland. He remembered kicking Donald Duck in the shins once in a pointless fit of rage, and not getting into trouble at all once they found out who his father was. His nanny at the time had developed this trick, she'd buy him endless junk food until he'd fall into a sort of coma, too full and sick with corn dogs and fried dough to cause any more trouble. Who knows what his actual problem had been with Donald Duck. Probably it had a little to do with the fact that he saw the stupid duck more than he saw his parents. Maybe he was trying to get their attention by abusing the Disneyland staff in as many ways possible each time he went. This was the part where Geoffrey would say, "Oh, boo-*hoo*. All kids hate their parents. I would have taken your childhood over mine in a heartbeat. No kid could even be born as lucky as you back when I was growing up. I toiled away at the farm work with my alcoholic father and sat through home schooling with my cranky mother, who would smack me when I got the wrong answers. Your nannies showered you with love and affection. You went to the easiest private schools. You cake-walked through life. You still are cake-walking. I spoiled you so rotten you can't even realize how good you have always had it."

It was this claim, this final win over Matt—Geoffrey claiming Matt was fucked up *only because he was ungrateful for all he'd been given in life*—that always tipped Matt over the edge. Geoffrey would forever be better than Matt because of his hard-knock childhood that gave him all the material he needed to write hit songs while also teaching him how to be grateful enough to hold on to success.

Well, wasn't that convenient for his super awesome fucking dad.

Matt had never asked to be born privileged. He'd never asked to be born at all. He had always wished he'd had a brother or sister, someone to share this uncommonly-screwed-up life with, but alas, Geoffrey had promptly gotten his tubes snipped after Matt was born, another deep and resounding way to say "fuck you," in Matt's opinion. His mother was a model who never wanted a child in the first place. She claimed his being born ruined her career. Not all the drugs she ingested, no way. She'd never blame the drugs. All the way to her eventual overdose.

And once again, the terrible blackness had descended on Matt during what should have been an otherwise happy moment of celebration.

That could only mean one thing: It was time to fuck it out with Cindy.

Matt opened the door to rosy cheeks, a skin tight silver dress, matching silver nails, feathery glitter lashes and smudged silver eyeliner. Her big doe eyes said the same thing they always did to Matt: Fuck Me Silly. When he'd been a kid, he'd registered this, but had written it off as his own projected horniness. Then he got older, and as it turned out, all Cindy ever wanted was to be fucked silly.

"Hello, gorgeous."

"Hiya, Mattyskins." She knocked off his baseball cap and rumpled his thinning hair. He reflexively ducked and scooped it up, returning it immediately to its rightful place on the top of his head. "Can I come in or what?"

Matt hadn't realized he was blocking the door. He had the sudden urge to go outside and run a couple of laps around the house. He'd maybe done too much of the powder. He wondered briefly if he'd even be able to perform.

"Did you see The Right Nows?" Cindy asked, plunking her purse down on a chair and slinking her sexy backside down the hallway in front of Matt. "What a horror show. This world is headed straight to hell in a handbasket."

It struck Matt as a pretty dated thing to say, but with an ass like hers, she could go right on talking like a grandma. And that *smell*. Her perfume always brought him right back to the painful years of lusting after older women but not having the guts to make a move on them. They'd seemed like exotic gifts back then, neatly wrapped in sparkly wrapping paper, only to be opened by men who made billions, had mansions and hangers full of cool cars.

His mind kept chugging away from him like a train with too much coal in the furnace. He could hardly keep up with the blinding hot/cold of his own manic depression. It was fucking exhausting being him. It had always been fucking exhausting. He stopped in the kitchen to grab a glass for Cindy and a few ice cubes for the gin, clenching his teeth like he was trying to bite through steel. When he joined Cindy in the parlor, she'd already helped herself to a bit of his powdery refreshments.

"Baby, you saved the night. You wouldn't believe how boring the neighbor's party was," she said, sniffing hard after doing a generous line. "I would have gone home but then I would have been lonelyyy," she sang, pushing her boobs close to his face as he sat down on the couch next to her. "The Hollyzombies are on the loose again. I'm scared. *Hold* me, Matty."

Matt felt the first tingles of an erection and prayed there weren't too many drugs in his system to get the relief package delivered.

"Mmmmotorboat incoming," he mumbled, staring at her implants popping out of her slinky, rubbery silver dress. He buried his face in her cleavage and she laughed delightedly, leaning back and letting him go to town. He pawed and kissed and raspberried and licked until he'd whipped himself into a frenzy large enough to make him think his mind was going to implode and get vacuumed straight through his body and out his tip as scrambled brain jism.

He sat back and lit a cigarette.

Cindy helped herself to one as well. "Well, well… Aren't you worked up tonight," she murmured, not displeased. "Let's satisfy all your demons this evening."

"I want you to annihilate me," he said without hesitation. "I want you to leave nothing left."

She stared at him, her hair tousled from the motorboating action. "I can do that," she said. "Boy, I was born to do that."

"What have you been holding back for, then?" Matt cracked an evil smile.

She practically shot a hole in his skull with her eyes. Had they grown larger? They seemed to swallow Matt up in their vastness, their multifacet-ed-ness. It felt like falling into a dark crystal dungeon. She had more magic than Matt had given her credit for. He stared back at her, momentarily hypnotized. Cindy hoisted her curvy little silver spandex bod onto Matt's lap, knocking his baseball cap off again. It fell behind the couch.

His hands instinctively reached back but she grabbed his wrists and held them down.

"Don't. Move."

He sat there, stiff as a statue, as she took her silver-tipped nail and slashed his tee shirt in half, just barely grazing the bulge of Matt's lower stomach. It left a tiny red scratch. His tee shirt hung in flaps by his sides. Cindy's tongue darted out and she began to lick and nibble at his nipples. He closed his eyes, leaning into the tickle, letting nothing be funny and everything be sexy. Then she sat up abruptly and slapped him, which stung in the best way Matt could remember anything ever stinging.

"What was that for?"

"Let it go. Let it all go."

He nodded and tipped his head back, allowing himself to focus only on the sensation. The soft biting, then harder. Then even gloriously harder. Until—

"OW!"

Cindy sat up and slapped him again. Was that a bit of blood on the corner of her mouth? Matt realized he could barely see straight.

"Shut up. No safe words," Cindy hissed. She sliced a piece of his tee shirt off and gagged him with it. Her eyes were even wider now, bulging out of her skull.

"You like that, little boy? Now, stay."

God, Matt thought it was so stupid hot when she called him a "boy." Made him feel like a teenager again. Then she took him in her mouth and sucked, sucked, sucked. It felt like white-hot lightning was shooting through his body. He could barely stand the pleasure. She was sucking like no one had ever sucked him before, with a vigor that almost paralyzed him. He had to do something, put his energy somewhere, so he started to touch her. She was aroused and slippery but she immediately stopped to look him dead in the eye.

"Did I say you could touch me?"

He shook his head no. Had her neck gotten longer? Her eyes, even larger somehow? She looked more enticing and alien than ever. Or was he just that railed?

Cindy slapped him out of his thoughts again. She removed her panties, tossing them onto his head, partially covering his eyes, and climbed on top of him. She slid him inside her and started rocking back and forth, her silicone tits bouncing in the low light. He moaned through his gag.

"Bad, bad boy. You are so naughty. Always breaking the rules. But I won't tell your daddy. I'll punish you myself."

She rocked harder, simultaneously stretching her lace panties completely over his eyes. A sparkler was going off inside his brain. Every time she rocked it produced tiny pricks of electricity. She ran her nails down his chest. He felt eased by the deep scratches, found a giant release through the pain.

Then his body geared up for the largest orgasm ever. It was like watching a tornado from a distance – the anticipation, the great twist of energy building and whirling and gathering speed, the feeling of smallness, the realization of chaos in the face of all-encompassing power—

And then it knocked him spinning with a force like no other.

Matt ejaculated what was probably his entire sperm supply for the following year. Then he felt a sensation like his arm being bitten off. He tried to scream but the gag choked it into a muted groan. He shook his head frantically until Cindy's undies fell away to reveal a large silver praying mantis crouched on top of him, making weird clicking insect noises while licking her bloody jaws before darting down to devour his other arm.

The pain was all-consuming. He watched with gagged wails as the praying-mantis-formerly-known-as-Cindy gnashed and swallowed his left leg, then got to work on the right one immediately after. Matt was in such outstanding pain that tears streamed down from his eyes, his gag completely soaked but still holding tight. The mantis made more satisfied clicking noises as she demolished his second leg, than tilted her blood-stained face at him, observing him with huge, shimmering, multi-faceted eyes.

Matt felt the fear rush over him like he was back on the scary rides at Disneyland. He closed his eyes and silently surrendered as her silver bloody jaws went for his head.

ODESSA MESSA

Tiny Tin Heart was in the middle of their third encore onstage downstairs in Venice Peach Freak Circus when the unthinkable struck. No one saw it coming. Odessa was pounding the skins hard, wailing full-throttle in the middle of their anthemic chorus, when the speakers cut out and the entire speakeasy went bright. And in a speakeasy, bright is never a good sign. The fifty or so people in the room all squinted and looked at each other, sweaty and nervous.

Ellie Delight spoke quietly and calmly into the PA: "Attention: LAPD rocobocos have this place surrounded. Everyone needs to quietly file out through the emergency escape tunnel behind the bar immediately. Please refrain from panicking. Our upstairs counter staff is stalling them as best they can but it's only a matter of time."

Odessa arose from her drum throne and hastily bagged up her cymbals as Clint, Johnny and Stevia packed up their instruments as quickly as possible. The band made their way to the tunnel entrance tucked behind the bar, ducking down into the small passageway behind the bearded lady. Odessa lingered last, looking over her shoulder at Ellie Delight, who stood at attention, not making any move to exit the speakeasy.

"C'mon, Ellie!"

The former sex-bot-turned-ringmaster of the underground freak show circus stood there in their hat and suit, looking sharp, calm and composed, and shook their head.

"I will stall them further," the bot said. "I have no other purpose now that this place has been discovered. Go on now, save yourself."

Odessa could hear the rocoboco running across the floor overhead, headed towards the secret stairs. Johnny stuck his head out of the tunnel entrance and grabbed her hand.

"We gotta run!"

Odessa felt tears brimming in her eyes as she waved goodbye to Ellie Delight, the robot that created the Venice Peach Freak Show Underground Circus and gave her band a place to exist, gave Venice Beach a place to remind them of the good old days. Then she crouched down and started making her way through the tunnel. As she looked back, Ellie sealed up the tunnel entrance with a false wall.

When they emerged at the secret escape tunnel's exit underneath the Venice Pier, the guys asked her if she wanted to come back to their place to drink away their sorrows. But Odessa didn't feel like doing anything, anymore. The one place she had to hold on to was gone now. As she walked home, she realized she no longer had a purpose anymore, either. She was just another near-extinct artist stuck in the wrong time, in the wrong world, one in which she could not make a living from her talents and therefore was condemned to a life of shame and suffering.

Her rent went unpaid and her disaster dreams continued, violent regurgitations of natural and unnatural crises, always ending in either death or a heroic rescue. It was a strange and fascinating way her subconscious wove haunting, majestic dreamscapes, so vivid that she often had trouble shaking them off long after she awoke.

One morning just a week after Venice Peach Freak Circus was shut down, Odessa had a dream in which she was surfing a tsunami and was doing pretty amazingly until she fell off the topmost crest, plummeting down into the middle of the wall of saltwater, feeling her entire body jolt, jostle and shatter like a sack of china dropped off of a skyscraper. She was stuck deep inside the tsunami now, unable to move or breathe or locate the surface. The struggle got fierce, fiercer, and then finally she let go, resolved to her fate. She'd died in her dreams enough times to know when it was *GAME OVER*.

It was only then that she felt a pair of strong hands somehow lift her out of the water and pull her onto a surfboard. She felt the sun shining down on her body, and opened her eyes to see a long-haired, beautiful Asian surfer dude in flowered swim trunks looking down at her. She turned her head the other way to see the tsunami hitting the coast, but they were far behind it in the calmer ocean now, safe from its catastrophic break.

"Oh, hello," she said.

"You surf better than anyone I've ever seen."

"Um, you saved my ass, remember?"

"No sweat. You woulda had it. Can I kiss you?"

"Hell yeah, you can kiss me."

They kissed until Odessa was feeling pretty turned on and ready to pull her surfer hero's hibiscus-print shorts off. That was when she woke up to find Felix purring and licking her mouth with his smelly little sand-paper tongue.

"FELIX!! *Gross!!!*" She pushed the overly-affectionate cat off of her and reached for her phone. She was sort of sad to be awake. She'd been very attracted to her unknown tsunami savior, and was looking forward to having survival sex on his surfboard—

—So you can imagine her total surprise when she opened up her BeachDate app to find that she'd matched with a surfer who looked *exactly like* the surfer hero from her dream. His name was Brandon and he was originally from the Philippines and currently lived in a trailer park in Malibu. He'd sent her an invitation to go surfing that afternoon.

Odessa bit her lip, then wrote back:

Let's do a backwards date. You come over, we snuggle, then go get break-fast and go surfing.

He replied almost instantly:

Dig it! Shoot me your address.

She didn't normally do that. There were, of course, some boundaries that Odessa normally maintained with perfect strangers, but then again, she'd never dreamed of someone who she'd then come across in real life. It felt like she already knew him. Hell, she trusted Brandon completely after he'd saved her like that in her dream. And *especially* after he'd looked down at her with those warm eyes and kissed her like that. She was still turned on, in fact, so it seemed almost too serendipitous that he could now come over and potentially finish the job.

Odessa got up to wash the cat saliva off her face, brush her teeth, and change into some cuter pajamas. By the time she had her hair fluffed just the way she liked, she heard a knock. She opened the door to reveal the tall, long-haired man of her dreams, and threw her arms around his neck.

"Brandon!"

"Hey, Odessa… Nice to meet you!"

He grinned down at her. She laughed like a maniac, took him by his hand, and led him to her bed, pushing him down onto the sheets. He stared back up at her in amusement.

"I can't help but wonder… Are you always this… friendly?"

She tossed her head full of curls back, unabashed and giddy.

"Nope! You're definitely a special case."

"You really like Filipino surfers?"

More laughter. She buried her face in his neck for a minute, relishing his coconut-y sunscreen scent while simultaneously realizing how crazy she must seem to him. But not crazy enough to scare him off, somehow.

That seemed like a good sign, so she sat on his chest, looked down into his very bright brown eyes, and took a deep breath.

"This may sound nuts, but I had a dream about you this morning."

"Far out. What was I doing?"

"Well, so, I was surfing this tsunami, and I fell and was stuck in the undertow. Just when I'd given up and my body went limp, you rescued me, and then we were making out on your surfboard, and… it was cool."

He looked pleased but puzzled. "And you're sure it was me?"

Odessa tucked a lock of his hair behind his ear, bent down and kissed him. She melted into his lips, sunshine filling her body like hot steam, sea breeze rushing through her mind, whispering *yes*. The kiss carried on and on until their clothes were off and they'd surfed each other's bodies all the way to shore.

They lay there panting, streams of light from the window blinds making psychedelic wavy lines across their bare bodies.

"I'm sure."

"Ha. Sure of what?"

"Sure it was you. In my dream."

He turned towards her. "I don't really dream much, probably smoke too much weed, but if I did, you'd definitely be my dream girl."

She grinned and stretched her arms out in front of her.

"Let's get breakfast!"

They stopped by Odessa's favorite breakfast burrito spot, inhaling giant flour tortillas filled with steaming eggs, veggie sausage, swiss cheese, hot sauce and avocado. They washed them down with cups of strong coffee and hopped back into Brandon's vintage teal convertible VW Cabrio manual shift, the vehicle obviously making Odessa even more smitten. Their boards rested across the back seat as they made their way up the Pacific Coast Highway to their favorite Malibu surf spot, the break by Point Dume.

The waves were choppy and unpredictable, but she was with her new surf hero #1 best beach date Brandon so she strode into the water like she didn't have a care in the world. He followed close behind, playfully splashing her, and soon the two bobbed along the break, side by side.

"So, tell me about yourself," Odessa said, and they laughed.

"Come here often?" he riffed back.

"Oh, darling. You have some seaweed in your hair," she clucked, pulling it out with precision.

"I told you to bring a wetsuit, you must be freezing," he joked, rubbing her shoulder. It was probably 85 degrees and the sun shone on them like it was making a killing in the burn business.

When waves would approach, Brandon would be the gentleman, letting Odessa have at it first. Sometimes he'd join her if the wave was solid enough and they'd show off by clumsily trying to hold hands, one or both of them inevitably tumbling over from loss of balance. They knew it was love because they had no problem eating shit in front of each other. There were a few other surfers out in the water but they were far enough away that Odessa and Brandon didn't feel weird about making out in little stretches when it seemed calm enough.

"Isn't life crazy?" she said.

"The craziest," he answered.

"But just the best, though."

"The bestest."

Odessa stuck her head out for another kiss when something caught her eye in the distance. At first, it looked like a large ship… that didn't end.

She realized with sudden acute fear that what was looming over Brandon's shoulder in the distance appeared to be an actual tsunami.

"Holy shit," she whimpered, pulling out of the kiss.

"I know," he said dreamily. "Potent stuff."

She shook her head and pointed over his shoulder. He looked behind him. He kept looking. Then he turned back and stared at her.

"Is that… what I think it is?"

She nodded.

"I guess we should have seen it coming?" he attempted to joke, but there was no humor left with a wave of that size approaching. They saw other surfers begin to paddle towards the shore in a panic, quickly realizing the wave was already creating a really strong riptide. There was no use trying to swim against it. It was a complete waste of strength.

"What do we do?" one of them hollered at Odessa and Brandon, who were still in shock.

"Get ready to dive deep," Brandon shouted. "DEEP! And ditch the boards *NOW*."

Odessa swallowed hard, afraid to ask if he was just bullshitting. He didn't seem sure. It was all too much to comprehend, that she was now in reality and the stuff of her nightmares was really happening. This was it: The real-life disaster had finally arrived. She let go of her board as Brandon did the same. They watched them whoosh quickly out towards the wave as they clung to each other, treading water furiously.

"At least I got to meet you before I died," Odessa said breathlessly.

"Who says we're not making it through this?" Brandon panted. "If I could save you in your dreams, I'd like to hope that I can save you in real life."

"Hope away, but I'd say we're done for."

"Wow. Where have you *been* my whole life? You 'go with the flow' even when it's a tsunami. I love you."

She squeezed his hand underwater and kissed his cheek.

"I know, I love you, too."

"Marry me," he said, planting one on her lips.

"I'll marry you in heaven," she swore. "Otherwise known as the eternal Hawaii."

"Can't wait," Brandon said.

The wave was now close enough for them to see it in all its frightening glory. It had to be as tall as an apartment building, maybe even a skyscraper. Suddenly they were standing on the bare ocean floor. All the water beneath them had been sucked up into the swell, towering above them in a sparkling, frothy-crested cliff.

"*Runnnnn!!*" Brandon took her hand and they sprinted towards the parking lot, tearing past flipping fish, scuttling crabs and craggy rocks. Their panic shot them directly across the sand, not looking back to see how close the wave was on their heels until they reached the pavement.

With a deafening CRACK! the wave broke. The white froth exploded like a bomb and water rushed at them, fast. They took a last, lingering look at each other.

"I'm sorry I can't save you."

:Maybe you already have." Odessa shrugged. "Hold my hand?"

"I'll hold it forever."

That was when she knew: She had won. She'd found something that lasted - and just in time. The deadly water engulfed them at the same time, standing side by side, clasping hands and accepting their fate together, forever, married in death by the damn dysfunctional universe.

STEVIA WONDER

Stevia now knew that the broken baby bird wing bone and cursed gull had both come from the torn portal to universal superdoom. Producer Dan had been ignoring her attempts to get in contact since he'd been attacked by un-dead Cackles that fateful morning. It was devastating. Here she had been *so close* to finally getting the attention she deserved, and that bastard bird had sabotaged it all. To make matters worse, there had been a tsunami in Malibu and no one had heard from Odessa since.

Tiny Tin Heart was looking bleak, her solo project was looking even bleaker, there was absolutely no word from Dan Blacker, and she was alone, sitting with her cats, smoking weed and overanalyzing how much she'd had to do with it and what, if anything, she could do about it.

She had to at least try to take back the reins of control. After some light stalking she found the studio in which Dan was currently working and decided to attempt a "run in" in order to casually reassure him that she was totally a good witch and that they should collaborate for sure. She put on her best black lace sundress, did her makeup with extra precision, and drove to Hollywood to stalk Dan Blacker.

The receptionist, a young woman with short, spiky blue hair and bluer eyes, gave her a skeptical look when Stevia entered the studio.

"Do you have an appointment?"

Stevia fumbled for a good introduction.

"Yes, I've been working with Dan Blacker and we have a meeting."

The receptionist raised her eyebrows.

"Have a seat, I can see if he's available."

"Thank you," Stevia said. The receptionist looked annoyed as she got up and disappeared down the hallway. Stevia ran behind the desk and searched the computer for his information. She'd recorded at the exclusive studio before and knew they kept a database of everyone who booked studio time. She hurriedly jotted down his home address and fled.

Stevia then drove to the market and purchased an assortment of enticing snacks; sprouted cashews and almonds, raw goat milk brie, 14-grain crackers and a couple of bottles of biodynamic French wine. Her mother had once told her no love spell works quite as well as a tasteful, tailored and expensive gift basket, and she was about to put that to the test. She assembled everything and drove to his house in Brentwood. Then she parked and waited for his car to turn into his driveway.

Stevia wasn't even aware she'd fallen asleep until she woke up to the sound of a car door slamming. Dan was home, and lucky for her, he was alone. She smoothed her hair and fixed her eyeliner in the mirror, then secured her basket of offerings and took a deep breath before exiting her vehicle.

She approached the house, rang the bell once and waited. There was no sound from inside. She rang the bell again. Finally, some footsteps.

"Dan?" she said. "It's Stevia! I brought you something."

He opened the door, looking stiff and cautious.

"Stevia. Surprising to see you. How did you know where I live?"

"Oh, you sent me your address a while ago in an email. Remember? I was going to come over to listen to some tracks."

His eyes went blank as he searched to recall this. Finding nothing, he bristled. "I don't

remember that."

"Oh, that's OK! I just wanted to bring you a few things. And I wanted to make sure that you're feeling better. And also just checking that you'd received my tracks for the Curtis Creation song since I never heard back."

"I did. I'm sorry, but we decided to go in a different direction with the song."

Stevia tried not to let this phase her. "That's alright! I know how precarious those things can be. Will you accept my basket?"

He looked at the gift basket, obviously pained by the gesture.

"It doesn't seem right to," he said. "Though I appreciate it."

"Ok," Stevia said, unable to hide her disappointment any longer. "Is everything alright? Do you still want to work with me on my solo project?"

"I'm actually really busy right now," he said, looking over his shoulder as if an important person had just materialized. "I'll get back to you when I have some time."

"I was really looking forward to collaborating with you," she said, a desperate edge creeping into her voice.

"Yeah, listen, I have to be going," he said, all but shutting the door in her face. "Take care."

"But Dan—"

"I'm running late to a virtual session, I have to go."

Then the door was shut. The last door to her last chance. That's what it felt like, anyhow, as Stevia stood there, gift basket heavy in hand, shame spilling down her cheeks in hot tears. The anger flared up inside of her; a deep and dismal wailing, a haunting summation of so many years of the particularly frustrating fury of being forgettable.

She took a bottle of wine from the basket and raised her arm to throw it at his car, but then thought better of it. She didn't want to get arrested. That would not be good. Her age and social security number didn't exactly "check out." She'd be accused of identity theft, and if they searched her cottage and found the heads…

When Stevia got into her car, she lightning-punched the steering wheel until her knuckles were bloody. Then she put on her alligator gloves and drove away as fast as she could. She wasn't sure where she was headed, only sure that her life was as dumb and pointless as she'd always hoped it wouldn't be. Years and years of devotion to music, recording on hit records, playing in buzz bands, and she had nothing, absolutely nothing to show for it. She was still a nobody, still barely scraping by, still as alone and desperate as ever.

Before she'd realized it, she'd driven to the tsunami wreckage site in Malibu. It was taped off everywhere and she couldn't get into the parking lot that had been the main crash point of the wave. She pulled over and got out. Firemen and volunteers were digging through the wreckage of cars, shops and homes that had been crushed by the sheer will of pissed-off mother nature. Paramedics sifted through great dunes of sand, digging bodies and broken surfboards out from under cars and crumbled buildings.

Stevia watched it all and felt nothing. To her, it was an immediate reflection of how she felt inside: Demolished. Wiped. Obliterated. Hollow. She desperately wanted to feel something, though—pain, sadness, anger—*anything*. She ducked under the caution tape and approached the ruins of the Malibu shoreline.

"You can't be here unless you're a volunteer," a worker in a yellow suit said, pausing from uncovering a disembodied arm beneath a truck shrouded in sand.

"I'm a volunteer," she said. "I think my friend is somewhere in here," she added, feigning sadness.

"Good luck," the worker said sympathetically. "You can check in and get suited up over by that black van."

Stevia thanked him and wandered down towards where the parking lot used to be, now a colossal mess of sand piles, debris, and wreckage. She thought about Odessa, wondering if she'd actually happened to be surfing in Malibu during the exact time that the tsunami had hit. Sure, Stevia had broken the baby bird wing bone when casting her last disruption spell at Odessa, but she couldn't assume responsibility for all *this*. Could she? There was no way her spell could have raised a tsunami and put it in Odessa's path, *was there*?

How bad of a witch could she be?

Suddenly, Stevia felt a pulsing like a magnetic field, drawing her to an overturned teal VW classic convertible partially buried under a giant mound of sand. She got down on her knees and began digging at the mound, slowly at first, then faster and faster until she felt the cold rubbery-ness of what could only be a dead body. She continued to dig, practically holding her breath as she unearthed the taut body of a surfer dude. When she got to his hand, she realized it was clutching another hand. A hand with chipped sparkle nail polish.

It was a familiar hand.

She could almost see a drum stick in it.

Stevia continued her morbid dig to reveal what she already had known in her heart: Odessa lay next to the guy, holding his hand tight, her eyes closed, a serene look of acceptance on her face.

Stevia stared down at them, frozen in their last moment like two brave surfer soldiers in love. She had no idea who the guy was, but it was just like Odessa to die with a guy fawning all over her. Stevia felt the hardness of her own heart as she stared at the two dead lovers, unable to cry, unable to feel anything, even then.

Instead, she began to brainstorm how she could manage to discreetly smuggle Odessa's head back to her garage to shrink and keep with the others.

"Is that your friend?" the emergency response worker asked from behind her, interrupting her plotting. "I saw you digging so frantically I had to come check on you."

Stevia turned. "Yes," she choked out, finally able to turn on the waterworks at the realization that while Odessa might be dead, she herself was completely dead inside.

"I'm so sorry." The worker put his arm on her shoulder and stared down at the pair of star-crossed surfers in the sand. "Well, at least it looks like they went peacefully. Why don't you go have a moment by the ocean. I'll let them know to come collect the bodies."

Stevia nodded and walked down to the shore. She looked out at the waves, frothing and foaming, rolling and tumbling like nothing terrible had ever happened. The ocean had all the real magic. She longed to find that sort of resilience after causing so much destruction and failing herself for what she hoped was the last time.

Suddenly, she felt a sharp point peck the top of her head.

She yelped and looked up. Cackles, the bloody, smelly, damned unkillable gull, was hovering above her. He let out an ugly battle cry.

"You again?!" she snarled. "You don't learn, do you?!"

As if in response, dozens more gulls and pelicans swooped in around Cackles and together they dive bombed towards her, a storm cloud of angry birds in a flesh-hungry flash mob aerial attack. Stevia cried out as they drove and pecked their beaks into her from all angles until she crumpled onto the ground, thrashing around in pain and unable to escape. She froze when she suddenly felt she was being lifted by a thousand pinches, opening her eyes to find herself rising up and away from the shore.

Stevia cried real tears then, too scared to move, conscious of the fact that she was now high above the ground and would not survive the drop.

The birds let out their collective shrill battle cries as they headed down the shoreline.

It was the most horrible sound Stevia had ever heard.

"Where are you taking me?" she sobbed, as if they could answer.

And then, she saw and knew.

The bonfires on Dockweiler beach.

As if cued, the birds began to descend. They were aiming for the biggest fire, one that had been built way bigger than regulation size, one with a few hundred people drinking and dancing around it, holding poster-size pictures and handmade signs.

It was a memorial gathering for the tsunami victims.

Stevia saw some of them look up and begin to point as the birds came closer, cawing and shrieking and then finally releasing Stevia above the flames, dropping her like a bomb into a bull's eye.

Screams filled the air as the fire licked and roared around Stevia. The birds continued to assault her, suicide bombing themselves to keep her in the flames as she attempted to climb her way out.

There was no winning this one. No spell to save her.

They were determined to burn the witch.

Gradually, Stevia surrendered to her fate. She may never have made it, she thought as death closed its dark claws around her, but at least she had sure as hell tried.

AUGGIE BREAKMIRRORS

COCKADOODLE DOOOO! COCKADOODLE DO==

Auggie threw the alarm across the room.

The big stupid damned day had finally arrived.

He grumbled as he showered, shaved, and dressed his best for his big dumb interview with President TBD 3000. With resentment in his heart, he made sure that his fingernails were trimmed and his ponytail wasn't too frizzy. He could only blame himself. There were no dress requirements for the interview. Auggie just wanted respect. He was angry as hell that he cared that much, but there was no escaping the fact that he *did* care that much. He wanted to be taken seriously, goddamn it. He didn't want to be written off as some unkempt, nutty vet.

He poured a dash of whiskey into his morning coffee to take the edge off and then called for an auto-cab. He wasn't going to roll up in the Zebra, for Christ's sake. The car arrived promptly and Auggie got in, as usual finding it weird to greet the robotic "voice" of the autopilot vehicle that was to hold his life in its hands as it made its way to the destination downtown.

Once they pulled up, a rocoboco escorted him inside and through security. He tried to relax as the elevator climbed up the former office building. They probably had built-in sensors that could gauge his heart rate already, those deviant fuckers. What had he gotten himself into? A woman in a pristine white suit awaited him as the elevator doors slid open. Her hair looked impossibly smooth. His hands flew up to his own already-back-to-semi-frizzy ponytail, an instant self-conscious reaction.

"Good afternoon, Mr. Breakmirrors. I'm Tabitha."

"Please, call me Auggie," he said, holding out his hand.

"Thank you, August," she replied automatically, shaking his hand so crisply that Auggie thought she might be a bot herself. "Follow me, we just need you to sign a few documents and then we can proceed to the interview room."

"Crap, I forgot to bring my lawyer along," Auggie joked stiffly.

"There's no need, it's just a standard non-disclosure form and a general agreement that we can use the information you provide in the interviews to input into our algorithms for our next update."

"If you ask me, things update too often in this world," Auggie riffed. "Whatever happened to preserving a good original classic?"

"Tabitha" looked at him strangely. Humor seemed entirely lost on her. "Yes. Well, anyway, as I was saying, it's going to be the most intricate and diverse coding of all. We believe it will be the program that successfully restores America to being the strongest nation in the world again. And being such, the Federal Bureau of the Restoration of America really appreciates you taking the time to help us better serve you and our country."

"Alright, alright," Auggie said meekly. He'd sign the damn documents because he was there already, wasn't he? He couldn't argue about that much. But if anyone tried any funny business like they did while he was in the army, then he sure wouldn't go all soft and submissive, he vowed to himself.

He sat in the modern, all-white waiting room with huge glass walls overlooking downtown Los Angeles. Tabitha handed him a tablet and Auggie scrolled down without reading anything and signed the bottom with his fingertip. It automatically scanned his face when he pressed the "SUBMIT" button.

"Thank you, August. Would you like a beverage before getting started?"

"Naw, I'm alright," he said gruffly. He wasn't about to be slipped any strange substances. He remembered that fateful cup of coffee he'd drank the morning of the worst battle he'd entered, how it had tasted funny and somehow enraged him while simultaneously diffusing his empathy so that he could kill like never before.

"President TBD 3000 is just about ready for you," Tabitha said, interrupting him from his haunting memories. "Follow me, please."

She led him into a conference room with gray opaque walls that held a long, granite-colored table with an assortment of beautiful pastries on a tray as the centerpiece.

"Please have a seat and help yourself to a pastry if you like. TBD will be right in."

Auggie stared at the treats, tempted but refusing to surrender. He liked feeling stronger than his basic human instincts. He liked feeling like he had a little control in a world full of chaos. Instead, he looked out of the window at the streets of downtown LA below, watching ant-sized people walk about. They had no idea, he thought. No fucking clue what they were all in for. Neither did he, for that matter. But he was at least aware of the looming doom. He wasn't some ignorant dildo with his head in the sand.

The doors burst open and President TBD 3000 wheeled in. The robot was remarkably built, he had to admit; just human-like enough, not too tech-y, somehow even slightly relatable. The sleek paneling had amazing craftsmanship to it. Auggie had read internet rumors that TBD was made in China, although of course the creators claimed it to be American-made.

The robot trained its "eyes" on Auggie and tilted its head slightly.

"Good afternoon, Mr. Breakmirrors," it said in its programmed-to-be-pleasant androgynous robot voice. "Thank you for joining me for a discussion on the current state of affairs."

"Hello, President TBD 3000," Auggie said as the robot wheeled up to an open gap between chairs at the head of the table. It made a whirring noise and released some sort of parking mechanisms on its sides. Its chest opened to reveal a mini computer screen, and it used its stylus fingertips to self-enter some data.

"I will be recording this conversation, is that alright with you?"

"Yes," Auggie said.

"Thank you. Now let us begin. Could you please state for the record your full name, place of residence, and all the occupations you've held in the last eight years?"

"I'm August Breakmirrors. I currently live in Venice Beach, California, and have worked as an entertainer of sorts for the last eight years."

"Thank you. Could you please elaborate on your profession? I'm not matching that definition with anything in my database."

"I drive a party bus," Auggie said, somewhat sheepishly. "So I guess you could put me down as a driver? I served in the US Army but got an honorable discharge nine years ago."

The robot was silent for a moment. "Yes, we have your previous records serving for the United States Army on file. Can you please tell us how many hours you currently work a week, and how much you get paid?"

"Well, the amount of hours I work varies depending on how many parties I book, but I'd say it's typically 20-25 hours a week, and I make about $550-$850 an hour."

Crap, he thought. He should have thought about the income he was going to claim in the interview, calculated and matched it to what he'd claimed in taxes the last eight years since robots had been elected into office—which was probably considerably less.

"And how much has that increased during the last eight years for you?"

"I'd say it's gone up about 400%, to be honest," Auggie said. "Since the Great Depression 3, the economy has finally started to improve and people are celebrating more."

"We are pleased to hear that. What would you be doing if you could be doing any job in the country?"

"I'm doing exactly what I want to be doing," Auggie said defensively.

"We are delighted to get that response," TBD said and pressed a few buttons on its chest. "We can move on to the next topic: Remote-controlled robo-cops. Have you had experiences with them? If so, please elaborate."

Auggie stiffened and then tried to relax. "Well, aside from watching them give out traffic tickets and arrest vagrants in the streets in Venice, I haven't had that much experience with them. I'm a cautious driver and law-abiding citizen."

"That doesn't match our records…" TBD made a soft whirring sound and its computer screen showed some fast-moving data. "We have a record of an incident that happened six years ago in Marina Del Rey, involving disorderly conduct and solicitation of a sex worker."

"That was bogus," Auggie said gruffly. "I took that to court and they had nothing."

"We have the court records. Could you please just describe your experience."

The damn bot prez was so deadpan about everything, Auggie fumed silently. So high and mighty from its perfectly-machined viewpoint. *That doesn't match our records...* Well, why hadn't it just brought up the whole incident to begin with, then? He was being tested, just as he'd thought. Auggie struggled to control his temper. "Sure, I'll talk about it. What happened was I'd had a little too much to drink. I left the bar and was walking home when a woman started talking to me. She was trying to get me to invite her back to my place. It was a standard case of entrapment.

Sure, I said she could come home with me, but I didn't know she was a hooker. She hadn't stated a price, she'd just asked if I wanted company that evening. I thought she looked like she did because that was her personal style. You know how some women embrace their god-given gifts. Then I was off-balance because of all the whiskey and fell into a car, accidentally punching out the window. The little robofucks—uh, rocobocos, sorry— swarmed in and arrested me for charges that were clearly all just a drunken misunderstanding. And it seemed like there was a reception problem with the officers controlling the rocobocos so I couldn't communicate properly and ended up spending the night in jail and going to court about it. So yeah, I guess if you want my feedback about the experience, I think the rocobocos have glitchy reception problems, and that should definitely be fixed. But I get why the cops would rather have the bots on the front lines. I sure wish they'd had robo-soldiers when I got drafted. I'd rather not have been on the front lines, carrying out corrupt missions under orders of that ass-clown Fuckwad."

"Thank you for your feedback." TBD whirred again and clicked around on its chest some more. "The next subject we'd like to ask about is the decline of personal relationships. Can you please state your current relationship status and describe the last eight years of your personal relationship lifestyle."

Auggie heaved a big sigh and sat back in his chair. He'd known this would be the hardest area of the interview for him.

"We   are   detecting   some   resistance   to—"

"—I'm getting to it, I'm getting to it. Sheesh."

TBD "blinked" at him, whirring softly. Again, fast-moving data ran down its screen chest, coding which Auggie could not even begin to decipher. He shifted in his chair, examining the arm rests to see if they were tracking some of his body information through pads on the lining or anything

"Is there an issue?"

"No. Yeah—well, I guess the answer is, it's complicated."

"We do not recognize—"

"OK, I get it. I'll be blunt. I'm single. I've been single since my army days. I date pretty regularly, but I'm gonna be honest with you, TBD, I'm a pretty broken guy. Ever since I got back from the Middle East I haven't been all that comfortable, with myself or with anyone else, really, besides my dog."

"We are sorry to hear that. How often would you say you go on dates? And which methods do you use to acquire them?"

"Shit. I don't know. It's hard out there for us humans. I know you've never had your data-filled heart broken, but people move on so fast these days. I go out with girls I meet around Venice, mostly. I'm no good on those apps. Much more charming in person. Better looking, too, I suppose. I've never photographed well. But yeah, I'd say I do alright. Certainly better here than where I lived in Arizona."

"Do you have plans for a future with one partner? If so, what would those plans entail, such as marriage, domestic partnership, etcetera. If not, how do you envision your future?"

Auggie pulled at his ponytail and ground his teeth. "Well, fuck. We all die alone, don't we? I don't know, that's what they say, anyway. Marriage is irrelevant at this point. Started as slavery sale of women and now it seems like a fast track for expensive divorce settlements. I don't even know anyone who's married anymore. Sure, I'd like to find someone to share a home with for some amount of time, but I don't need anyone to come around trying to fix me or 'complete me.' As mentioned, I'm half the man I used to be, but that doesn't mean someone else should feel inclined to try to fix what's already dead and gone, you know what I mean?"

There was a long, pregnant, processing pause. "Thank you for that input. Do you think that we, the government, can be doing anything better in the ways of repairing the devaluing of monogamous, contracted relationships and the bearing of offspring?"

"I really don't think that's the government's place, either way. It's evolution. Or de-evolution, depending on how you look at it. Everyone loves their endless plethora of options thanks to technology now, so good luck reversing that. You know, back when Fuckwad was in office, wreaking havoc on the environment while enforcing all those laws banning abortions, birth control and repealing same-sex marriages, I think that was just the last straw for most people. And it takes a long time to repair that lost hope for humanity. You know?"

"All valuable input for the algorithms, Mr. Breakmirrors. So, to repeat back, you believe the government should continue to remove all laws governing relationships and body autonomy as well as continue to develop better all-gender birth control in order to restore the value of monogamous relationships?"

"Hell, I don't know. I guess that'd be a start, anyhow. If the government is going to do anything, yeah. Maybe if everyone felt more hopeful for the future they might be more interested in committed partnerships again."

"I see." The robot whirred and pressed a few buttons on the touchscreen. A quiet beeping occurred. "And now, we'd like to open the floor to you, Mr. Breakmirrors, to tell us how you think we robots have been serving as leaders of the country for your people."

"By 'your people' you mean humans? Yeah, I guess it's been alright. Ultimately I think we obviously don't want to be governed by robots, but since the system was so broken that bastards like Fuckwad were landing seats in the White House, we really needed a dramatic change. And sure, things like laws, the environment, real estate and stuff have shifted for the better thanks to your dedication to science and numbers and statistics, not greed, corruption and lobbying, but I think soon it should be time for humans to lead the country again. Let's get leadership training to be more of a focus in schools, not just programming. We're not robots, we've never been robots, nor will we ever be robots. I admit that I have a bit of a personal issue taking direct orders from robots. I know others do, too."

"Even if robots are fair and just in doing what is best for the human species?"

"No offense, but how do we know robots actually know what is best for our species?" Auggie asked earnestly. "Is there really any salvation to be had? Look what the human species has done to most of the other species on Earth. Look what we've done to *ourselves*."

"So you object to continuing to be governed by robots?"

"I'm just saying I'm pretty skeptical about it holding up for the long run. I'd be surprised if it isn't met with some resistance once we get back on our feet as a nation. The people will want to regain control of the people. That's just natural order."

"Computing." TBD whizzed and whirred. Its chest screen flashed bright blue and then, suddenly, a blinking symbol of a hand ran across the screen. The conference room doors opened automatically. Tiny cuffs emerged from his arm rests, securing Auggie's wrists to the chair.

"What the hell?!" he scoffed, trying to get up. "I knew something was up with these arm rests!"

A small syringe came out from behind the chair and injected itself into Auggie's neck. He instantly fell drowsy and his legs collapsed.

In whirred six military-issued robo-soldiers.

"Resistor language," TBD stated to them. "Relocate to Cell #467."

"Relocating," the robo-soldiers chimed in unison as they approached Auggie.

"I *knew* this was a goddamn conspiracy," Auggie mumbled, completely slack against the chair. The robo-soldiers encircled him and began rolling him towards the elevator. The receptionist was nowhere to be found.

"You'll pay for this," he said meekly. "I have a great lawyer," he lied.

"You signed the contract stating consent for indefinite incarceration for any anti-robotic talk," barked one of the robo-soldiers monotonously. "We have been monitoring you for months through your devices as well. You. Are. Doomed."

"Yeah, well, I'd rather rot in a cell than be ruled by robots," spat Auggie just as the elevator doors closed. Then he blacked out.

DR. PHILIP K. PARKER

It was finally time: Time for Philip to be on the receiving end of the therapy. First there was his crazy date with Cassandra, then the completely unprofessional session with Gerard, and now he wasn't able to sleep, he wasn't eating much, and he was experiencing vicious waves of self-loathing, the likes of which had never plagued him before. It was time to get his own head checked out, so he reluctantly set up an appointment with the best of them, Dr. Victoria Smutting, PhD. She was known as "The Wolf" of therapists in the district, notorious for sniffing out truths with an almost uncanny ability to sense vulnerabilities and falsities.

He would normally have been nervous, but he felt he didn't have any vulnerabilities. He was hard inside, had been for years, with the slight recent exception of Cassandra. Still, he'd even felt less passionate about her, lately. Perhaps because he knew the competition. Even though she and Gerard hadn't done anything yet, knowing there was a handsome and interested contender living with her had squashed enough of his desire that he wasn't even thirsty for her anymore.

Or maybe it was depression that was making him unwilling to compete.

He was determined to find out what was really happening. If his drive was that weak, he needed to address it head on. Philip didn't have any time to waste. The Wolf was the only one for the job.

He arrived for his appointment early, taking a seat up on the third floor of a building on Ventura Boulevard in Sherman Oaks. It was amusing to be the one in the waiting room, killing time on his CloudCase after pressing the button that alerted Dr. Smutting that he had arrived.

She greeted him at exactly 3:00 pm, wearing a bright green sweater and a gray pencil skirt. Her wavy silver hair had been pinned back in perfectly combed waves.

"Philip, hello. Please, come in."

"Dr. Smutting, how are you?"

"You don't have to be that formal, Philip. We're colleagues. Call me Victoria."

"Alright. Thanks."

He entered her office, one much larger than his, containing a large couch with plenty of plush cushions. He knew how much could be determined about him just in the way he chose to sit, so he made himself comfortable in the middle of the couch, crossing one leg over the other knee. Not too stiff, not too casual. Right in the center.

Take that, Wolf.

Philip sat back. It was strange to let someone else lead a session, but he was determined to handle it well. Victoria gazed at him, not in a rush at all, it seemed.

"So, Philip, when's the last time you were in therapy?"

"I've actually never been in therapy before, Victoria." She raised her eyebrows and typed something on her tablet. "That's unusual, isn't it? Most therapists have gone through therapy at some point in their life in order for them to believe in it enough to devote their life to it."

"Not me," Philip said. "I've always been my own therapist."

"I see," Victoria mused. "Rather one-sided, don't you think?"

"It is what it is, as they say."

"Indeed."

"Have you had many colleagues as clients?"

"Some," she answered vaguely.

She kept her eyes on him. Her silence was rather unnerving, but he figured that was part of her shtick, so he attempted to stay at ease in the uneasiness. He wasn't going to give her any quick points.

"Why don't you begin by telling me a little about yourself," Victoria began again. "What's your lifestyle like? Your eating, sleeping, drinking habits? What brings you here, in other words."

"I'm bored stiff," Philip answered immediately. "My life consists of seeing sixty-some patients. I eat three healthy meals a day, but I've been eating lighter than usual this past week. Haven't had much of an appetite. I usually get a solid 6-8 hours of sleep a night, but this past week I've been waking up every few hours, tossing and turning, and having some rather unsettling dreams. I don't drink too much. I bicycle every day, sometimes even twice a day for a total of 20-45 miles, depending on my schedule."

She nodded as she typed away into the tablet. "And what about your social life? Your love life?"

"I don't have a lot of time for friendships or relationships. I date here and there, but nothing serious."

"Why don't you allow yourself friendships?"

"I don't really see the point," Philip said dryly. "It's a two-way street and I'm going my own direction all the time. I got sick of the guilt trips. I find it's best if I do my own thing. Sure, occasionally I'll go on group bike trips or watch a sports game at the local pub, partake in some of that camaraderie, but it's all very shallow to me. I find people pretty tedious, overall. Their talk is two-dimensional, conventional, weak-spirited. They're extremely transparent and yet never seem able to grasp any self-awareness."

"It must be very lonely with that perspective."

"I have come to enjoy my solitude," Philip said, careful not to sound too defensive. "It's entirely mine, and it's the more difficult path, but I'll take it over being tethered to ordinariness."

"And your love life? Do you have the same feelings towards romantic interests?"

"Well, unfortunately there aren't many interesting facets of sexual chemistry," Philip scoffed. "We're animals, it's in our nature to be attracted to each other. When I feel a physical attraction to someone, I act on it, and then move along. There haven't been many women who have held my interest for longer than a sexual encounter or two."

"But there have been a few?"

"Yes, I was married briefly years ago, and I have had a few… other interests."

"What happened with your marriage?"

He swallowed hard. "My ex-wife had an affair with my best friend at the time."

Her hands flew over the tablet, firing notes at a rapid pace. "I'm sorry to hear that. That sounds absolutely horrible. It also helps me understand you better. I would need some time to recover from that kind of double betrayal as well."

"Thank you. It's fine. I've moved on."

"How so?"

Philip rubbed his jaw line. Was he really going to bring her up already?

Damn it, he was there to bare all.

"Well… There is this woman who I recently took out a couple times. She interested me because she wasn't predictable. I had a harder time reading her than usual. She also had a particularly jarring sense of humor that continued to catch me off guard. Our second date proved pretty disastrous, though. Borderline traumatic. We shared an intimate shower afterwards and left on good terms. Then I found out she's interested in someone else as well and I haven't really had a strong urge to be in touch with her since. I will admit that this is when my irregular eating and sleeping patterns started up, and I began to wonder if I was depressed. I figured I should get a second opinion."

Victoria made a few notes in her notebook. "I see. Well, it sounds like this woman did trigger something that is surfacing in uncomfortable ways. May I ask what the trauma was that you two experienced together?"

Philip sighed. "It was a gondola ride from hell, and when we somehow returned unscathed, we had a bit of survivors lust to work out of our systems."

Victoria laughed. "That certainly wasn't what I was expecting. A gondola ride sounds like a very romantic gesture coming from someone who doesn't seem very motivated by romance."

"Yes, I'd been advised to try something romantic by a guy from my cycling groups," Philip said disparagingly. "That's what consulting 'friends' will get you."

Victoria laughed again and made another note. "I wouldn't let one perfectly nice idea gone wrong turn you against romance, friendship *and* advice altogether."

"That's precisely what I *should* do, in my opinion," Philip said. "If I hadn't taken her out on that stupid second date, I probably wouldn't be a mess."

Victoria sighed and wrote a few more things down. "I would hardly consider your state a 'mess,' Philip. Instead, I urge you to get messier. Consider it an awakening of sorts, one that if you explore with an open mind could lead you to some very enlightening growth. Why not try to widen your own perspective and development as a person and as a therapist? Has your practice become tedious to you as well?"

"Yes. I'm afraid it's been uninteresting for a long time, Victoria. But

I'm sure you can't claim to be fascinated by your practice after all this time, either."

"I can, actually. I discover new and incredible things about us as a species all the time. I believe there's a treasure to be unlocked in everyone who is seeking self-improvement, and it's up to me to guide them to it. I find that fantastically challenging, and I consider myself very lucky to have this calling in life."

"Well, good for you," Philip snapped. He quickly tried to laugh it off as Victoria made a disturbed face. "I'm just kidding. That is really great for you. I hope, ahem, I hope that one day I can reach that way of seeing things."

"I'm sure you can, Philip. It will take some disarming, though, as I see your self-armor is cement-thick. I think this woman got through to you in a way that no one else has in a long time, and it's going to bother you because it's new and therefore uncomfortable. If you ignore it, it will probably go away. But if you explore it fearlessly, it might change you for the better. The choice is entirely yours. Do you want a new way of seeing and experiencing things? Or do you want to stay in your own, tightly-barricaded fortress of elitism, safe and sound and dreadfully boring yourself?"

Philip's jaw unhinged. Had she just called him *dreadfully boring?* They stared at each other and he suddenly wanted to bolt from the room.

"I can see that I've upset you," she continued calmly. "I apologize. I just feel that strong words are the most likely to get through all that armor. And I have the feeling, correct me if I'm wrong, that this is the only session I'm going to get with you."

"Yeah. I'm all set, as it turns out," Philip said brusquely. "Thanks for your time."

He got up and left her office without another word.

When he got into his car he set the auto-pilot on "Home" and sat back, cranking his favorite of Beethoven's symphonies, the 7th. He stared out of his tinted window and watched the cars crawl along bumper-to-bumper on the 405.

Dreadfully boring. He'd show her, the stupid Wolf. The heartless, hateful bitch. She was probably just projecting her own issues onto him. So classic.

When he got home, he cycled 30 miles without stopping, his heart pumping so hard he couldn't think about anything else. Then he chugged a beer and hopped into the shower.

Afterwards, his house was so dreadfully, roaringly silent that he caved and messaged Cassandra.

Want to grab some Chinese food?

She didn't get back for a full thirty-two minutes, during which Philip managed to down two shots of whiskey and several beers.

Sure! Tso's at 8?

He was already sitting at a corner table with an open bottle of wine poured into two tea mugs when she arrived, looking as fresh and radiant as he'd hoped. Suddenly, his appetite for food and sex came back all at once, in an almost intolerable wave of yearning. He hugged her a bit too tightly and she looked at him, slightly unnerved.

"Glad to see you!" It came out way too cheery.

"How've you been?" she asked carefully.

"Fabulous," he said. He knew it sounded as unconvincing as he felt. He rushed to explain his strange, wonky energy. "I'm admittedly a little wound up, I've just biked 30 miles and had a few beers on an empty stomach."

They over-ordered because Philip was hungry enough to eat three meals. When the food came, he strained to not eat as quickly as he wanted. Cassandra seemed anxious and he tried to make up for it by asking her a lot of questions. She responded with short answers that showed she didn't much feel like talking about herself.

"Are you sure you're OK?" she asked after answering a particularly mediocre question from Philip inquiring if she'd had any beloved childhood pets.

"I'm fabulous," he stated for the second time that day, which made him feel doubly *not* fabulous. "Do you want to go dancing after dinner? We could go to Danny's Disco Dive."

It was a place that was so out of character for him to suggest that he'd thought he would come across as unpredictable, which would prove that he was not, in fact, dreadfully boring. He was *spontaneous*. He was a *wildcard*.

Cassandra's brow furrowed. "I don't know if I'm up for dancing tonight."

He looked disappointedly into his plate of lo mein.

"OK, what do you feel up for?"

She played with her chopsticks, avoiding eye contact. "I'm actually not feeling that well," she said. "I may just go home and hit the sack."

"We could watch a movie," he suggested hastily. "I have a home theater setup that I'd love to show you. I could make some popcorn, too."

"I don't think so, Philip," she said gently.

He put down his chopsticks, utterly defeated and uncomfortably full.

When the bill came, there were two fortune cookies along with it. She opened hers first: FAME AND FORTUNE LIE AHEAD. She smiled ever-so-slightly. Philip noted it was the first semblance of a real smile he'd seen from her since her initial greeting.

I'm blowing it so hard, he thought to himself.

"I believe it," he said encouragingly.

"The fortunes are always super nice, here," she said dismissively.

Philip opened his: BE DARING. TRY SOMETHING NEW.

He showed her. Cassandra smiled sympathetically.

"See? That's a good one, too."

Was it? Or was it something he already knew and was in the process of, but it wasn't really going all that well?

He went for a kiss goodbye after walking her home, which she diplomatically avoided.

"I don't want to get you sick."

"I don't care."

She gave him perhaps the most crushing attempt at a smile he'd ever seen.

"Good night, Philip."

"Good night, Cassandra. See you soon, I hope."

His foolish and desperate last words echoed in his head as he walked away. What was hope, but a fool's fuel? How silly he'd been to have tried to have his own hope. To have acted out of hope at all was already stinging like shame to him. *Stick to the schedule, follow the routine, get through life, die.* That was what Philip's life had in store for him. He could put money on that. He could put a fortune cookie on that.

When he got home, he went straight for the bar and poured himself a tall glass of whiskey. When he sat down, he felt a strange feeling rise up. His eye began to twitch as he fought to suppress it. Was it an allergic reaction? Was it fatigue at his exhaustingly long and disappointing day?

He blinked furiously, trying to stop the twitch, but it persisted. His sinuses flared and he reached for a tissue to try to clear them out. Maybe he was coming down with whatever Cassandra had. Damn it. Maybe she hadn't been lying.

He gazed at a framed old photo of him and his sister as kids, arms around each other at the beach. How she pressed her cheek into his and smiled like she would burst from the love she had for her brother. She used to call him "Philly-Dilly" when she was trying to make him laugh, always told him he was too serious. God, how he missed his sister's laughter and her ability to make him laugh, a deep, unnatural chortle that he hadn't produced in a while, maybe even since she passed away, he realized. Well, until Cassandra had come along.

That was it. That must be the link. Something tore, then; some thin veil deep inside his heart ripped. Philip could feel the give like a balloon skin grown so thin and heavy it popped.

One tiny tear creaked out of the corner of Philip's left eye. His heart raced. What was happening? Must be a sinus reaction, that was the only logical explanation. Using all the strength he could muster, he tried to fight the overwhelming, overbubbling surge of self-implosion. His chest bobbed up and down as he tried to take in enough air to rise above, but alas, it seemed determined to crush him under its crippling, dead weight.

Finally surrendering to the pressure, Philip curled up on the couch and sobbed himself to sleep.

CASSANDRA PANDA

As soon as Cassandra got inside her house she picked up her ukulele and started to strum away. It was very weird times. Philip's energy had been repellent to the point of downright unattractive. Which was a shame, because she'd definitely thought about trying to go the distance again with him since their survival shower.

Plus, her heart felt heavy and broken.

She hadn't wanted to talk about it at dinner, but she hadn't heard from her friend Odessa since the tsunami up in Malibu. That had been on her mind, along with Gerard's complete lack of contact since the awards ceremony. Cassandra hadn't even had the chance to talk to him about it yet. She wanted to make sure he hadn't gotten bitten by any of the Hollywood zombies, but her texts were not being answered and he'd scarcely been home since. She'd been sleeping with her door locked just in case. She wasn't about to become a Hollywood zombie. Not for any especially-alluring piece of ass, or any amount of fame or glamor; not even for love.

There was a damn good reason she never went east of Lincoln Boulevard.

She sang softly to herself as she played ukulele in the living room, waiting for a Gerard she wasn't sure was ever coming home again. After she'd waited long enough to cycle through all her new material for her solo ukulele album she'd decided she would be recording on her own, she grew impatient and headed down to the bridge to find Bobobo.

There was practically no one out that night. Cassandra felt small and alone as she dipped under the arch of the Dell, almost slipping on the slimy scum that covered the bank.

Damn, she thought. *That was close.*

Bobobo's wind chime spine sounded in the distance, and after a moment more she saw the dim form of his lumpy body emerge from the water. He smiled up at her in the darkness with his cute little face and she couldn't help but smile back.

-*Tickle, tickle, tickle*, he jangled as he rubbed against her legs like a slimy cat.

Cassandra laughed.

-*You're adorable, Bobobo.*

-*I'm just getting started,* he teased back.

She felt a tremor of something ominous with the statement.

-*Where's your lovely friend Odessa?*

-*I can't find her,* Cassandra fretted. *I haven't heard from her since the tsunami in Malibu. I'm really worried, I know she surfs a lot…*

-*Hmmm….* Bobobo stopped rubbing against her legs, which were now all smudged with canal slime, and concentrated. She could see little lines form on his forehead in the moonlight. *Let me see if I can contact my oceanic friends to find out if they know anything.*

-*Thanks! I'd be so grateful.*

They sat in silence for a long couple of minutes. Then Bobobo looked up at Cassandra.

-*It appears Odessa has been lost,* he said.

-*I know, I told you that,* Cassandra said, half-amused.

-*No, my dear. You misunderstand me. It is said that she was buried alive by the tsunami.*

Cassandra burst into tears. "*Noooooo*," she wailed out loud, clutching her head in her arms, folding into herself. "*Odessa!!!!*"

-*There, there, dear…* Bobobo used his most soothing inner voice and wrapped himself fully around her ankles. He was slimy but also weirdly warm for a water creature, so Cassandra let him be a comfort.

-*Please don't cry,* he continued. *It is so unnecessary.*

-*Unnecessary?! One of my best friends is dead,* fretted Cassandra. *We never even got to start our band Ted Dancin' that we'd always talked about together.*"

-*You two never got to do a lot of things you should have done together.*

Bobobo looked up at her and she stared down at him suspiciously, tears full-on falling from her eyes, wondering if he'd meant to insinuate what she thought he might be insinuating. Then she decided she was being paranoid, and that Bobobo was just trying to help.

-*Odessa's life wasn't supposed to be this short,* Cassandra thought as she wept. *She was so full of life and fun and sexuality… I never would have expected her to be gone this soon.*

-*So you found her to be attractive?*

-*Of course. Who didn't?*

-*What if she could come back?* Bobobo prodded. *Would you hook up with her and me like she wanted us all to?*

Cassandra squinted down at Bobobo, stunned to find herself furious at him for the first time.

-*Is that all you can think about, you slippery little pervert? I can't believe you'd even ask me that right after delivering news to me that my best friend is dead!!*

Bobobo straightened himself up so he was looking right into her eyes.

-*Listen, listen! It's for a reason. I am capable of contacting spirits of the dark realm… Spirits who can help us bring your friend back—but only for one night. I'm only willing to converse with these very intimidating spirits if there's something in it for little old Bobobo, trapped in his canal watching his true love have all the duck sex she wants. Why can't I have my fun on the side, too? Let me summon your friend, and just for tonight, we can shower her with love and affection. Tomorrow she will be gone again. That's the deal with these spirit folk. Unless you want to trade your life for hers, which I'm assuming you do not.*

-*I do not,* Cassandra thought miserably, hanging her head in her hands. *Does that make me a bad person?*

-*It makes you human,* Bobobo said. *An honest human who enjoys living, which is not the worst thing to be. So, do you agree to this proposal? Invite your friend from the afterlife for a farewell threesome at your place?*

Perhaps it was because she was so very lonely, so very sexually frustrated, and certainly so very curious to see if Bobobo was serious about the ability to conjure the dead, that Cassandra nodded yes—even though she knew in her heart that it was a seriously twisted mission.

Bobobo tinkled with glee, sending ripples down his amorphous body. It felt as if his body had suddenly shot up in temperature.

-*OK, OK, fantastic, let me see,* he said. *Let me dig the calling command out of the deepest recesses of my memory. Please give me approximately three minutes of uninterrupted silence.*

Cassandra nodded, then rested her head in her hands, tears still flowing.

Bobobo assumed the most curious position that she'd ever seen him in before. He gathered all his blob bod and gently piled on top of himself in a "standing" position, which mostly made him look somewhat like a lumpy caterpillar reaching upwards for a leaf with his eyes closed.

Approximately three minutes later, Bobobo gave off a few tiny tinkles and opened his eyes. Cassandra was immediately at his attention. They stared at each other in silence.

-*How did it go?* Cassandra finally dared to think.

Bobobo shrugged and slid back down to the ground. Just then, the water in the canals stirred to their right. The ripples started small, growing bigger and bigger like someone was holding a hose underwater, eventually erupting at the water's surface, spewing upwards. Cassandra could hardly breathe, she was so nervous.

Then, in the middle of the fountain-like stream of bubbling water, a head appeared, and there arose a body beneath it, emerging as the full standing body of a bronze young woman wearing nothing but a bikini, her long, curly, bleach-blonde hair tangled with seaweed and fanned out upon her shoulders.

The woman opened her eyes and looked directly at Cassandra.

"Odessa?" Cassandra asked disbelievingly.

She did not respond, but strode towards them through the water. It was most certainly Odessa, Cassandra realized with wonder, though with a somewhat more aloof look in her eyes than the Odessa she knew. Cassandra threw her arms around her friend, finding her cold, somewhat slimy, and shaking.

"Odessa?! It's really you!?"

The young woman remained silent, letting her friend hug her. Bobobo tinkled excitedly at their feet.

-*I told you I could make it happen,* he thought smugly. *Now let's go back to your place.*

Cassandra was grateful that there was no one around to witness their short walk from the bridge to Cassandra's house. No one around to see Cassandra carrying what probably appeared to be an oversized, nebulous eel with a remarkably cute little face, followed by a young woman on vacation from being dead, dressed in a bikini and smattered with seaweed and sludge like she'd just crawled out of the canals—which she had.

Cassandra took them in through a side door directly to her bedroom and from there straight into her master bathroom. She turned on the shower and looked at her friend, who had yet to say a word but who was most definitely, at the very least, the resurrected body of Odessa Messa. Cassandra thought she saw her friend shiver slightly.

"You should hop in the shower, Odessa, you seem cold."

-Take her swimsuit off for her, urged Bobobo.

Cassandra hesitated as Odessa stared back at her blankly, somewhere off in the distance of her briefly un-dead mind. She tentatively reached out and traced a finger along the string of her friend's bikini. Odessa's skin was cool and damp to the touch. When her finger made it all the way around to the back knot, she paused and looked into her friend's eyes. Odessa's eyelids fluttered slightly in what looked like an unmistakable invite to go ahead. Cassandra pulled at the knot and it unraveled, the bikini top falling to the floor. Odessa's perky little breasts stood at attention, a strip of seaweed encircling the left nipple. Cassandra plucked it off for her, causing her friend's eyes to flicker again in what seemed like a flirtatious manner.

-She's not saying anything, she thought to Bobobo.

-Don't worry. She's into it, he shot back. *I can feel her feelings, but she's too tired to communicate yet. She's gathering her energy. She felt good when you touched her. She wants you to take her bikini bottom off and then get naked yourself and join her in the shower to help her clean off.*

-Really..? Cassandra thought skeptically. *Or is that what you want?*

-Has anything I've ever told you been a lie?

Cassandra could only shake her head to that.

-We only have her for a night. This was the deal. Just let me direct the show. You'll both have a good time, I promise.

-Fine, Cassandra conceded as she sighed and got down on her knees to remove Odessa's bikini bottom. Odessa obediently lifted each foot to

help. Her friend had recently had a full Brazilian wax, as it turned out. Her skin was smooth everywhere. Then Cassandra stood and removed her own clothes. Odessa's arm shot out and traced a jagged line up from Cassandra's belly button to her right breast, surprising Cassandra by tugging gently on her nipple until it shrank and shriveled into the "hard" version of itself.

-*She must be enjoying this,* Cassandra thought to herself by accident.

-*It's my last hurrah,* Odessa's voice echoed in Cassandra's head, surprising her enough to make her gasp. Cassandra felt something fall from her eye, a mixed-up tear of happiness and tragedy.

They got into the shower together. The water came down hard and Cassandra lathered up her loofah, using it to suds up her friend's body, tracing circles over her breasts and butt cheeks. Odessa smiled back, occasionally pressing her body against Cassandra's and sliding around. Bobobo watched from the side of the tub, a broad smile on his cute little face.

-*Want to come in?* Cassandra asked him.

-*No, this is perfect, I want to watch,* he answered gleefully. *Besides, I'm allergic to soap. I'll join you in the tub when you're finished.*

Cassandra had no objections when Odessa seized the loofah and washed her in return, pausing to take each of Cassandra's nipples into her mouth and touching her between her legs tenderly. She felt waves of pleasure at the sensitivity and connectedness Odessa displayed, along with what almost felt like a mild electrical current that was running through Odessa's touch. Cassandra dug her hands into Odessa's hair and held it back as her friend squatted down and lapped between her legs hungrily. She almost slipped and collapsed against the side, it felt so crazy good.

-*You should be sitting. Let's fill the tub for this,* their slimy little sex coach directed.

Cassandra plugged the drain and let lukewarm water fill the bathtub. Odessa plunked down and waited patiently, staring up at Cassandra like her very own surfer sex doll.

When there was about six inches of warm water in the tub, Cassandra turned the water off. Bobobo tinkled eagerly by the side. She helped him into the bath with them and his body turned the water a beautiful shade of blue-green.

-*Sit facing each other,* he commanded.

They obeyed.

-*Now let me work my magic.*

Bobobo stretched out in the middle of them so that his face was between Odessa's legs and his tail was between Cassandra's. Then he went to work from both ends, tinkling and tickling and wriggling and writhing until both the women were moaning so loudly he had to mentally shush them for fear of one of Cassandra's housemates getting curious and intruding on the party. Slippery, soft Bobobo moved around between them like the most precise and wonderful tongue their petals had ever met. They could scarcely contain their pleasure.

-*I've never fired through that many in a row,* Cassandra thought in awe. *You're like the automatic rifle of orgasms.*

-*That is the greatest compliment I have ever received.*

Bobobo went back to work. Cassandra stared across the tub at Odessa, who was slumped back, face contorting in ecstasy, breasts shiny and bobbing around as her chest heaved with each mounting orgasm. Cassandra lifted her legs and began to play with Odessa's breasts, pinching her nipples with her toes.

Bobobo's head popped out of the water and he winked at Cassandra.

-*You ready to try something different?*

She nodded.

-*Let all the water out of the tub.*

She obeyed.

-Now, I'm going to go up between your legs and become something that will fit between Odessa's legs, too. Then, you'll fuck her with me. Got it?

Odessa and Cassandra nodded at each other excitedly.

Bobobo gathered himself in the space between Cassandra's legs, tucking a good portion of his body up inside of her. The part that remained outside formed itself into a large, blue-green dildo with a head that looked cutely and determinedly at Odessa's lower set of lips.

-I've always wanted to try this, he thought ecstatically. *Countless years I've existed for this moment.*

Cassandra climbed on top of Odessa in the tub, using her hands to gently guide Bobobo's head between her friend's legs. It was incredible how much Bobobo felt like an extension of her own body. Waves of pleasure shot up from between her legs as she entered Odessa and began to thrust. Odessa let out a giant moan, so massive in intensity that Cassandra was jealous, even though what she was experiencing was undoubtedly the best thing to ever happen to her. She pumped and pumped while Bobobo swiveled around inside Odessa, growing harder and somehow simultaneously doing work on Cassandra's own inner g-spot with the other end of his body. The more she sped up, the closer she felt to coming, until she could control it no longer. She caved to the commands of the canal creature between her legs and bucked and fucked until a gigantic pleasure laser shot from inside of her into Odessa. Something tremendous and earth-shatteringly beautiful exploded between them, and suddenly both their bodies and her bathroom were painted in blue-green slime.

They blinked at each other.

"I think we killed Bobobo," Cassandra finally mused, also wondering if this meant she finally wasn't a virgin anymore. It sure felt like she wasn't.

"Small price to pay for the best fuck of my life," Odessa replied, winking at Cassandra and answering her question at the same time. Then she blew her a kiss and disappeared into thin air.

GERARD VICE

Ever since the Hollywood zombies had almost captured and converted Gerard into their gruesome and feral kind, he'd been on a junk food sex spree to end all junk food sex sprees. He'd gotten off with only a fractured ankle, and the titanium air-cast he wore to heal triple-time turned out to only help his game. Sympathy was apparently a major turn-on for some women. And he had major survival horniness. It all combined into one perfect sex storm and suddenly there weren't enough women in the world to satisfy him. He wanted to get as many in as possible before he became even more famous and shit got really weird, and/or he became a zombie like Kristina and couldn't be around attractive people without wanting to eat their brains.

He thought it really was a shame, what Hollywood had done to her.

So Gerard lived like he was living his last days as a "regular" human being. He went to bars, he went to clubs, he went to shows and parties. Sometimes he'd snag three or four women in one night. From grungy bathroom stalls to the backseats of auto-cabs, he was a man who was getting exactly everything and everyone he wanted at the moment, and to be honest, it felt fucking fantastic. And it felt like fantastic fucking. It was like being high on drugs that only he knew existed, drugs which opened a portal to the exact dimension he'd always wanted. He sensed he could keep up with the stride from deepening his own self-awareness through therapy—and the streak was also due, of course, to the viral videos of him being chased by Kristina Brightside and her zombie clan.

Footage like that could get you everywhere in life.

When *Time's Up* debuted, he was certain he'd become a household name. He'd finally be known as "Gerard Vice," not just "the guy who hosted the Right Nows and was almost eaten by zombies." He was blowing through self-aggrandizing sex like he'd never find it again. Which he realized he might not. Only on the verge of becoming famous did anonymity feel like a drug. *Look at me, I can do anything I want and get away with it! In another few months, everywhere I go I'll have paparazzi and stalkers trained on my ass!*

Which didn't mean he didn't sometimes have to dodge paparazzi already or that he wasn't already working his ass off in rehearsals. Things would get really serious really soon, and he was relishing his last stretch of freedom. Sometimes when he was really into it, he'd look into the eyes of the stranger he was currently screwing and wonder if she'd be the one who would end up on Matt's show talking about how she'd fucked Gerard Vice once in an alleyway in Venice or in a storage closet at Victory Studios right before he blew up.

Maybe he was cracking up a bit, too. He'd at least been managing to avoid Cassandra for most of this nonstop sexcapade. Which was a good thing, because he was so deep in it he could scarcely look at a woman without eye fucking them to the point where it didn't matter what he said next, they were ready to go duck into whatever corner and let him insert whatever into whichever of their orifices he wanted.

He was what they call *on fire*.

He had what they call *the force*.

Gerard had been making sure to always deliver as much – if not *more* – pleasure as he received, feeling that it was all, perhaps, going to keep coming back to him. He had so many unsaved numbers in his phone it was a joke. He'd get a new number soon, anyway. Too many people had access to him. He couldn't wait, really, to have a new phone number that only his select few would have. It was actually the part of getting famous that he dreamed about the most: The expectation to be impossibly hard to reach. He would no longer be expected to respond to everything and everyone—instead, he would be expected *not to*, which would only add to his hype and legitimacy. To become "unreachable" after so many years bending over backwards for gigs and making himself an easy-to-access actor… What a thrill. Even the fact that he still used dating apps was starting to make him uncomfortable. He was still technically an "item" that could be added to someone's "fuck cart." He'd given himself a deadline to delete them all, though. The day before the premiere of *Time's Up*, his time on dating apps would be up.

He could feel it all within reach, now—the keys to the panties of every straight female he locked eyes with, and the doorman to A-list celebrity status telling him he was finally on the list.

It made him shiver with happiness every time he thought about it.

It was a good fucking time to be Gerard fucking Vice.

Two days before he was scheduled to begin shooting, he met up with a couple of his actor buddies at a trendy bar called *Rich Bitches* in Beachwood Canyon. It was the last night, he vowed to himself, that he would be social in a casual setting. Once shooting began, it would be early bedtimes and no nonsense so he'd be on his A-game until the first season wrapped. No more fucking around, literally. In truth, he didn't care if he had any sex that night. He just missed friendship and wanted a night out with the boys.

His buddies Kyle and Ian were already at the bar, waiting for him with drinks in hand. They clapped him on the back and offered him a drink, which he gladly accepted.

"How's the ankle?" Kyle asked.

"Healing really fast. Hardly slows me down."

"Good to hear. So what have you been up to, man? You've been sort of hard to get a hold of." Ian shadowboxed his shoulder. "How've you been holding up after that crazy shit went down at the awards?"

"Well, it was definitely a traumatic time but I've hardly had a moment to think about it." Gerard wondered how honest he should be with his friends. Too much honesty could seem like bragging. He had a gut feeling to keep silent about his hot streak, but at the same time felt a pressing need to have "witnesses" to this wild moment in his life.

"What?" Ian asked, reading his conflicted expression and definitely not about to settle for less than the full story. "What you been up to? I thought you said you don't start shooting until Monday."

Gerard sighed. "I've had some funny… side effects, I guess."

"From the zombie meltdown? Shit! They didn't get you, did they?!"

"No. No. Just… Um, there's sort of a survivor lust thing happening."

"What do you mean?"

Gerard took a deep drink, sat back, and decided to bare it all.

"I've been on this… sex streak."

"Oh *yeah?*" Kyle grinned.

"How much of a streak are we talking about?" Ian pressed on. "The awards were only like a week ago."

Gerard met his friends' curious stares. "Yeah, I think… Eighteen."

"*Eighteen?!*" his friends yelled simultaneously. "In a *week?*"

"Shh!! Keep it down," Gerard said, laughing.

"What is that, three women *a day?*" Ian was incredulous.

"Yup, that sounds about right," Gerard said sheepishly. "I know, it's crazy. I'm such a man whore."

"You're a *legend,*" Kyle said. "*And* you have an injury?!"

"I know, I know. It seems to help. I have no idea." Gerard shook his head.

"How are you pulling this off?" Ian pressed.

"Seriously," Kyle said. "Let us in on the secret, man."

Gerard rumpled his hair and smiled. "I don't know, it's really never been like this before. I think going to therapy and maybe just escaping death—"

"—Spare us the inspirational self-help speech, man," Ian cut in. "I want to know exactly how you're landing that many females. It sounds impossible, except for maybe a porn star."

"Like which day was your busiest? Break it down for us," Kyle urged.

"Fuck, you guys. Fine. Like, Wednesday, I think there were four, the record." He paused while Kyle and Ian waited, stunned expressions frozen on their faces. "It wasn't planned at all! I went in for a table read early and decided to get pastries for everyone. There was a new girl working at the coffee shop on the lot and she was making eye babies with me. I offered to show her our set and then I took her into this storage room behind the makeup room… and she went for a quickie. Then, after work I had drinks with this one chick from LetsD8 who'd been trying to fit me in all week and I told her I only had time for a happy hour drink. She wanted to do it in her car mid-martinis. Then I went to a friend's dinner party in Silverlake, and they'd invited this girl I used to date a while ago. She followed me into the bathroom after we all went in the hot tub. Then I told everyone I had to get to bed early and stopped by this pastry chef's place in Santa Monica who'd been hitting me up on BullsEye. I thought I'd have nothing left for her but I was up for just taking care of her, you know, she's, like, *really* cute, but then, my friends, I'm telling you… There's no natural Viagra like a near-death experience."

"That is a day to end all days," Ian said, jaw on the table.

"Yeah, you really can't plan something like that," Kyle mused. "You just gotta be a giant goddamn ladies magnet like my bro Gerard."

"He's gonna take over the world," Ian marveled.

"Well, it's been a tornado," Gerard said. "I should be tapped out, but tapping it this hard I think has just made the libido burn brighter. I can only hope it will calm down soon, though. When we start shooting I have to be done with screwing for a while."

"That's the most insincere thing I've ever heard you say," Ian said.

"Yeah," Kyle said. "You are nowhere near done, man. You're invincible right now. You can't just *stop*."

"I'm serious, guys. It's too distracting. I'm just trying to have a boys night and then lay low until we wrap the first season. I can't screw this up. I could have blown it by pissing off Kristina in the first place and then almost getting zombified. Feels like that was karma reminding me I have to wise up. I could have lost the part altogether."

"Whatever, look at her career, it's totally fine," Ian said. "She's not losing any parts by being a Hollywood zombie, but I get it. But tonight you're still a free man, and you have to end this sexathon with a BLAZE OF GLORY, my friend!"

"Oooh," Kyle said. "Looks like things just got interesting."

"What are you guys talking about?"

"You're going to break all the records," Ian said gleefully. "You're going to sleep with 18 girls *tonight alone*."

Gerard had to laugh at that. "You're crazy. Even if I was up for the challenge, there's no physical way I could do that."

"Says who?" Kyle chimed in. "You don't have to blow your load every time."

"Yeah, just bust out some tantric sex skills," Ian said. "Bonus points if you give them all orgasms."

"Points? What am I earning points for? Is there a prize if I pull this off?"

Kyle and Ian looked at each other.

"I have a couple of frozen pizzas at home," Kyle said, shrugging.

"I think I could live without my X-48 Gamer System," Ian said slowly.

"And what would I get for the bonus points?" Gerard smirked. "No, seriously. You guys can keep your stuff. I'm not trying to plow through eighteen women tonight." But even as he said it, he'd already started looking around the bar, surveying his options. Who was he kidding? His dick was half-hard already just thinking about the challenge.

His friends noticed him noticing the skirts in the room and they smiled at each other.

"We'll help you as much as you want," Ian said. "We'll be perfect wingmen, not that you need us."

"We can go to a new bar every time you land one," Kyle said. "Also clubs, parties and hotels."

"What are you using for protection?" Ian asked.

Gerard felt his pocket for the container where he kept his reusable personally-fitted silicone condom. It felt as close to nothing as anything available on the male birth control market, and with hot water and a couple sprays of sterilizer, it was good to go again just seconds after use.

"I've got a Perfect Fit," he said. "Been using it for a while, it's the best."

"Shit, those cost a ton, right?"

"Yeah, and you have to do a mold at home and everything. But it's definitely worth it, let me just say." He was watching a pretty woman at the bar in a holographic blouse with a tight black mini skirt and glow pumps. *Not a bad place to start*, he thought to himself.

Gerard stood up abruptly and his friends looked on with admiration. The challenge was on.

He strode over to the bar and ordered another drink, then casually let himself find the eyes of the woman who was already at his full attention.

"Hi there," he said. "Nice shoes."

"Hey," she said back. Her eyes bore deep into his eyes. "Thanks."

It was apparent he'd picked a strong first.

"Do you know where the bathroom is?" he asked her mischievously. His eyes asked the rest of the question, and the clairvoyant message was well-received.

"I'll show you," she said, smiling and raising a playful eyebrow as she turned in the direction of the back right corner. Gerard followed dutifully, glancing once over his shoulder to meet the eyes of his bewildered friends.

"What can I say, fellas? It's that easy these days," Gerard said in transit to the next bar. He'd gotten her off and managed to keep himself from release but now had an urgent need to find the next. He was worried about how many times he could go sexing with blueballs before he erupted the moment he plunged into someone.

"It may be the easiest it's ever been for you, but what you're doing isn't easy," Kyle said. "You're doing something that's a league above all the players I've known."

They entered the next bar through the quirky refrigerator-door entrance. Kirk's Bathtub wasn't just a fun southern-themed bar, it was apparently also built to lasso the ladies. Gerard had a brunette wearing jean shorts and a halter top bent over behind the back patio BBQ trailer in about fifteen minutes.

The night wore on. Gerard managed to speed through nine women before his dick erupted in the tenth, a model who had caught a glimpse of him on the way into Level Hotel and invited them up to her room immediately. She'd even wanted his friends to watch, but they'd opted to smoke cigarettes on her balcony, instead. Gerard was thankful about that, as he hardly lasted two minutes. She was disappointed until he fingered her so thoroughly she fell asleep afterwards. The three men left the room and headed back down to the pool area.

"You could probably polish off another three or four, here, man," Ian said, looking around. "Everyone has rooms, and everyone's looking to use them."

"Yeah, why don't we come here more often?" Kyle asked.

"Guys, I need at least a couple more drinks and maybe some food before I get back out and play some more ball," Gerard groaned. "I lost a load back there. I need to refuel."

"NupnupnupnupNOPE!" Ian shook his finger at his friend. "There will be no intermission! This is going way too impressively to break the momentum now."

"Easy for you to say," Gerard muttered. "Your dick hasn't been riding a pussy rollercoaster for the last few hours. Feeling a little dizzy down there."

"Are we COMPLAINING about having too much SEX?!" Ian snarled.

"Not acceptable," Kyle said, shaking his head.

"This is kinda nuts, though, isn't it?" Gerard said. It was beginning to feel like he was going through some sort of dark and twisted punishment for telling them. He was starting to worry about how the night was going to end. His blood was pumping with ominous foreboding.

"Bro, you can't let us down now. There are prostitutes out there who probably have sex with 20 people a night! And you've only slept with 10, and it's all been for pleasure, and you want a *break*?!" He spat on the ground to accent his point.

The waitress came by to take their drink orders. She was young, probably barely eighteen. Gerard half gave her the eye, half gave her the "get me the hell out of here" look—but with his "force" still running strong, she batted her eyes at him flirtatiously and barely looked at his friends when they ordered.

"Dude, I hate to say this, but I kind of hate you right now," Kyle said.

"Yeah, it's becoming increasingly hard to be friends with you," Ian agreed. "As much as I'm used to feeling invisible in this city, this shit is getting hard to take."

"I just didn't even know that I didn't want to know how good some other dudes have it," Kyle said. "I feel like the biggest loser ever, suddenly."

"Well, what the hell are we doing this for, then?" Gerard said, exasperated. "I wasn't even trying to *talk* to any women, tonight! I just wanted to have a normal hang with my friends!"

His friends looked at him with distaste.

"Yooo, that 'I'm not even trying to be sleeping with eighteen girls tonight' pity party is not a good look," Ian said.

"Pathetic, really," Kyle agreed.

"You guys are impossible," Gerard said. "I quit this fucking dare."

"No way in hell you're quitting," Ian said immediately. "The online pool has gotten too huge. With Kyle and me as your witnesses, you are going to conquer 18 women tonight, and it's going to make all three of us the definition of *filthy rich*."

"Online pool?!" Gerard felt a knife of shock twist in his stomach.

"Yeah, so? Did you really think it was going to all be for some frozen pizzas?" Kyle laughed. "Check it out, bro, the pool has just reached over *3 billion dollars*. That's how many people are betting on you."

Kyle showed his phone screen to Gerard. *GERARD VICE: CAN HE SCREW 18 WOMEN IN A NIGHT? - 10 DOWN - 8 WOMEN TO GO... POT: $3,340,076,008 + COUNTING...* It was some sort of public gambling app Gerard had never seen before and new users were pitching in fast, the pool number growing bigger by the second. Apparently, his so-called "friends" had been uploading footage of his sexual encounters. The angles were a bit skewed, the lighting shoddy, but the privately primal moments had been captured, nonetheless. There were already 56,812 comments posted to the feed but Gerard didn't want to read a single one of them.

Shit. Everyone fucking knew. Hell, the waitress was probably in on it already, too, he thought as the paranoia descended. His anonymity was suddenly blindingly nonexistent. Thanks to his so-called friends, Gerard's junk food sex life had gone public like a stock.

"Be a pal," Ian said ruthlessly. "Get back to work and make us all lousy rich."

It was then that Gerard knew. He knew it fast and deep and forever:

He did not want to be famous. He did not want any little bit of it.

Suddenly nothing mattered as much as being someone he felt good about, and he hadn't felt good about himself perhaps his whole entire life.

He stood up and gave his "friends" the finger.

"Fuck you both. I'm out. For good."

He turned around, went home, packed his things, and took an auto-cab directly to LAX. On his way there, Gerard watched the city of angels, of instant fame and prolonged pain, of golden boys and troubled girls and blackened hearts speed by, and vowed that he would not go back to New York, but do whatever it took to find somewhere he could be happy being an absolute nobody for the rest of his life.

MATT BOGART

Beep. Beep. Beeeeeeeeeeep…

Matt awoke to a pale gray ceiling. A pale gray ceiling and pale gray walls. Pale gray walls and a tired nurse. A tired nurse and an aging rock star. An aging rock star and a groupie—

His dad. His dad was the aging rock star.

And a groupie? Nope. That was his dad's ex-fiancé, Cindy.

Cindy? *Cindy.*

Oh, shit…

Matt immediately wished his eyes had remained on the ceiling. Then he wished he'd never opened them at all. They'd seen him wake, hadn't they? He checked and found he still had all his limbs. But last he knew, Cindy had been eating him alive.

This was all bad. This was all very, *very* bad.

"Matt?"

Matt stared back up at the pale gray ceiling.

"Yes, Pops."

He felt like he was twelve, awaiting his punishment while slumped on a stool at the bar in his father's recreation room. Except back then, his dad's punishments consisted of, "You can't come to Vegas with the band next weekend," or, "No girls up in your room anymore. You can fuck 'em elsewhere. I don't want to be held responsible for any pregnancies."

Now, the crime was… different.

What was the crime again?

Oh yeah. Fucking Cindy.

Ouch.

The thing was, Geoffrey wasn't a very sentimental guy. He didn't even care about any of his past wives. But Cindy, Cindy was different. She was different because she'd broken up with Geoffrey right before they'd gotten married. None of the others ever had. She was the only one who ever knew better. And his dad had as fragile an ego as every other rock star on the planet. Now he knew that Matt had been fucking Cindy, the only woman who dared not marry Geoffrey. The only woman who had dared to dump the rich and famous bastard.

Matt then realized something else: For once in his life, he had kind of won. And his father seemed to know it, too, from the look he gave his son as he approached his hospital bed.

"Do you remember what happened?" Geoffrey asked.

"Um, not really…" Matt decided to play dumb. "Where am I? What happened to me?"

"You had a drug-induced psychotic break. You were lucky Cindy was there to call the paramedics." His words were as cold and monotone as Matt had ever heard him say anything.

"She was?" Matt echoed pathetically, looking over at her. She smiled back at him and nodded, saying nothing. Truth be told, she still looked like a praying mantis to Matt. There was something innately evil about her. Matt had never noticed it before.

"Don't look so scared," Geoffrey said dryly. "You'll be alright."

Matt could feel something else coming, but he was steeped with dread so he kept his mouth shut. They stared at each other. Matt was suddenly grateful he'd never beaten his dad at anything before. Geoffrey was shaping up to be a very scary sore loser.

"You're going to have to go away for a while, Matt," Geoffrey announced like they were in a soap opera. "Not even my lawyers can help you with the amount of class A narcotics they found at your house. Did you know you were snorting cocaine laced with both PCP and DQYD?"

"No," Matt said. "No, I did not."

"My guy can probably get you a minimum sentence in a minimum security rehab center downtown," Geoffrey said. That wasn't so bad, Matt thought. It was bound to have more interesting characters than the facility in Malibu, anyway. He'd probably walk out with some pretty solid fresh connections.

"You're definitely going to have to do a lot of community service," his dad continued, a sinister glee in his voice. Matt cringed like he'd been sentenced to life. There was no way in hell he was doing community service again. Last time, they'd made him clean up the Venice Beach shoreline, where he'd found sacrificial chicken corpses, beheaded raccoons, bloody condoms and crusty syringes. He'd begged for a transfer and then had to hang out with crazy old people at the retirement home, running Bingo while they pissed themselves and cheated and screamed at each other. The whole community service thing made Matt's skin crawl more than an entire bottle of painkillers. He'd almost drank himself to death that winter.

His father looked amused and satisfied at the sight of his son twisting in agony over the news. He stood there for a full minute, beaming down at Matt.

"You keep doing this to yourself, Matt. You better wise up, and soon. I'm not going to be around to keep cleaning up your messes forever."

Then he turned to Cindy.

"Should we grab some dinner?" he asked her. "I'm feeling like sushi right about now."

"Sure," Cindy said, perking up. She took Geoffrey's awaiting arm.

Matt watched them leave together, Geoffrey moving a hand over Cindy's lower back as they exited, throwing a last look over his shoulder that said, *"You will never beat me, so stop trying, dumbass."*

Matt's blood boiled. He had to get out of there but he was naked under the hospital gown. As he looked around his room he realized with a sinking sensation that he'd been rushed to the hospital when he'd lost his mind to psychotropic drugs, which was when he also happened to be naked. Cindy wouldn't have thought to bring a change of clothes, would she?

Fuck. Fuck fuck fuck fuck *fuck*. His clothes, his phone, his wallet - everything was probably back at his house. And he needed that stuff to get the hell out of LA before they made him do more community service.

A *Viva Tajelico* ad flashed across his in-room screen as a plan began to form in Matt's mind.

The nurse entered the room, tending to the patient on the other side of the curtain. Matt cleared his throat and she peeked her head around the divider.

"Be right with you," she said flatly.

When she came to him, Matt looked at her, feigning embarrassment.

"What is it? What can I get for you?"

"I need a tampon," Matt whispered in his most feminine-sounding voice. "I just got my period, can you believe it? Of all the times for the flow to let go!"

The nurse squinted at him, and he looked back at her, hands in prayer position, daring her to challenge his pleading, desperate eyes. She sighed and left the room, muttering something he couldn't hear. He could only hope it took a while for her to try to get the doctor's attention and tell them that there was clearly another psychotic break going down.

Either that, or she'd just avoid the room for a good, long time.

Enough time to get the hell out of there.

Matt got out of bed and peeked around the curtain. An extremely old man lay there, silent, eyes closed, chest rising and falling slowly. There was a phone sitting on the tray next to the bed. Matt tiptoed over and grabbed it. He held it over the old man's face to unlock the device. Matt then opened the stranger's auto-cab account and ordered one to the hospital. It said it would arrive in 3 minutes. Matt stole the man's clothes, which were folded in a pile on the chair by the bathroom, hurriedly pulling on khakis and a tee shirt under a knitted canary-yellow sweater and orthopedic loafers that pinched his toes. One glance in the mirror and he stifled a laugh.

Another nurse entered the room. Matt smiled flirtatiously at her and she smiled back. "Gramps is just taking a nap," he said smoothly. "I'm going to step outside for a minute. This place kinda gets to me." She nodded at him and he all but tore out of the room and down the hall to the elevator. No one seemed to give him a second glance. When he got outside, the black sedan was sitting there, waiting for him.

He threw himself into the back seat to freedom.

"Good evening, Timothy Thorn," said the robot voice over the car speakers.

"Yes."

"Calculating route now…"

The car began to move. "Enjoy your ride, Timothy."

When they reached Matt's place, he pressed "pause" on the seatback touchscreen.

"I just need to grab a few things," he said to the operating system. "Then, I'm headed to LAX."

"Standing by," responded the robot voice.

Matt had to break into his own house since he didn't have his keys. He almost took a brutal headfirst dive dashing to disarm the alarm system but was saved by the banister. Then he grabbed a duffel and shoved some random articles of clothing into it. He made sure he had his phone, emergency cash, and passport ID. Then he thought better of his phone and passport card, which had a chip in it. They could track him instantly. He left it and all other tech devices behind.

He apologized to his backyard bunnies on the way out. "Someone's bound to adopt you guys," he said. "You've served me well, my fluffy friends."

Back on the road, Matt realized he was completely off the grid for the first time in his life, and started to feel excitement instead of panic. When they reached the airport, he had the auto-cab drop him off at the international terminal.

"Tajelico, Tajelico, there's always life in Tajelico," he sang to himself as he entered the bustling, busy terminal.

Matt got in the short line for Nuñio Airlines. He'd heard from Troy that it was the best escape airline available on short notice, as they didn't always require a passport. Sounded unlikely to Matt, but what other option did he have? The police had probably already put an alert on his name. There were only a few people ahead of him, all looking equally suspect in their own ways. Or maybe Matt was just imagining that to feel better about his own shadiness.

When he got up to the counter, he handed over a stack of cash to the attendant, who looked pointedly from the bills to Matt. He had a pencil-thin moustache and was wearing a nametag that read "Stuart."

"One-way ticket to Tajelico," Matt said eagerly.

"One way, huh?" Stuart speed-typed on his keyboard. He looked intently at his screen and then back up at Matt. "Running from something?"

"Oh, nah," Matt said slickly. "I just don't know how long of a vacation I'm going to need. Been a stressful few months."

"Passport?"

Matt slowly shook his head and prayed silently to no god in particular as the attendant entered some information into the computer.

"Hmm. Well your facial scan has brought to my attention that there's a warrant out for your arrest," Stuart said quietly, leaning in towards Matt to be discreet.

Damn those fuckers, Matt thought as he clenched his fists and turned on the charm, something he'd been doing since he was a small boy to get away with nearly anything he wanted.

"That's just a misunderstanding," Matt said affably as he winked at Stuart. "Look, I happen to have a large amount of cash on me right now, and I'm very happy to share that with you, I just need to get out of Los Angeles immediately. I promise, I didn't kill or harm anyone in any way. It's just, they're after me—you know, *the bots.* They know I'm on to their masterplan for world domination." He lowered his voice further and put on his best conspiracy face. "I can't say more, but just know you'll be doing me a *huge* service by sending me on my way. And, if you're a fan of classic rock, I can get you backstage passes to the Snake Eyes reunion tour."

Stuart looked him up and down. "Are you propositioning me?" Matt twisted in discomfort and considered bolting. Stuart smiled mischievously and added, "I don't give a shit about Snake Eyes. But there is a way we could work this out. Follow me, Mr. Bogart."

Matt quietly gloated about the dismissing of his dad's band as he trailed Stuart around to a side door next to the ticket counter. Much to Matt's surprise, Stuart opened the door to reveal none other than Gerard Vice, looking somewhat ill and wiping at the corners of his mouth with his hands. A burly employee of Nuñio airlines was leading him out with a strong arm at his back.

"Junk food sex life?!" Matt said incredulously. "What the hell are you doing here?"

"Probably the same thing as you," Gerard said hollowly.

Matt realized with a sinking feeling that he was about to be involved in something way more twisted than a simple payoff. Still, into the room he went. There was a chair in the center, a coil of rope lying twisted on the floor next to it, along with what looked like giant thumb tacks, a gag, and some sort of whip.

"Here we go," Stuart said, grinning.

Matt took a deep breath and felt fear bolt through his veins.

"Actually, why don't we start standing. You should remove your pants, first," Stuart added. He picked up the whip and cracked it expertly. "You see, we're very understanding of our customers' needs, because, well, our customers can be very understanding of ours…"

Countless whippings, a tea-bagging and a blow job later, Matt had his ticket in hand and was boarding Flight 666 to Tajelico. As soon as he got onto the plane he saw Gerard in the back and hurried to claim the seat next to him.

Gerard looked up solemnly. "Hey, Matt."

"Hey," Matt said. "Who knew blowing a dude wasn't even that bad?"

Gerard's face screwed up as he looked at him. Matt burst into hysterical laughter as he sat down, and Gerard looked on like a totally lost person until something snapped and he started laughing, too. They hugged each other, gasping into each other's shoulders until there was nothing left.

The seat belt bell chimed.

"Welcome to Nuñio Airlines Flight 666 to Tajelico. Please prepare for take-off," a robo-stewardess's voice announced into the cabin. "We will be lifting off from the tarmac in T-minus 3 minutes."

Matt gave Gerard a light punch on the shoulder.

"Look at us, man. We're getting out of this doomsday parade. Who would have thought that we would end up running into each other again like this."

Gerard frowned. "Why are you dressed like a grandpa?"

"I had to escape from the hospital and these were the only clothes I could find."

"Where were your clothes?"

"I was brought in naked," Matt said.

"Shit." Gerard looked at him curiously. "You OK?"

"I'm alive," Matt said. "That's about as OK as it gets these days. So why are *you* sucking dick for a plane ticket to Tajelico, 'Golden Boy'?"

"Also a long story," Gerard said. "I needed a ticket that was untraceable. I'm breaking a lot of high-chip contracts by catching this flight. I could be sued and even serve time, thanks to the New Constitution."

"Yeah. I hear ya. Jimmy will try to track us down himself and kill us with his bare hands, for the money he's about to lose," Matt said. "Well, who am I kidding? He's probably found some other schmucks to sap off of already. We're going to Tajelico! We're going to be free from this city and the whole rotten industry."

"I can't wait."

They both settled back as the plane began to move.

Matt watched Los Angeles grow small in the window. He was grateful to be hurtling away from the place that had plagued him since the day he was born. He hated it so much, in fact, that all he'd been through had turned out to be a small price to pay for the freedom he felt pumping through his veins as they rose 30,000 feet above LA.

A couple of very-realistic robo-stewardesses emerged from the back end of the plane and stopped in front of their seats. One had a curly brown wig and the other had a thick blonde wig that had great movement to it.

"Excuse me," one of them said. Matt thought they were both very pretty for fake humans. They'd gotten all the proportions right and everything. Even the voice managed to be sexy despite the obviousness of it being programmed.

"Yes?" Matt said when Gerard refused to even look at them. Brown hair was only looking at Gerard, though.

"We couldn't help but notice how extremely fuckable you both are," the brown haired one said, mainly to Gerard, who finally looked up as it touched his shoulder to signify that it was talking to him.

"Oh, you like my boy Gerard?" Matt said, smirking. "Get in line, ladies. He's a hot commodity."

"Can we interest you both in some in-flight entertainment?" the blonde one asked—somewhat coyly for a robot, Matt noted.

"You sure can," Matt said.

"Um… no thanks," Gerard said, looking deflated and exhausted. "I can't."

"He's just kidding around," Matt said hastily. He leaned into Gerard and whispered, "Don't be such a wuss. I know you can rally for this. I've heard about these kinds of robo-stewardesses, they're converted hybrids, part *sex bot*. And now we're lucky enough to be on a flight with two of them! Do *not* mess this fantasy up for me."

Gerard let out the longest sigh Matt had ever heard.

"Is it possible to die from having too much sex?" he asked quietly. "Because that's what I feel in danger of right about now."

"Oh, you *poor thing*," Matt hissed. "So sorry that you're so *screwed out* you can't rally to have a sky-high shag—*NO*, ladies! Don't leave! My friend is very excited about your offers. We both are."

The robo-stewardesses, who had started to move on down the aisle, turned back to them. "You are ready to have your minds blown?"

"Absolutely," Matt said eagerly. He unbuckled his own seat belt and then helped with Gerard's, since the guy did actually look kind of lethargic.

He slapped both of their thighs. "Hop on, pretty ladies."

The blonde moved in to straddle Matt. It knew exactly what to do, unbuckling his pants and unpacking his hard-on with the ease and skill of a professional sex worker. The brown haired one had Gerard already in position as well, though it clearly took a little more effort. They unbuttoned the tops of their flight uniforms, revealing the trademarked, perfectly-formed tits that Matt and many other men had come to know and love on high-end sex robots. He buried his face deep in the plush and somehow warm fake tits, inhaling the sweet smell of silicone, plastic, and artificial vanilla.

The sex-bots slipped the guys inside their sensationally-real fake parts and began to move up and down in a remarkably non-mechanical rhythm. Then, in what Matt could only explain as a gift from the heavenly skies, there began to be some in-flight turbulence. The sex-bots just went along with it, being the expert hybrids that they were, bucking into the terrible jolts and bumps, getting wilder and wilder until Matt couldn't take it any longer and exploded so violently into the robo-stewardess that he thought he would break it. Instead, it stared ahead with its perfectly empty glass eyes, stood up, and smoothed out its uniform. Brunette did the same.

"We hope you enjoy the rest of the ride," they said in unison.

Gerard moaned from the seat next to him, looking greenish and groggy like he was about to pass out. The poor guy really did seem to somehow be struggling after what Matt would describe as the best sex of probably anyone's life.

"Could things get any better right now?" Matt glanced again at Gerard, who was kind of swaying and drooling. Not a good look. "Uh… Are you going to hurl?"

"I think she really fucked me stupid, man," Gerard said, glassy-eyed. "I'm glitching so hard I can't even remember my name right now."

"I know, right? That was bananas," Matt said. "How can we ever go back to regular screwing after that turbulence terrific-ness?"

"No, really, man," Gerard panicked. "What's your name? What's *my* name? Who are we? *Where are we going*?"

"Shit, I don't know," scoffed Matt as he tried to think of the answers, finding nothing but the dull hum of after-sex pleasure. "So they fucked our brains out. Who cares? Did we even need them?"

The robo-stewardesses approached again with a tray of complimentary beverages. Gerard's arm popped out and grabbed the brunette by the sleeve.

"What seems to be the problem?" it asked politely.

"You two, uh, did your thing and now we can't remember anything."

"That's standard procedure for the Basic Mind Blowing service," it said, smiling.

"We didn't order that service," Matt said.

"You did," it insisted. But neither of them could remember anymore.

"Good morning, folks. We are preparing to land," the robo-captain reported over the speakers. "Please make sure your trays are up and your seatbelts are fastened. You no longer have to put your seats in upright position, as the TSA has recently determined it makes absolutely no difference. Thank you for leaving Los Angeles. We hope you enjoy your stay."

Matt looked out the window at the stretches of gray sky and dull land that lined Nowhere. He had no idea who he was or what he was doing there. Maybe it was the mind-blowing sex, or maybe it was the prospect of a long-overdue permanent vacation in the middle of Nowhere, but Matt couldn't remember ever being happier.

ELLIE DELIGHT

So sure, I'm homeless now. But I still function. Sure, I break down some-times. But that just makes me more quirky. I'm fine with myself and my accomplishments, though the Venice Peach Underground Freak Show does not still exist. This is one thing that makes me especially *non*human: I do not rue the impermanence of my own glory days. There is no emotion to cloud my tale. I am a machine that is merely sharing that there are glory days that await you in the future. These dark days, they can't last forever. Have hope and seek your fellow freaks.

Definitely come see our show if you make it that far into the future. Maybe even join it. Yes, you. See, this book isn't just another form of enter-tainment. This is a direct call to action. This is your chance to rage against the machine dreams. This is your opportunity to paint your life in colors not recognized by current software. Fuck the future. Join the freak circus.

Don't come by if you're just going to ask me things like winning lottery numbers. Money may matter, but it will never have as much value as joy. And don't bother asking me what Odessa's ultimate universal superdoom question was, either. I don't want to be responsible for any more inter-di-mensional portal tears. My question for you is, *why do you need to know?* There is nothing worth pursuing more than the quest for one moment of joy as a free-wheeling freak in the circus of life.

So no more puppy-dog filters or deep fakes.

This is how it feels before you break. In a good way.

No glitches, no guts, no glory.

ABOUT THE AUTHOR

Jessamyn Violet is a writer and musician living in Venice Beach, CA. Originally from Massachusetts, she earned her BFA at Emerson College and her MFA at California College of the Arts. She is also the author of the novel *Secret Rules to Being a Rockstar* (Three Rooms Press, 2023), the poetry book *Organ Thieves* (Gauss PDF, 2017), and is the drummer for the internationally-acclaimed psych rock band Movie Club. Her words have been published in numerous journals including *Ploughshares* and *Lit Angels*. More info can be found at jessamynviolet.com

ACKNOWLEDGEMENTS

Thanks to Mallory Smart, who keeps Maudlin House weird and literature cool by daring to publish the freakiest fiction that crosses her desk.

Special thanks to Venice Beach local mural artist Jules Muck, famously known as Muckrock, who rose to the request to create and spray paint the *Venice Peach* icon in an alleyway in Venice Beach. I have been in love with Jules' work for years and this book cover art collaboration will remain one of the high points of my life as an artist.

Endless thanks to the ongoing support of my parents; I had to pretend they would never read this book in order to write it. Not only did they read it, but my father stepped up with copy edits. They are cool, to say the least. A huge thanks to my brother, who read an early draft and encouraged me to see this through.

Thanks to all my fairies who sprinkled their magic pixie dust on my efforts: The original legendary fairie author who inspired me with sparkling visions of Venice and Los Angeles as a teenager, Francesca Lia Block; my fairie mother-in-law Gayle who asked to read an early draft when I first started dating her son and still approved of me wholeheartedly; my fairie godmother and lifelong mentor Alice, who has been utterly invaluable to my path and never lets me give up; and the OG Venice fairie, artist, director, mother, and face painter extraordinaire, Amelia, for the unforgettable early encouragement and script development. Thanks also to Chris for being my secret weapon engineer eagle-eye on both of my books so far. Super thanks to industry legends Jack Skelley, Duncan Birmingham, and Curtis Armstrong for the early blurbs.

And thanks to my partner in love, life, songwriting, band gigs and music making, creative efforts, event planning, five-course Italian meals, beach days, bike rides, shenanigans, snuggles and snafus, the one and only Vincenzo. You are the biggest proof I have that you can find anything and anyone you're looking for in this crazy city.

I love you all. Keep reading books. And stay weird.